Nell
AND
Lady

ASHLEY FARLEY

Text copyright © 2018 by Ashley Farley
All rights reserved.

Published by Lake Union Publishing, Seattle

www.apub.com

Amazon, the Amazon logo, and Lake Union Publishing are trademarks of Amazon.com, Inc., or its affiliates.

ISBN-13: 9781503903005
ISBN-10: 1503903001

Cover design by PEPE *nymi*

Printed in the United States of America

Nell
AND
Lady

ALSO BY ASHLEY FARLEY

Sweet Tea Tuesdays
Saving Ben

Magnolia Series

Beyond the Garden
Magnolia Nights

Sweeney Sisters Series

Saturdays at Sweeney's
Tangle of Strings
Boots and Bedlam
Lowcountry Stranger
Her Sister's Shoes

Scottie's Adventures

Breaking the Story
Merry Mary

To the nurses on Six West of ART at MUSC

CHAPTER ONE

LADY

Present Day

Adelaide Bellemore was known to family and friends as Lady, although no one considered her a lady, least of all her mother. She stood at the sixth-floor window of the medical center, admiring the orange horizon as the sun set over Charleston Harbor. Clusters of nurses, dressed in cobalt-blue scrubs with totes slung over their shoulders and lightweight coats and sweaters draped across their arms, migrated past her to the bank of elevators. She studied the faces of the men and women—young and old, black and white, blond and brunet, slim and heavyset. Would she recognize Nell in this passing parade after thirty-one years? Nell was her sister, bound forever with Lady by legal documents but not by blood. They were no longer friends, hadn't been for years. The close friendship they'd shared from birth, the cherished memories of carefree childhood days, had come to a tragic ending as a result of the events of Lady's sixteenth birthday party on a rare snowy night in January of 1981.

The sound of more voices from around the corner soon brought another group of nurses into view. Lady spotted Nell among them, her lovely caramel skin and thin brows arched high above eyes the color of cognac. She wore a long-sleeved white T-shirt beneath her scrubs and her glossy hair pulled back into a tidy knot at the nape of her neck. She'd grown from a scrawny little girl into a stunning middle-aged woman. They locked eyes for an instant. Nell's posture stiffened, her jaw tensed, and she quickly looked away.

Lady crowded into the elevator with the nurses and eavesdropped on their conversation as they made plans for the evening ahead—the household chores and children that needed tending, the sleep required to refuel their bodies and minds before returning for another grueling twelve-hour shift at seven the following morning. The sign on the elevator wall, which hung high above their heads, served as a constant reminder to hospital personnel not to discuss patient care in public spaces.

The elevator doors parted, and everyone stepped out one by one. Lady trailed the nurses at a respectful distance through the vast lobby and across the open-air connector. Inside the parking deck, they bid each other good night as they separated. All but Nell disappeared into yet another elevator that would carry them to other levels where they'd left their cars. Lady followed Nell past three rows of parked cars to a sleek silver Mercedes sedan.

Nell clicked the unlock button, opened her door, and tossed her things inside. She turned to Lady, her lip curling slightly as her eyes traveled Lady's body. "What do you want?"

Lady felt herself cringe under Nell's scrutiny. She was no longer the beauty she had been in her high school class with her white-blonde hair, her pert nose, and a body all the boys lusted over. But mirrors don't lie. That perky nose now looked out of place among the broken capillaries, wrinkles, and age spots. She drew her tattered cardigan tight around her body to hide the muffin top spilling from the waistband of her jeans. "Nice car," she said, her words competing with the sound of vehicles bumping over concrete grooves in the exit ramp.

"My husband gave it to me for my fiftieth birthday three years ago. He's an anesthesiologist."

Lady nodded. She needed no further explanation. Everyone knew that anesthesiologists made the big bucks.

"Why are you here, Lady?" The nickname rolled off Nell's tongue with a tone of condescension.

Lady coughed to clear her throat. "Willa sent me. She's dying." She paused to let the news set in. "And she wants to see you."

~

Lady palmed the steering wheel as she emerged from the parking deck. "Damn it! I can't go through this again." Her words sounded hollow inside her mother's 1991 Buick Riviera. "If it were anyone but Willa . . ."

A tear sprang to Lady's eye at the thought of her mother dying. Growing up, Lady's friends had called her mother a freak behind her back. But Lady preferred to think of Willa as unconventional, an eccentric old kook. But a lovable one most of the time—not that they didn't have their issues like all mothers and daughters. Willa lived life by her own set of rules, regardless of what anyone thought of her. Most of the time, Lady humored her by letting her have her way.

From the moment Lady had uttered her first words, her mother had insisted she call her Willa. The same held true for Lady's daughter, Regan.

"I'm too young to be a grandmother," she'd declared when Regan was born seventeen years ago. "She'll call me Willa, like everyone else."

Lady never referred to Willa as *Mom* or *Mama* except when she was angry or needed to get a point across.

Willa's one dying wish was to see her adopted daughter one last time. Why would Nell refuse to see her? Willa had done so much for her. Not only had she provided food and shelter when Nell had nowhere

3

else to turn, but she'd also paid for Nell's education all the way through nursing school.

Lady took a left onto Calhoun Street and worked her way over to the Battery. She rolled down the window and gulped in the fifty-degree air. She fumbled in her pocketbook for her pack of cigarettes, lit one, and took a deep drag, tasting the stale tobacco as the nicotine calmed her nerves. She rarely smoked but kept a pack on hand for times of crisis.

She turned onto Water Street and parked in the driveway alongside her mother's house. Her parents, as newlyweds, had purchased and lovingly restored this antebellum home. Willa was a wealthy woman, although she lived like a miser. She'd inherited a fortune from her parents and a considerable amount of life insurance when her husband, Patrick Bellemore, died. But when Lady's meager alimony from her stingy ex-husband ran out, which happened on a monthly basis, Willa refused to float her a loan. Never mind that Willa kept the exterior of their house in pristine condition. Her priorities were obvious, signified by the absence of rotting wood or peeling paint on the shutters or wooden facade.

The single house, with original gray siding and black shutters, was the width of one room street side but stretched deep to the rear of the property. A spacious two-story porch, which Charlestonians referred to as a piazza, ran the length of the longest side. A glass-and-wooden structure, a hyphen, now connected the main house with the building, or dependency, that had once included the kitchen house, servants' quarters, and stables. The rear addition featured the family's den, which Lady had claimed as her own hangout growing up, and a small apartment upstairs where Nell had once lived with her mother, who had been Lady's parents' housekeeper.

Lady entered the house and went straight to the kitchen cabinet where she kept her martini supplies. She removed a chilled martini glass from the freezer and dumped several cubes of ice into a metal shaker.

She poured a healthy amount of Tito's vodka over the ice and added a splash of vermouth.

Sensing her mother's presence behind her, she fastened the top on the shaker and shook it. The sound of ice cubes pinging against metal filled the room. Lady watched through the kitchen window as the neighbor next door took out his trash with his Jack Russell terrier barking and nipping at his heels, and she thought back to another night thirty-seven years and sixty-seven days ago. Same house. Different neighbor. Different barking dog. The night that had forever changed her life.

She strained her martini into a glass and turned to face her mother.

"You've been smoking again," Willa said. "Why would you smoke those nasty old cigarettes when your poor mama is dying of lung cancer?"

Lady lifted her glass to Willa. "Ironic, don't you think? When you never smoked a cigarette in your life. Or did you smoke marijuana during your hippie days?"

Willa, a self-proclaimed leftover from the hippie movement, still wore long flowing dresses with Birkenstocks on her feet. Of all the silver-framed photographs that adorned the grand piano in the drawing room, Lady's favorite was of Willa, taken with her bridesmaids at their luncheon the day before her wedding. Wearing a Pucci minidress with a crown of daisies on her head, Willa stood out like a sore thumb among her bridesmaids, who were all dressed like Doris Day.

Willa raised a brow. "Did you find Nell? What'd she say?"

"She said to tell Miss Willa she'll be praying for her."

Nell's message caused Willa to stumble backward. She gripped the table beside her and lowered herself into the chair. "Did you say what I told you to say?"

"Mostly. I asked her to come see you. I did not ask her to come nurse you. She has a full-time job. We're doing fine on our own anyway. At least for now."

Lady had nursed her mother through two chemo treatments, with two more to go. Each treatment left her vomiting for days. Willa's long gray hair was falling out in clumps, like a dog with mange, and she appeared to be shrinking in size by the minute.

"I don't understand why she won't see me. Did she offer an explanation?"

"She said that no good could come from dredging up the past."

Lady turned away from her mother's pained expression. She refused to cover for Nell or sugarcoat her words. Lady wasn't dredging up anything. She lived in the past every single day. She was a character in a movie with a worn-out theme—waking up every morning to repeat the same traumatic day over and over again.

She drained her martini and refilled her glass as random thoughts ran through her mind. The interior of her mother's home was as equally well kept as the exterior. In exchange for food and board, it was Lady's job to make certain everything was polished to perfection—that windows sparkled, silver and brass gleamed, and random-width oak floors were buffed to a sheen. Although the exterior and interior surfaces of the house were kept in mint condition, the furnishings—drapes and Oriental rugs and upholstery—were circa Betsy Ross. That included the kitchen with its original General Electric appliances and wallpaper with bouquets of orange and yellow daisies. Much had transpired in this kitchen over the years, and Lady felt at home at the worn pine table surrounded by green Formica countertops and white metal cabinets.

She moved to the table and sat across from her mother. "I don't get it, Willa. You did so much for Nell after Mavis died. It hardly seems fair for her to treat you this way."

Willa's blue eyes clouded over, and Lady followed her gaze to the linoleum floor in front of the stove where Mavis—Nell's mother, Lady's nanny, and Willa's maid and beloved friend—had suffered a stroke and drawn her last breath on a sweltering summer day in August of 1979.

"I'm not giving up hope just yet. Nell always was slow to come around."

"That's true," Lady said, and they sat for a moment in silence while she sipped her martini.

"I've never gotten a straight answer from you about what happened all those years ago," Willa said. "Whatever you did to Nell to ruin your friendship is the reason she shut us out of her life and why she refuses to see me now."

"I resent the way you assume it was me who drove Nell away." Lady waited for her mother to respond, but she remained silent. "My answer hasn't changed since the last time you asked that question, but I'll give it to you anyway. I don't know what happened. Nell didn't trust in our friendship enough to tell me."

The door banged shut, and Regan rounded the corner from the dining room into the kitchen still dressed in her school uniform—plaid skirt and hunter-green polo with the logo for All Saints Prep School embroidered on the upper left breast. Regan barely glanced at Lady as she pulled a rocker up close to her grandmother and plunked down. She removed her laptop from her backpack and opened it on the table.

"Is it time?" Willa asked, rubbing her hands together in anticipation.

"Almost." Regan checked the time on her computer. "Nine more minutes."

Lady's mother and daughter were kindred souls. They even resembled one another—small in stature, with dimples on their cheeks and bright blue eyes that sparkled with life. Like her grandmother, Regan fashioned her golden hair, the same color as Willa's in her younger days, in a single braid down her back. Lady felt guilty for resenting her mother and daughter's close relationship. If only they didn't irritate her with their whispered secrets and inside jokes.

"Nine more minutes until what?" Lady asked.

Regan's fingers tapped the keyboard. "Until I find out if I got accepted to Chapel Hill. Today is notification day."

Lady ignored the pang of disappointment. Why hadn't her daughter told her about the notification date?

She had long since given up arguing with her daughter over her choice of colleges. Lady thought UNC too big, but Regan was determined to attend her father's alma mater. As if becoming a Tar Heel might somehow make him pay more attention to her. Lady worried her daughter was setting herself up for more heartache where her father was concerned. Letting her daughter make her own mistakes was the hardest part of parenting.

Far be it from her to be the party pooper. "All right, then." She clapped her hands. "The countdown is on! It just so happens that I have a bottle of bubbly. This seems like as good an occasion as any to drink it."

She got up from the table, and while her mother and daughter whispered with their heads pressed together and their faces planted in the computer, she retrieved three crystal champagne flutes from the breakfront in the dining room and popped the cork on a bottle of Barefoot Bubbly she'd purchased at the Harris Teeter.

She was topping off the third glass when cheers erupted from the table. She smiled to herself. Despite her belief that UNC was the wrong choice for her daughter, she was proud of Regan for working so hard to get into the college of her dreams. Regan had little interest in sports or boys. Although there was one boy in her grade, Booker, whom Regan spoke of often but whom Lady had never met. She sometimes wondered if they were more than just friends, but Regan assured her their relationship was all about healthy competition to get the best grades.

"This calls for a toast," Lady said, handing each of them a flute. She raised her glass to her daughter. "To ACC football, sorority sisters, and dates with handsome frat boys."

With her glass held high, Regan countered, "To an undergraduate degree in political science from UNC, a law degree from UVA, congresswoman by the time I'm thirty-five, president of the United States by age fifty."

Lady clinked Regan's glass. "That's my girl!" Her daughter was hell-bent on fixing everything she deemed wrong with the country, but Lady secretly considered Regan too reserved to endure being in the public spotlight as president.

Willa beamed. "I'd say you're off to a good start. You're president of your senior class, and you'll graduate with honors as valedictorian."

Regan set her glass down without taking a sip. Her daughter wasn't much of a drinker anyway, but Lady suspected something else was bothering her.

"Did I say something wrong?" Willa asked, her face pinched in concern.

"I hope you won't be too disappointed if I'm not valedictorian," Regan said, staring down at her computer. "Right now, Booker's GPA is a fraction below mine. He could catch up at any minute, and he seems determined to."

Lady lifted her daughter's chin toward her. "There's more to the selection than just grades, sweetheart. You have an impressive résumé. All the community service you've done and the leadership positions you've held will pay off."

"I'm not worried about a thing, sweetheart. You've always come out ahead," Willa said.

Lady, who had never come out ahead on anything in her life, winced at Willa's sarcasm, knowing it had been directed at her.

Willa gulped down half a glass of champagne and smacked her lips. "Yes siree, Bob! I will die a happy woman watching my granddaughter deliver her valedictorian address."

CHAPTER TWO

NELL

Nell sat paralyzed in the driver's seat, both hands gripping the steering wheel, long after she saw Lady's taillights retreat to the lower levels of the parking garage. Seeing Lady again had brought on a torrent of emotions. Guilt, for not visiting Miss Willa or calling or sending her a Christmas card. Shame, for taking advantage of Miss Willa for so many years. Regret, for never showing her adopted mother proper appreciation for saving her from foster care. Heartache, at the memory of her own mother's death. Fear, at the thought of having to return to that house. Anger, at the atrocities she'd suffered in the downstairs den. Fury, at Lady for not stopping it from happening. Humiliation, over the whole sordid affair. The intensity of the last emotion took her by surprise—provoking an ache in her chest and a torrent of tears. She was heartbroken at the thought of Miss Willa dying.

Why was this happening now, when things were going so well for her? She was on track for a promotion at the hospital. Her son, Booker, was about to graduate at the top of his class and be accepted at an Ivy League college. And her husband was finally noticing her again.

Nell had told her husband very little about her upbringing. And she'd told her son lies.

Her phone pinged in the center console with a text message from Booker. Did you forget to pick me up again?

She quickly thumbed a response. On the way. Got held up at the hospital.

She backed out of the parking space and exited the parking deck.

Booker was waiting for her in front of the library, his backpack slung over his shoulder and his fleece zipped tight under his chin against the chilly late-March evening. She wondered, as she did at least once a day, if her son would grow any more. At seventeen, he'd yet to reach Nell's height of five feet six. The doctor promised that he had the potential to grow seven or eight more inches. Her husband claimed that he didn't top out at six feet until his second year in college.

Booker climbed in the car and buckled himself into the passenger seat. "Drive fast! I don't want to miss it."

"Miss what?"

"Seriously, Mom. We've talked about this a gazillion times. Harvard is posting acceptances tonight at eight o'clock."

"Oh, right." She glanced at the clock on the dash. Seven twenty. She'd planned to stop at the grocery store on the way home. Oh well. Her son and husband would have to settle for leftovers again.

"You know, Mom, our lives would be so much easier if I had my own car."

Nell ran her hand over the top of his head. "Hang on a little longer, son. Graduation is in two months." She put the car in gear and pulled away from the curb.

"I don't understand why I have to wait for graduation. It's not like it's a surprise or anything. You already told me you're buying me a car." As they drove through town and across the Cooper River bridge toward Mount Pleasant, Booker presented his argument, outlining all the reasons his parents should give him his promised graduation present early.

He'd worn her down by the time they arrived home. "Let me talk to your father."

"Thanks, Mom." Booker hopped out of the car and hurried inside.

She gathered her belongings, entered the house through the front door, and passed through the center hallway to the family room–kitchen combo. Booker, perched on a barstool with his elbows propped on the granite countertop, was staring at his open laptop.

She set her bag and lunch box on the kitchen table. "Well? Did they post anything yet?"

"Not yet. Thirteen more minutes. What's for dinner?" he asked, his eyes glued to the screen.

She opened the refrigerator and surveyed the contents. "You have two choices—jambalaya or jambalaya."

He groaned. "Ugh. Not again."

"Sorry. You were in too big a hurry to stop at the grocery store."

"See!" he said, his pointer finger aimed at the cathedral ceiling. "If I had my own car, I could've stopped at the store for you on the way home from school."

"Give it a rest, son. I've had a long day."

Nell dumped the leftover container of jambalaya into a casserole dish and slid it in the microwave to reheat. She poured herself a glass of pinot noir and took it outside to the porch to enjoy the last few minutes of twilight. She sat down in a rocker and gazed across their dock to the glistening waters of the Wando River. She and her husband, Desmond, had started construction on this house the same month she'd discovered she was pregnant with Booker. Back when their marriage was solid and both their careers had taken off. My, how good things had been for them back then.

Growing up, she'd always dreamed of one day owning a home like the Bellemores'. She'd gotten the big house. But she'd known from the beginning that something was missing. Something that had nothing to do with the problems in her marriage. That something was the love she'd experienced as a child in the Bellemores' home. Back when her mother was still alive and Lady was her best friend. Nell of course loved her son with her whole heart. They shared a close bond, as special as any mother and son she knew. But the love that had filled that house on Water Street was tender and sweet and kind. She understood now what a rare gift it had been.

When the sky grew dark, with only two minutes left until the appointed hour, she left the porch and returned to the kitchen. Standing behind Booker, she peered over his shoulder at his applicant status portal for Harvard.

She nudged him with her elbow. "Are you excited?"

"I'm scared to death. I can't look." He closed his eyes. "Tell me what it says."

The notification appeared, and her heart sank. Wait list. She sighed inwardly. Why had they denied her son admission? This had to be an error. He'd been accepted everywhere else he'd applied—USC, UGA, UVA, Duke. His college guidance counselor had assured them he would be a shoo-in for Harvard.

"Well?" Booker asked, his eyes squeezed tight.

"They must've made a mistake," was all she could think to say.

Booker opened his eyes and read the announcement. "Dang it!" He pounded the counter with his fist. "I can't believe this is happening."

"I'm sorry, son. I know you're disappointed." She rubbed circles on his back. "I felt certain you'd get in."

"Why, Mom, because I'm black?" he said and buried his face in his hands.

"No, not because you're black. Because your grades and SAT scores meet the criteria." The fact that he was a minority certainly didn't hurt, of course—she'd factored that in—but Nell wouldn't admit that to her son, at least not now when he was so upset. "Duke is a fine school, your father's school. He'll be so proud."

"I don't want to go to Duke," he said, his voice muffled by his hands. "I want to go to Harvard."

"Well, a wait list isn't a flat-out rejection. Maybe there's a chance . . ."

His head shot up. "You're right, Mom. I'll wait it out, until August if I have to." The lines in his forehead creased, and his fingers flew across the keyboard as he conducted a Google search on the wait list statistics for Harvard. "They'll take me off the wait list once they see my grades this semester and I'm selected valedictorian."

"That's the fighting spirit." She tugged on his arm. "Let's get ready for dinner. You'll feel better after you've eaten something."

Booker was setting the table and Nell was mixing a green salad when Desmond arrived a few minutes later. She smelled the sickly sweet floral perfume the minute he walked through the back door. The smell brought on a wave of nausea that made her want to vomit. She'd been so hopeful that this time would be different. True what they said—once a cheater, always a cheater. She wanted to claw his hazel eyes out and smack the smug look off his handsome face, but she would save the argument until later. Booker had experienced enough disappointment for one day.

Dinner was a solemn affair. Booker picked at his food while his father extolled the virtues of Duke University.

In a sweet voice that sounded fake even to her own ears, Nell said, "Gee, Des, if you ever get tired of being a doctor, you could apply for a job in their admissions office."

"I just want the boy to feel good about his decision," Desmond said.

"I didn't make this decision, Dad. The decision was made for me." Booker pushed back from the table and snatched up his plate. "You wait. I'm going to find a way to get off that wait list." He dropped his plate in the sink with a clatter and stormed off to his room.

"Who is she, Des?" Nell asked when they were alone.

He stared at her over a forkful of jambalaya. "Who is who?"

"The woman who wears that god-awful perfume." Nell pinched her nose. "It would've been wise of you to take a shower before coming home to your wife and child."

He set his fork down. "Baby, I—"

"Save it, Des." She stood abruptly, knocking over her chair.

He jumped to his feet, but she shoved him back down and righted her chair. She glared at the man she loved so much who had cheated on her time and again over the past ten years. "I really thought we had a chance this time. We were in such a good place."

Walking her plate to the sink, she rinsed both hers and Booker's and placed them in the dishwasher. She refilled her wineglass and stood with her back to her husband, her thoughts racing through her head as she looked out into the dark night.

Where do we go from here? she wondered. They'd tried everything. Counseling had worked for a while, until Desmond stopped showing up for the appointments. There was no fix for whatever was wrong with their marriage. Trying again would only prolong the agony. She needed to get out while she still had some semblance of dignity. While she could still look herself in the mirror in the morning.

"I can't do this anymore," she said with her back still turned to him. "Our marriage is over."

After a long moment of silence, he sighed and said in a resigned tone, "As much as I hate to admit it, I agree. This isn't working for me anymore either."

She spun around to face him. "Did our marriage *ever* work for you, Des?"

He stood up and crossed the room to her. "Of course it did, baby. You and I were good together in the beginning."

"I have one question for you. Will you at least do me the courtesy of answering it honestly?"

He nodded. "I'll try."

She took a gulp of wine for courage. "What is it about me that turns you off so, that has driven you time and again into the arms of other women?"

He studied her face as though trying to decide how to respond. "You asked for honesty, so I'll give it to you. It's that chip you carry around on your shoulder. Something bad happened to you in your past that you refuse to talk about." He cupped her cheeks in his hands. "I know the pain it causes you, Nell. I hear you crying out in your sleep. That anger and bitterness is eating you up inside. Get some help, Nell. Find a good therapist. Releasing your burden will set you free."

"I want you to leave, Des," she said in a soft voice, almost a whisper.

A wounded expression crossed his face, and he dropped his hands. "Can I wait until after graduation? I don't want to spoil this happy time for Booker."

Booker's relationship with his father was strained at best, but divorce would be hard on him, as it was on most children regardless of the circumstances. But Desmond staying in the house meant pretending nothing was wrong. And she couldn't do that. She couldn't sleep in the same bed, do his laundry, and cook his dinners while he was having an affair with another woman. They would undoubtedly fight the whole time, which would turn Booker's last two months of high school into a living hell.

"I'm not the one spoiling it, Desmond. You did that all by yourself. I want you out of the house tonight."

CHAPTER THREE

N ELL

1979

Nell remembered the day as clearly as if it had been yesterday—that sweltering afternoon in late August of 1979 when her world had come crashing down upon her.

Eager to tell her mama about her first day of high school, she'd rushed home from the bus stop. She was also eager to share her day with Lady, but Lady was staying late at her school for tennis team tryouts. They would have to wait until they'd had supper and finished their homework before they could stretch out on the cool floor in the downstairs den and compare notes. They had each set goals—with challenges of a vastly different nature—for the coming school year. Lady's goal involved a new crush she had on a boy in her class, Phillip something or other, while Nell had committed to making the dean's list. Over the long, boring summer, as she'd watched her mama slave away over another woman's laundry and cooking and cleaning, she'd made a silent vow to make something of herself. What that something was, she'd yet to figure out. But she'd determined getting good grades was a step in the right direction.

As she rounded the corner into the driveway, she expected to see her mama—her face as dark as night with her white uniform gaping open across her ample breast—waiting for her on the back stoop. But her mama was nowhere in sight. The kitchen door was open, and through the screen Nell saw a pot boiling over on the stove. Butter beans. She smelled them from where she stood. She dashed inside and dropped her book bag on the floor. As she moved toward the stove to turn it off, she tripped over her mama's body crumpled in a heap on the floor.

"Mama! Oh God, Mama!" She knelt down beside Mavis and tapped her cheek. "Get up, Mama. Open your eyes. Oh God. What am I gonna do?" She placed her index and middle fingers on Mavis's wrist like she'd seen the paramedics do on TV. Relief rushed over her when she felt a pulse. "Hang on, Mama. I'm gonna get you some help."

Nell jumped to her feet. "Miss Willa, come quick! Something's wrong with Mama."

She raced about calling for Miss Willa—up the stairs, to the drawing room at the front of the house, and back to the kitchen. Then it dawned on her that she hadn't seen Miss Willa's car parked outside when she came up the driveway. She raced outside to double-check. The driveway was empty. She darted across the tiny lawn to the neighbor's house and pounded on the door, but no one answered. Returning to her mama's side, Nell placed both hands on her mother's heart and pumped with all her might, even though she knew she was doing it all wrong. If only she'd paid attention when they taught CPR in health class last year.

She went to the black rotary-dial wall phone and dialed 911. "Help! Please help me!" she cried to the operator. "My mama's passed out and can't get up." Nell babbled out her name and address before hanging up.

She stretched out on the floor beside Mavis, draping her arm across her body. "Please don't die, Mama," she whispered over and over. But as the sound of sirens approached from a distance, she felt her mama's body go still.

Paramedics soon swarmed the room.

"Please help her! I found her like this when I got home from school."

One of the paramedics, a man with kind brown eyes, said, "We're gonna do everything we can for her," as he fastened an oxygen mask to Mavis's face.

They lifted Mavis's body onto a stretcher and began working on her as they wheeled her out the back door.

Nell followed them outside. "Where are you taking her?"

"To the emergency room at MUSC," the kind paramedic said. "Are you here alone? Is there anyone you should call?"

She glanced toward the street and noticed Miss Willa running up the driveway.

"What the devil is going on?" Miss Willa asked as she fought to catch her breath.

"She's dead, Miss Willa. I think my mama is dead."

"She can't be." Willa looked to the paramedic for confirmation.

"Every minute counts," he said.

"Then what are you waiting for?" She stepped out of the way of the ambulance. "We'll follow you in our car."

"Come on, let's go." Willa took her by the hand and dragged her down the driveway to her green station wagon parked by the curb. As she stumbled along beside her, Nell noticed Miss Willa's honey-colored braid was wound on top of her head in a bun, and she was dressed in the proper suit—yellow polyester with a white ruffled blouse—that she reserved for church, instead of the flowery smocks she wore around the house.

Willa turned on her hazard lights and raced her wagon through the downtown streets to the medical university. They entered the emergency room and identified themselves to the receptionist, who summoned a nurse to show them to the back. As they burst through the double doors, Nell saw her mother's gurney in the hallway surrounded by a team of doctors and nurses. She watched in horror as one of the doctors drew a white sheet over her mama's sweet face.

Nell, rushing over and pushing through the tight circle, threw herself across her mama's body. "No! Please, no!" Nurses on either side of her took her by the arms and led her down the hall away from the gurney. Cooing words of comfort, one of the nurses draped a warm blanket around her shoulders, and the other handed her a bottle of apple juice. Their kindness, at a moment in time when she needed it the most, had a profound effect on Nell, although she wouldn't realize it until much later.

After a short discussion with the doctor, Miss Willa came to collect Nell, and they walked out of the emergency room together. Judging by her pale face and quivering chin, Nell knew Miss Willa was fighting to keep herself together.

"I don't understand how this happened," Miss Willa said on the drive home. "We ate lunch together, only hours ago, before my garden club meeting. Life is tragic that way. One minute you're fine; next thing you know you've suffered a fatal stroke." Her eyes filled with tears. "How will I ever survive without her?"

Nell gaped at Willa but held her tongue. *How will you survive without her? The bigger question is, how will I survive without her?*

Miss Willa removed a tissue from the travel pack she kept in the side pocket of her car door. She took a tissue for herself and handed the pack to Nell. "Mavis told me a little about her background," she said, dabbing at her eyes. "As far as I know, she doesn't have any other family."

She shook her head. "No, ma'am. My grandparents are dead, and Mama didn't have any siblings. I'm the only one left in my family." She'd never met her father. Never even knew who he was. But admitting that to Miss Willa seemed like she was betraying her mama. Her mama and Miss Willa were close. If Mavis had wanted Miss Willa to know about her daddy, whoever he was, she would've told her.

When they got home, Nell retreated to the dingy rooms at the back of the house where she lived with her mama. The apartment, the only home she'd ever known, featured a bedroom they shared with twin beds, a minuscule bathroom with a rusted tub, and a living area. One wall of the main room boasted a kitchenette, complete with small refrigerator, hot plate, and single-bowl sink.

She sat on the edge of her bed. Her mind buzzed, her limbs felt numb, and her heart ached. But as hard as she tried, no tears would come. She heard the back door slam and Lady call, "I'm home." Nell waited and listened for the sound of her friend's footsteps on the stairs outside her room. But two hours passed before she appeared at her door, still dressed from tryouts in her white polo and tennis skirt, her eyes puffy and her face tear stained.

"I'm so sorry, Nell," Lady said, wrapping her bony arms around Nell. "I would've come sooner, but Willa thought you needed some time alone to mourn."

Time alone is the last thing I need right now. I have the rest of my life to be alone.

Lady held her at arm's length. "I know how you must be feeling. Well, not exactly. Losing a father is way different than losing your mama. This is so unfair." She buried her face in the crook of Nell's neck and sobbed.

The tables turned, as so often happened with them, and Lady became the star of the show, with Nell in a supporting role. Nell stroked her back and whispered in her ear until she finally stopped crying.

"Willa said to tell you supper's ready." Lady pushed away from her, wiping her eyes with her shirttail.

The thought of food made Nell sick to her stomach. "Tell her I'm not hungry."

"Okay, then. If you're sure." Lady turned toward the door. "I'll come back later and check on you."

Alone once again, Nell lay down on her mother's bed and buried her face in her pillow, inhaling the scent of Irish Spring soap. Finally, the tears came, soaking the pillow as she cried herself to sleep. Miss Willa awakened her sometime later with a supper tray. Nell's stomach churned at the sight of the runny eggs and greasy bacon.

"I'll eat later. I'm not really hungry right now." She took the tray from Miss Willa and set it down on the coffee table.

"I haven't been up here in years." Miss Willa gave the room a once-over, her mouth twisted with distaste. She perched herself on the edge of the sofa and patted the cushion beside her. "We need to talk about your mother's funeral."

Nell sat down next to her.

"If it's okay with you, I'd like to bury Mavis in our family plot at Magnolia Cemetery. There's plenty of room. I think she'll be happy there."

Nell stared at the woman. *You think she'll be happy there? She's going to heaven, not on a cruise.*

"Unless, of course, you have other plans."

"No, Miss Willa. That is mighty kind of you. Mama would be grateful."

Willa stood to go. "Leave everything to me. I'll take care of all the arrangements."

～

Nell insisted on going to school the rest of the week. She couldn't bear the thought of staying in her apartment all alone, and she didn't want to get behind in her schoolwork so early in the semester. Her commitment to making good grades was more important than ever. She was only fourteen with no means of supporting herself. Maybe the people in her church could help her find a place to live. She would need to be careful to avoid social services, though. She knew what happened to kids who were placed in foster homes. The feeling of helplessness haunted her through the long days at school and the even longer sleepless nights.

Miss Willa arranged for the funeral to take place on Friday, with the minister of Mavis and Nell's Baptist church presiding over the graveside service. About a dozen people attended—some of the help from other houses on the street, a few members of their church, and several of Miss Willa's friends. Nell's friends, not that any of them would've come, were all in school. Aside from going to church every Sunday, her mama had never been one for socializing. She was a shy woman, never had much to say and never talked about herself. She had no family, no husband, few acquaintances, and only one true friend—Miss Willa, her employer.

They sang a few hymns, said a few prayers, and listened to the preacher read passages from the Bible and talk about what a strong Christian woman Mavis had been. After the service, Miss Willa and Lady waited in the car while Nell stayed behind to watch the cemetery workers lower her mama's mahogany casket into the hole beside Mr. Bellemore.

Lady's daddy had been a man of great mystery in her life, sneaking in and out of the house under the cover of darkness. When he wasn't working long hours at his investment firm downtown, he had been either playing golf or sailing on his boat. Two years ago, he'd had a massive coronary on the way home from the marina and had run his car into a telephone pole. Nell could still see the policeman's somber face when he'd come to the house to deliver the news. It had taken time, but life had eventually moved on for Miss Willa and Lady. Nell didn't see how life could possibly go on for her without her mama.

Back at the house, she excused herself to go to her room. Lady found her there an hour later, folding her clothes and arranging them on the bed in neat piles.

"What are you doing?" she asked, her blue eyes wide.

"What does it look like I'm doing? I'm packing."

"But for what? Where are you going?"

"I'm going to live with a friend," Nell lied.

"No!" Lady stepped between Nell and the bed. "You can't leave me, Nell. First my daddy and now Mavis. I can't lose you too. I just can't." She slumped to the floor. "Please don't go!" she hollered over and over.

Willa came running up the stairs at the sound of Lady's carrying on. "Get up, Lady." She pulled her daughter to her feet. "Whatever the matter is, it can't be all that bad."

"Nell's leaving us," Lady sniffled. "She's going to live with a friend."

Miss Willa cast a suspicious glance at Nell. "What friend?"

"Just a friend from my church," Nell said with a shrug. "You don't know her."

"Now, Nell," Willa said, draping her arm around her shoulder, "your mother and I never actually discussed it—we never thought we needed to—but she would want me to make certain you ended up with the right people. We've all had a difficult day. We need to give this some thought. You can stay here until we figure something out."

"Yes, ma'am," she said to appease her, even though she had no intention of staying.

"Good. Then that's settled. I'll have supper ready in fifteen minutes."

"Yes, ma'am." In the five days since her mother's death, Nell had grown to despise Miss Willa's cooking. Willa desperately needed a cook and a maid. There was already talk of hiring someone to take Mavis's place. And that someone would need a place to live.

"Come with me, Lady. You can help me get supper on the table," Miss Willa said, and bustled her daughter out of the apartment.

Nell scurried around the apartment gathering toiletries and tokens to remember her mama by. She stuffed everything, along with her clothes, into paper grocery bags. With no idea where she'd go or how she'd get there, she started down the stairs. She stopped in her tracks when she heard her name mentioned as she passed the doorway to the kitchen. She pressed herself against the wall and listened.

In a shrill voice, Lady said, "I don't understand why Nell can't live here with us. She's like family."

"Your father would roll over in his grave. Our friends and neighbors would think I've lost my mind."

"Since when do you care about what other people think?" Lady asked. "Please, Mama."

There she goes, calling her Mama, thought Nell. *She must be really sad or want something real bad.*

Silence ensued, and Nell imagined Miss Willa's face all scrunched up in thought. "You have a point. I do like to stir the pot."

"Nell says she's going to stay with a friend, but that's a lie. I know for a fact she doesn't have any."

Ouch. That hurts. I have a few friends. Just none I would invite to come home with me.

Lady rattled on, "You can't throw her out on the street. It's not right. She's lived here all her life. Mavis would take care of me if something happened to you."

"That's true," Miss Willa said in a soft voice. "I owe Mavis this much, after all she did for us. Not only was she the best friend I ever had, she was the kindest person I've ever met. It's true what they say about the good dying young. Nell is a sweet girl, and she doesn't deserve this. Still, I need time to think about it. This is a big decision that will affect a lot of people."

"We don't have time to think about it. If Nell leaves us now, she'll never come back. And I can't live without her. Please! Say yes, Mama. Please, oh please," Lady whined. Nell smiled as she pictured her best friend bouncing on her toes with her hands in prayer formation.

"Lord have mercy, Lady. Anything to make you stop calling me *Mama.*"

"Is that a yes?"

"That's a yes," Miss Willa said. "At least for now. I don't see any harm in giving it a try."

CHAPTER FOUR

WILLA

Willa couldn't remember the last time she'd gotten a full night's sleep. It'd been decades, at least. She'd come to think of two o'clock as the witching hour, when her past came back to haunt her. She'd learned a long time ago that it was better to face her ghosts than allow them to torment her. Slipping on her pink chenille robe and her fur-lined slippers, she shuffled down the stairs and into the kitchen. She filled the teakettle with water and placed it on the stovetop to boil and then set two cups in saucers, dropping a chamomile tea bag into each cup. When the kettle whistled, she poured hot water over the tea bags and let them steep for four minutes. She added a lump of sugar to one and a dribble of milk to the other. She set the sweetened tea at her place at the table and the other cup next to her. Planting her elbows on the table and her head in her hands, she blew on the tea to cool it down. When the tips of her fingers felt the smooth skin of her bald head, she drew her hand away and gaped at the fistful of hair.

"Tell me, Mavis, what exactly am I supposed to do about this?" she asked, holding the clump of long gray hair out to the ghost occupying the empty seat beside her. "I should probably have a stylist shave it all off, but I wouldn't know where to go. I haven't been to a beauty parlor in thirty years. I could find out where my friends have their weekly blowouts. I can see it now, the pity in their eyes when I march out of the salon with my bald head."

Willa twisted the hair into a tiny ball and set it on the table.

"Why didn't you take me to heaven with you, May May?" Willa hung her head as she sipped her tea. "Don't say it. I already know what you're thinking. One of us had to stay down here to take care of the girls. You would've done a much better job than me. You were counting on me, and I failed you."

Willa reached for the metal tin of cheese biscuits in the center of the table. She removed the lid and held it out to May May. "No? I don't blame you. They're not nearly as good as yours. Shhh! Don't tell Regan. She made them. Followed your recipe to a T, but something's missing." Willa popped a cheese biscuit into her mouth and returned the lid to the container.

"I don't have the strength to fight anymore, May May. And I don't mean my cancer. You're up there watching us fools down here. You know what I'm talking about. This world has gone nuts. Plumb crazy. Mass shootings nearly every day. Crooked politicians and their unethical politics. Nobody cares about tradition anymore. Being politically correct is more important than doing what's right. We live in a different world now from when you were here. Where did we go wrong? God gave us this big beautiful planet. The least we can do is live together in peace."

Willa blew her nose into her napkin. "I got just enough strength left in me to watch Regan deliver her valedictorian address. After that, I'm gonna leave this world behind so I can be with you. We'll have ourselves a fine old time in heaven. Just like we used to do here."

Willa slumped back and folded her arms over her chest. "Back in the day, we spent many a night together at this table talking about life and how we wanted to raise our girls. Do you remember our first tea party? I do. It was the night before Thanksgiving in 1964, and you'd only been working here a month. I couldn't sleep for worrying about cooking my first turkey. After hours of tossing and turning and fretting over Mr. Turkey Bird, I left my husband sawing logs and ventured downstairs in search of the Harlequin romance I'd left in the drawing room. When I saw the light on in the kitchen, I tiptoed in here and found you sitting at the table knitting."

Willa closed her eyes and rested her head against the back of the chair and thought back to the night that had changed everything for them.

～

Willa plunked down at the table across from Mavis. "Lord have mercy, Mavis, my mama has gone off on a shopping spree to New York City and dumped Thanksgiving in my lap. Christmas too. What do I know about hosting the holidays? When I called her to find out how to cook the turkey, she told me I'd learn better if I figured it out on my own. The nerve of her."

Without looking up from her knitting, Mavis said, "Don't you worry about a thing, Mrs. Bellemore. I'll cook your turkey for you. All the fixings too, if you want. Mashed potatoes. Sweet potatoes. Oyster stuffing."

"I was hoping I could count on you. My cooking's so bad I'm liable to give my guests food poisoning." With one hand on her belly, Willa eyed the tiny pink booties in Mavis's hands. "Are those for me?"

"No'm, they're for me." Mavis's face grew darker as she stared down at her knitting.

Willa gaped at Mavis, her blue eyes bulging. "Are you saying you're pregnant?"

Mavis's gaze met hers. "Yes'm, I found out last week. I've been meaning to tell you."

Willa's mind raced. As far as she could remember, when she'd hired Mavis a month ago as a live-in maid, she hadn't mentioned a husband. "I didn't know you were married."

Mavis wound the yarn around her needles and laid her knitting on the table. "I'm not."

"Oh. In that case, I'd better make us some tea." Willa hauled herself up and went over to the stove. An awkward silence fell on the room as she prepared the tea. She didn't know what to think of the situation. She'd hired and fired a handful of maids before she found Mavis. She approved of the quiet and efficient manner in which she performed her duties, and she hated to lose her.

When the tea was ready, Willa returned to the table with the tray. "Do you know who the father is?" she asked as she filled two cups with tea.

"Yes'm, we lived together for three years." Mavis added a drop of cream to her tea. "He didn't treat me well, if you know what I mean."

Willa brought her hand to her throat. "You mean he beat you?"

Mavis nodded and looked away. "I couldn't leave him until I found another place to live. I was so grateful when you hired me. You gave me a job and a home."

"Does this man know where you are? Are you in any sort of danger? Are *we* in danger?" Willa worried about her own safety. She had her unborn child to think about.

"No'm," Mavis said. "He would've beaten me dead before he let me go. I packed my bags and snuck out of the house while he was at work. I heard through the grapevine that he's gone back to his family up north."

"That's a relief," Willa said, slurping her tea. "How far along are you?"

"Three months, according to the doctor. But they gotta run some tests to be sure."

Willa remembered Mavis asking for an afternoon off the week before to go to the doctor. "I see."

"You gotta believe me, Mrs. Bellemore. This ain't what I planned. And I know you didn't bargain for no pregnant maid. Can you please give me a little time to find another place to live?"

"Let's not get ahead of ourselves. I'm sure we can figure out a solution that'll work for everyone." She went to the pantry for the tin of cheese biscuits that had become a staple on their shelves since Mavis had started working for them. She popped cheese biscuit after cheese biscuit into her mouth as she walked in circles around the kitchen. "Do you feel okay to work? At least for a while."

"Yes'm, I feel fine. As long as my health is good, I plan to work right up until the baby's born. I'll be back on my feet a few days afterward."

An idea formed in Willa's mind as the logistics of their pregnancies fell into place like pieces of a puzzle. "This could actually work in our favor. When the time comes, I planned to hire a nanny. Would you be interested in the position? After you've recovered from childbirth, of course. I could get a housekeeper to come in twice a week to relieve you of the heavy cleaning. That way, your primary responsibilities would be taking care of the babies and doing the cooking. What do you think?"

Mavis's lips spread into a wide grin. "I think you just answered my prayers, Mrs. Bellemore. But shouldn't you ask Mr. Bellemore first? He may not approve of me living here with my baby."

"That won't be necessary. Mr. Bellemore trusts me to take care of the household." Willa returned to the table and sat back down. "How old are you, Mavis?"

"I'm twenty-eight, ma'am."

"Then you're the same age as me. If you're going to be my nanny, it hardly seems right for you to call me Mrs. Bellemore. I want you to call me Willa."

Mavis shook her head with vehemence. "Oh no, ma'am. I couldn't do that. It ain't proper."

"How about Miss Willa, then?" Willa suggested.

Mavis thought about it a minute and then nodded reluctantly. "If that's what you want."

Willa touched her teacup to Mavis's. "Then we have a deal." She fingered the booties. "Why pink? You can't possibly know it's a girl already."

Mavis set her cup down and picked up her knitting. "I just have a feeling."

"I don't have any intuition about the sex of my baby," Willa said. "Do you think that means I'll be a terrible mother?"

"Not at all. You're a kindhearted soul, Mrs. . . . uh, Miss Willa. You're gonna make a fine mother for your baby, whether it's a girl or a boy."

"Problem is, that kindness has to share my heart with a lot of self-centeredness. My ego is fragile, Mavis. I hate getting fat, and the thought of having my child suck on my breasts repulses me."

Mavis chuckled, the first laughter Willa had heard from her since she started working for her. "Ain't you heard? Breastfeeding is out of style for women like you."

Willa let out a little squeal. "In that case, let's stock the house with baby bottles. I refuse to let this baby cramp my style. My child will grow up self-sufficient."

Mavis shot her a quizzical look. "I don't mean to be personal, Miss Willa. But did you plan to have this baby, or was it an acci—"

"Lord no, it wasn't an accident. I've always wanted to have children. At least one child anyway." Willa placed a hand on her belly and felt the baby moving around inside her womb. "I already love this little pumpkin seed like crazy. I just don't want my life to change any more than it has to. This baby needs to adapt to me, not the other way around. Do you think that's too much to ask?"

"No'm. It ain't too much to ask for a woman in your position who can afford to hire full-time help."

"Let me ask you something, Mavis." Willa settled back in her chair with her arm propped on her belly and the teacup dangling from her finger. "What will you tell your daughter when she's old enough to ask about her father?"

Mavis's eyes remained on her hands as they adeptly wrapped the thread around the wooden knitting needles. "I'll lie to her. I'll tell her he's dead. God might strike me dead, but I can't have her running off trying to find him. He'll bring her nothing but misery like he done me." Her hands grew still, and she looked up at Willa, her face pinched in pain. "Please, Miss Willa, if anything ever happens to me, promise me you won't tell her what I told you about him."

Willa placed her hand over her heart. "You can trust me, May. I'll carry your secret to my grave."

CHAPTER FIVE

NELL

Nell called in sick for work the following day, the first time ever since she'd started working as a nurse. Unaccustomed to seeing his mother ill, Booker offered to get a ride to school so she could sleep in. She dozed after he left, her sleep plagued with restless dreams. Of Desmond making love to a woman with voluptuous curves and no face. Of Willa on her deathbed with a gnarled hand reaching out to Nell. Of Lady as a child playing hopscotch on the sidewalk in front of their house, back when they were best friends. The last dream—a figure lurking in the dark on a snowy night—awoke her with a start.

Her eyes sought the clock on Desmond's nightstand. *It's already past ten. Time to get up!* She tossed the covers back and threw her feet over the side of the bed. *Time to face your new reality.*

She went to her closet for her robe, but when she saw the empty rack where her husband's clothes had hung for nineteen years, she fell back against the doorframe and slid to the floor. Tucked in a fetal position, she sobbed her guts out, not for the pain and suffering of recent years but for the loss of the future she'd entrusted with her heart and soul. She and Desmond would not experience retirement and old age together. They would not travel the world or buy a condo in Florida. They would not host Thanksgiving dinners for Booker's family or take their grandchildren to Disney World. She would do all of those things alone while Desmond was doing them with someone else.

Finally, spent, she forced herself to get up. She changed out of her nightgown, now soaked with tears, and into her exercise clothes. Staggering to the adjoining en suite bathroom, she brushed her teeth and washed her face. "Get a hold of yourself, Nell," she said to her weary reflection in the mirror. "You need to be strong for Booker's sake. Take one step at a time. One day at a time. And the first step on this first day is coffee."

Tying on her running shoes, she went to the kitchen and brewed herself a cup of coffee. She was peeling a banana when her phone vibrated on the granite countertop with a text from Desmond. Sorry. Can't make tonight after all. Have dinner with a client.

Desmond had waited until their son fell asleep before leaving the house around midnight the night before. He'd promised to return that evening for dinner to break the news of their divorce to Booker.

Nell picked up her phone and hurled it across the room at the fireplace. The phone crashed against the stone and tumbled to the hearth.

"How stupid do you think I am?" she screamed, her voice echoing off the cathedral ceiling. "You're an anesthesiologist. You put your so-called clients to sleep for surgery. Oh, wait. I get it. You're having Chinese takeout delivered to the OR to eat while you monitor their vitals." She dropped the banana down the disposal. "This is just great! Now I'm talking out loud to myself. I must be losing my mind."

She took her coffee to the fireplace and picked up the phone. A spider's web of cracks stretched across the screen, but the phone still functioned. She started a nasty response to Desmond but then deleted it. He was a coward, unable to face his son and admit he'd cheated on his mother yet again. He was missing an opportunity to make things right. So let him make his own mistakes. She'd warned Desmond countless times that his noncommittal attitude toward their family could be detrimental to his relationship with Booker. But Desmond's actions no longer concerned her, any more than she needed his approval on matters regarding their son. Or any other matter. She would break the news to Booker gently, right after she told him she was giving him his graduation present early.

Pocketing her broken phone, she stared up at the oil painting above the mantel. The graceful limbs of live oak trees stretched out over the inlet at Desmond's family's waterfront property in McClellanville. She'd chosen the artist and commissioned the landscape herself as a gift to Desmond for Christmas three years ago. They'd spent the happiest times in their marriage on that farm, and even though the painting rightfully belonged to Desmond, she would have a difficult time parting with it. As she would most of the pieces in their collection of art that was decades in the making. She wondered what process couples used for divvying up their possessions when they separated. Half the contents of their garage—golf clubs, tennis and squash racquets, scuba equipment—belonged to him. She entered the adjacent room, his study—a man cave with dark paneling, leather furniture, and sliding glass doors leading to a bluestone terrace with an outdoor fireplace. He would undoubtedly clear these shelves of his rare book and vinyl jazz collections, but what about the theater-size television mounted to the wall? Surely it belonged to the house.

He would take all the contents, but he couldn't take the room. She would strip off the cheap paneling, paint the walls a bright color, and turn the space into her own private studio with a desk and comfortable seating for lounging with a good book on the days she didn't have to work. There would be enough room to set up an easel if she ever got around to signing up for the art classes she'd always wanted to take. She moved to the window and gazed down at the dock. She had no use for a thirty-foot cabin cruiser. Take it! As long as he left the seventeen-foot skiff for Booker. Except that Booker would go away to college in five months, and she'd be stuck taking care of a boat. If he got off the wait list at Harvard, he'd go away to Massachusetts and never come home.

Then she'd be left in this big house all alone. She wrapped her arms around herself. She hadn't felt so alone since her mother died. What a terrible time that'd been for her.

No one could take the place of her mama, but Willa had been an amazing substitute. She'd clothed her, fed her, and educated her. She'd done her very best to treat Nell the same as her own daughter. But Nell wasn't the same as Lady. She was a black girl living like a white girl in a white woman's house. And that had felt wrong to Nell. It wasn't until she went off to Spelman College where the majority of students were black that her life began to change. During those four years, she began to develop friendships and returned home to Charleston only two or three times, for the rare Christmas or Thanksgiving when she wasn't invited to one of her friend's houses. She and Desmond Grady had met while she was conducting her clinical training at Emory Hospital her senior year. By the time graduation rolled around, she knew he was the one. She'd finally figured out where she belonged—in his big, strong, capable arms. They were planning their future together. And that future did not include Lady and Willa Bellemore.

~

After a long, brisk walk and a bowl of tomato bisque for lunch, Nell spent the afternoon on the phone. She called every Toyota dealership in and around the Charleston area until she found a salesman she felt she could trust.

In a rich baritone voice, Orlando Holland said, "You realize you're looking for what everyone else wants. Low mileage, newer-model 4Runners aren't easy to come by. I can find you one, but it might take a couple of weeks. In the meantime, would your son be interested in test-driving a new one?"

"He's driven a friend's once or twice, but it wouldn't hurt to be sure this is what he wants. I'm working all weekend. Tuesday would be the earliest we could get out there. Will that prevent you from starting the search?"

"Not at all," Orlando said. "I'll get on it right away."

Nell experienced conflicting emotions that evening as she drove to Charleston to pick up Booker at the library. Her excitement to tell him about the car was equal to her dread over breaking the news about the divorce.

Booker tossed his backpack into the back seat and climbed in on the passenger side. "Do you feel better? I don't ever remember you being sick, which is surprising considering you work in a hospital."

Nell's heart ached at how much her son reminded her of his father as a younger man, a compassionate doctor full of concern for his patient.

"I feel much better, thank you. And you're right. I haven't been sick in years. I have a strong immune system, a by-product from working in the hospital." She waited for him to buckle his seat belt before pulling away from the curb. "How was your day?"

"Long. And I have a ton more homework to do when I get home."

"You don't mind stopping for a quick dinner on the way home, do you? I didn't make it to the store today."

"Ugh! Can we at least get it to go? I'm going to be up until midnight as it is."

She shook her head. "Sorry, bud. I need your undivided attention for a few minutes. I have a couple of things I need to talk to you about. I made a reservation at Grace & Grit."

The mention of his new favorite restaurant brought a tentative smile to his face. "I guess it's okay, then, since the service there is usually pretty quick."

She play punched his arm. "You need to take a break from studying anyway, to refuel your mind and your body so you can finish your homework later."

Nell's stomach churned as she took a left onto East Bay Street and headed back toward the bridge. She questioned her decision to break the news to Booker about the divorce in a restaurant. But telling him at home, with just the two of them sitting at the kitchen table, seemed dismal. Besides, her son wasn't the type to cause a scene in a public place regardless of the circumstances. And she planned to soften the blow by telling him about the car first.

Grace & Grit was hopping, with a large crowd of rowdy young professionals taking advantage of the craft beer happy hour at the bar that took up one whole side of the restaurant. They were seated, as Nell had requested, at the red leather banquette adjacent to the wall-size black-and-white image of men and women casting their shrimp nets. The waitress appeared within minutes, and they ordered without looking at the menu—scallops and a glass of Mas Fleurey rosé for her, and the she-crab chowder to start for him with the sweet tea–brined pork chop as his entrée.

Nell waited for his appetizer and her wine to arrive. "Let's start with the good news. I spent the afternoon on the phone with Toyota salespeople about finding you a car."

Booker froze, his soup spoon suspended in midair. "Are you serious?"

She nodded. "You won me over. It's silly for us to wait two more months when we will both benefit from you having the car now."

His eyes lit up like Yankee Stadium. "When can I get it?"

"Hold your horses, cowboy. The salesman warned me that it could take a couple of weeks to find what we're looking for. I have to work this weekend, but I thought we could go out to the dealership for a test-drive early next week."

Forgetting about the spoonful of soup, he tossed his hands in the air. "Oops," he said when the soup splattered on the back of the bench seat behind him. He wiped most of it up with his napkin, leaving traces of she-crab soup smeared across the seat. "Do I get to pick the color?"

"We're not in a position to be picky. We'll take what we can get unless it's a color you absolutely despise. It's more important to find one in good condition with low mileage."

"That makes sense. The color doesn't matter that much to me anyway." He picked his spoon up and lowered it into the soup. "What's the bad news?"

Nell took a big gulp of wine. "There's no way to sugarcoat this, so I'll come right out and say it. Your father and I are getting a divorce."

She watched closely for his reaction, but his face remained impassive.

After a long moment of silence, Booker asked, "Did he leave you, or did you kick him out?"

"We are in mutual agreement on the divorce. He wanted to wait until after graduation to move out of the house, but I couldn't continue to live with him knowing our marriage is over. I'm sorry, son. I know you're disappointed. As am I. I worked hard to make the marriage work."

He pushed his soup bowl away. "He doesn't deserve you, Mama. I love him because he's my father, but he's a womanizer. Why isn't he here with you now? Is he too afraid to look me in the eye and admit he ruined our family?"

Nell was tired of making excuses for Desmond. "I don't know, son. Maybe." She sipped her wine. "As for him ruining our family, he doesn't have that power. You and I are fortunate to have a close relationship. And I promise you, that's not going to change. You mean the world to me, sweetheart."

His posture sagged. "Thanks, Mom. I really needed to hear that right about now."

"We're gonna make it through this, son. The past few years have been hard for you and me. Let's try to put all that behind us and forge onward. I don't know what our new lives will look like just yet, but we'll be able to focus on ourselves without having to constantly worry about him."

CHAPTER SIX

LADY

After breakfast on Thursday morning, Willa dragged a small settee over by the window in the drawing room in anticipation of Nell's visit. Lady made multiple attempts to entice her away from the window. She offered to take her to any number of hot-spot restaurants for lunch, but Willa turned up her nose at all of them. "I'm not hungry for fancy food. Just fix me a scoop of chicken salad and a slice of tomato."

"After we eat, we could walk down to the seawall or take a drive out to Johns Island."

"I'm not leaving the house," Willa said with a determined set of her jaw. "I don't want to miss Nell."

"Why don't you at least move outside to the piazza and get some fresh air?" Her suggestion was met with an icy glare.

As she carried on her household chores that afternoon, Lady invented reasons to enter the drawing room to check on her mother. Willa dozed off and on, but she never left the window. Lady brought her a cup of lemon ginger tea around five o'clock. "Spring is in full bloom today. The birds are chirping pretty as you please. Would you like to walk around the garden for a bit?"

"Stop pestering me, Lady. Go away and leave me in peace," Willa said, shooing her out of the drawing room.

Lady knelt down beside her. "I can't do that, Mama, not when you're so upset. I warned you last night. I don't think Nell's going to come."

"Of course she's not coming!" Willa said in a shrill voice. "If she wanted to see me, she would've come to visit years ago. I blame you, Lady, for turning her against me."

Lady slunk off to her room with her bottle of Tito's and curled up in the wingback in the corner by the window. After her divorce, when she moved back in with her mother, she'd used her own money to redecorate Nell's old room with new carpet and fabrics in shades of gray and pink for Regan. But she'd done little to change her room since she was a girl. The same eyelet comforter, now yellowed with age, covered her bed. Her green carpet was worn in places, and posters of the Rolling Stones and Van Morrison still hung on the pale-pink walls.

She unscrewed the cap from her vodka bottle, brought it to her lips, and took a healthy swig, feeling the burn and relishing the numbness. She was sick of being the scapegoat for Nell's actions and tired of her mother walking all over her like a doormat. If it weren't for Regan . . . well, no point in going down that road, because she would never leave her daughter alone in the world with a father who paid her no attention and an elderly grandmother to take care of. The sun set, and the room grew dark as she took swigs of vodka and considered a way out of her dead-end life. She was blissfully intoxicated when Regan brought her a ham-and-cheese sandwich around eight.

Lady muttered a slurred thank-you as she took the plate from her. When she stepped sideways, away from the door, she tripped over her Dansko clogs, catching herself on the post of the mahogany rice bed. The plate tilted, and the sandwich slid to the floor. "Oopsy daisy." She dropped to her knees, slapped the ham and cheese back on the bread, and smooshed the sandwich down on the plate. With the plate in one hand, bracing herself against the side of the bed for support, she struggled to her feet, staggered to the nightstand, and set the plate down with a clatter beside the vodka bottle. Lady eyed the bottle, the taste of vodka on her lips.

"I think you've had enough," Regan said.

"You're probably right." She collapsed on the bed and fell back against the pillows.

"Here, Mom, let me help you get ready for bed." Regan approached the bed and tugged off her mother's shoes.

Lady kicked her away. "Stop fussing and go do your homework." She rolled over on her side, placing her back to her daughter.

"Why don't I make you a fresh sandwich, one that doesn't have carpet fibers stuck to it," Regan suggested.

"I'm not hungry, sweetheart." Lady waved her off. "Go on now. Leave Mama alone. I'm just gonna rest for a minute before I get ready for bed."

Lady closed her eyes and woke to the sound of floorboards creaking under her mother's weight as she crept downstairs to have tea with Mavis. The room was dark, and her comforter was drawn up over her fully clothed body. *Regan.* Her head throbbed, and her stomach churned. She hadn't eaten anything since breakfast. She blinked her eyes several times until the digital numbers of the alarm clock came into focus. Time noted—2:08. She typically waited twenty minutes before going to the kitchen to help her mother back to bed.

Lady slid open the drawer on her nightstand and fumbled around for the familiar feel of the prescription pill bottle. She unscrewed the lid and swallowed one of the painkillers left over from when Regan had her wisdom teeth out during Christmas break. *That should take care of this awful headache.*

She lay in the dark and watched the minutes click by on the clock. At 2:28 she got up and went downstairs. She followed her mother's voice through the dining room and listened from the shadows of the kitchen doorway. Her one-sided conversation with Mavis was always the same.

"I've let you down, May May. The first years after your death were hard for Nell. She never complained, mind you. But I saw the grief in her eyes. She worked hard in school and helped out around the house. We settled into a comfortable life, and the girls seemed closer than ever. Then something bad happened, and everything changed almost overnight. I know it's unfair of me to blame Lady, but I feel like she's responsible for that bad thing happening. I don't understand what the rift in their friendship has to do with me. Why does Nell dislike me so? Was her life with us that unbearable? If only I could see her one more time to tell her how much I love her and how sorry I am for the way things worked out. I miss her even after all these years. I can't go to my grave in peace until I know what I've done so I can say I'm sorry. I thought if I told her it was my dying wish to see her . . ."

Her mother's voice trailed off, and within minutes Lady heard the sound of soft snoring. She tiptoed into the kitchen, nudged her mother awake, and helped her back upstairs to bed. Returning to her own room, she opened the french doors onto the piazza and stepped out into the balmy night. Moving to the corner of the porch, she stared down the street past the seawall to the harbor where ripples of water shimmered beneath the full moon.

She lit a cigarette and inhaled a deep drag. She had only one cigarette left in her for-times-of-crisis pack, which she'd purchased just three days ago. This business with Nell was dredging up a lot of pain and sorrow that Lady thought she'd worked through years ago.

Her mind drifted back to the months following Mavis's death, when gloom had settled over the house and its inhabitants moved through their days in a daze. Lady had been grateful when Willa agreed not only to allow Nell to live with them but when she'd decided to legally adopt her. Despite her grief over her beloved nanny's death, Lady had been ecstatic when her very best friend in all the world officially became the sister she'd always wanted. But her elation had been short-lived. Her mother had never criticized her before, but suddenly Willa began measuring Lady's own mediocre performance in school against Nell's academic success. Lady had always been average at everything—academics, athletics, extracurricular activities. Her appearance had been the only positive thing she had going for her back then. And she'd used her good looks to entice the most eligible bachelor in Charleston to marry her. She'd never loved him. She'd figured that out by the time they'd returned from their honeymoon in Bermuda. Why had she married him? To please her mother? Or to spite Nell? Regan was the only good thing that had come from her marriage.

Tension in the house had been at an all-time high when Lady and Nell left for college. Lady had been secretly relieved when Nell didn't come home that first Thanksgiving and Christmas. And she'd been even more relieved when Nell hadn't invited them to her graduation four years later.

Every afternoon for weeks, Willa had waited for the mailman, much like she'd waited by the window today. Her mother had never waited for Lady for anything. Willa had refused to accept that Nell had purposely opted not to send them an invitation to her graduation, especially when she'd partially funded those four years of education. Confident the invitation had gotten lost in the mail and in spite of Lady's protest, her mother had insisted they attend the graduation anyway. Lady, ever such the dutiful daughter, had gone along with Willa. But she'd dreaded watching Nell march down the aisle in her cap and gown, dreaded even more listening to her mother sing Nell's praises and criticize Lady for dropping out of college after her junior year.

CHAPTER SEVEN

LADY

1987

The trip to Atlanta for Nell's graduation was doomed from the start. Twenty miles outside of town, a radiator hose blew in Willa's sky-blue wood-paneled Buick Estate wagon.

Lady and Willa stood on the side of the highway, watching steam billow out from under the hood. "It's god-awful hot out today," Willa said, blotting the sweat from her brow with her linen handkerchief. "I should've known something like this would happen."

"The temperature outside has nothing to do with our blown radiator hose. You bought this land yacht the same year I was born. It has long since been ready for the car graveyard."

"Don't be ridiculous, Lady. Bertha is a 1974 model, only thirteen years old, which is new by my standards." Willa stroked the front side fender of the car where it wasn't too hot to touch. "This land yacht and I have been through a lot together, and she still has plenty of good years left."

"Oh, for Pete's sake, Willa. It's a car, not a person." Lady turned her back on her mother and started off in the direction they'd come.

"Where're you going, Lady? You can't leave me standing here all alone."

"I'm going to use the pay phone at the convenience store we passed a half mile back." Lady walked backward while she spoke to her mother. "I'll call a yellow cab for us and a tow truck for your Bertha. Don't talk to strangers, and whatever you do, don't hitchhike."

"Make sure you contact a reputable company," Willa called after her. "I don't want anything to happen to her."

The tow truck arrived ahead of the taxi. After hooking up the wagon to his truck, with still no sign of the taxi, the driver offered them a lift home.

Willa scrutinized the driver. "Maybe we should wait . . ."

"Do you want to make it to graduation in time or what? Come on." Lady took her mother by the hand and helped her climb into the front seat of the tow truck.

The driver dropped them at home on his way to deliver Bertha to the filling station down the road for repairs. After watching them go, Willa and Lady jumped into Lady's orange VW Bug and chugged off down the street.

"My air conditioner's broken," Lady said with a sideways glance at her mother's linen church suit. "You might want to take your jacket off. I warned you it was going to be a hot day. You should've worn a sundress like me."

Willa deviated from her hippie attire only for church, garden club meetings, weddings, and funerals. And the occasional graduation. Lady approved of her bubblegum-pink linen suit. She looked like a real mother for a change.

Willa smoothed out the fabric of the skirt. "I'll be fine." But within minutes she was tugging off her suit jacket and complaining, "Why didn't you get the air-conditioning fixed in this dag-blasted tin can you call a car?"

"Because you refused to pay for it, remember?" Lady said, her mouth pursed in a self-satisfied smirk.

"You need to get a job, Lady. Or go back to school and finish your degree. At this rate, you'll never find a man willing to marry you."

Lady shot her a dirty look. "What's that supposed to mean? Am I that ugly?"

"I'm suggesting you need to make something of your life. No man wants a woman who lies around the house all day. And I haven't seen too many vying for your affections lately. And don't be ridiculous. You know you're not ugly." Willa grazed her fingers against Lady's cheek. "You're quite lovely, actually, the spitting image of me when I was your age."

Lady shook her head at her mother's conceit. "Let's roll down our windows. Maybe that will help."

They rolled the windows down and made the five-hour trip with hot air whipping through the car. They arrived at Spelman College with only minutes to spare. With no time to run to the restroom, they freshened up as best they could in the car. Taking turns with the rearview mirror, Willa tugged her messy hair free of its braid, raked her hands through it, and fastened it at the nape of her neck into a loose bun. Lady smeared mauve-colored lipstick on her lips, brushed stray blonde locks off her forehead, and wiped road grime from her face with Willa's handkerchief.

"You've ruined my handkerchief, Lady!" Willa opened the wooden handles of her Lilly Pulitzer Bermuda bag and dropped the soiled handkerchief inside. "How will I dry my eyes when I cry?"

"Don't cry, and you won't have a problem." Lady climbed out of the car and slammed the door behind her.

A multitude of folding metal chairs were set up on the lawn in front of the school's chapel. An usher handed them a program and showed them to the two remaining vacant seats in the last row. For the next two hours, as they baked in the midday sun, they saw nothing and heard little until the end when the crowd roared every time a graduate's name was called. Willa moved to the edge of her seat, clapping and cheering like a proud mama when Nell's name was announced.

Lady examined her sunburned shoulders during the closing remarks. She leaned close to her mother and whispered, "Can we go soon? We have a long drive home, and I'm fried to a crisp."

"Not until I've seen Nell. I have a present for her." Willa removed a small box wrapped in silver paper from her Bermuda bag.

When the graduates began recessing down the aisle, Lady stood and held a hand out to her mother, pulling her to her feet. "Let's make it fast, then. What'd you buy her anyway?" she asked as they fell in line behind the last of the graduates.

"I didn't buy her anything. I'm giving her your grandmother's pearl earrings."

Lady's stomach hardened. "Those earrings are mine, Mother. Granna left them to me."

"She left you the pearl studs, sweetheart. I'm giving her the tear-drops, the ones she left to me."

In Lady's mind, regardless of what was written in any will, her grandmother's jewelry rightfully belonged to her. Lady was Granna Bellemore's namesake and the reason her parents had decided to call her Lady. According to Willa, when Lady was born, Granna had complained, "Two Adelaides is too confusing," but secretly she'd been pleased to have her granddaughter carry on her name. Granna had died when Lady was only eight, years before Willa adopted Nell.

Lady struggled to keep up with her mother as she squeezed through the crowd. She spotted Nell clustered with a group of her classmates. Nell's face fell when she saw Willa and Lady from afar. She left her friends and made her way over to them. "What are you doing here?"

Willa held her head high and her shoulders back. "We came for your graduation, of course. Our invitation never arrived. The mail delivery is so unreliable these days. I called the school, and they told me the date and time."

Nell stared down at the black graduation cap in her hands. "The invitation didn't get lost. I never sent you one. But there's a reason for that."

Willa appeared stricken. "I don't understand. We're your family. Why wouldn't you want us here with you to celebrate your big day?"

"I thought you might feel uncomfortable," Nell said.

Willa's eyes narrowed and then grew wide again. "Oh, you mean because we're the only white folks here. You know that kind of thing doesn't bother me. Here." She thrust the gift-wrapped box at her. "These belonged to my mother. I hope you like them."

Nell ignored the present. "It's awfully hot out here. Why don't we go inside where it's cool so we can talk in private?" She turned away from them and walked off.

Willa and Lady followed her across the lawn to the student center, where long tables of refreshments awaited the graduates and their guests. Lady helped herself to a cup of punch.

"You're not supposed to drink that," Nell said. "The reception hasn't started yet."

Lady lifted the cup to her lips and downed the punch. "Sorry, but I'm thirsty. We drove for five hours with no air-conditioning and have been sitting in the sun for the last two hours."

Nell returned her attention to Willa. "I'm seeing someone, Miss Willa, a medical student. And . . . well, it's serious between us."

"How wonderful for you. I'd like to meet him. Is he here?" Willa stood on her tiptoes as she surveyed the graduates and guests who were flowing into the building.

Lady grabbed her mother by the elbow. "You're embarrassing yourself, Willa. You don't even know who you're looking for."

"He's not here. He had to work. Why don't we move out of the way?" Nell steered them to a far corner of the room, away from the crowd. "He doesn't know about y'all."

Confusion crossed Willa's face. "What do you mean, he doesn't know about us?"

"He knows my mother died when I was fourteen and that I've been living with my adopted family, but—"

"He doesn't know your adopted family is white," Lady said, finishing her sentence.

Nell looked away, unable to meet her gaze.

"What are you trying to tell us, Nell?" Willa asked. "Are you saying you don't want us to be a part of your life anymore?"

"I'm not sure what I want, honestly. It's complicated. I've finally found happiness with Desmond. He's my future. I consider him my family now."

In a desperate voice, Willa said, "Please, Nell, I'm begging you. Don't shut us out. We need to have ourselves a big heart-to-heart talk. I realize things haven't been good between you and Lady for a long time. But we can work it out, whatever it is."

"It's not just that. Although that's part of it." Nell turned her golden eyes on Lady for the first time all day. The hurt and anger were still present, raw as ever.

"Can't we at least try?" Lady said in a soft voice to the young woman who had once been her dearest friend. "I'd like to know what it is that I did to you."

"None of that matters now. It's all in the past, and I want to focus on the future." Nell opened her arms to Willa and gave her a warm hug. "I don't mean to sound ungrateful, Willa. I appreciate everything you've done for me. You've way more than fulfilled your obligation to Mama. I just think it's time for all of us to move on with our separate lives."

~

During the months that followed Nell's graduation, Willa slipped into a deep depression, akin to the one she'd suffered after Mavis's death. She neglected her garden and refused to eat. She'd lost ten pounds by the end of that first summer. She transitioned through the phases of grief—denial, anger, bargaining, depression, and acceptance. It was during the anger phase that she packed away every shred of evidence that Nell had ever lived in their house. For years, she refused to speak or hear Nell's name. She softened around the time her insomnia started, and Lady suspected that her mother's one-sided teatime conversations with Mavis helped her come to terms with the truth. That Nell was never coming back, but that it was not Willa's fault. It was Lady's.

CHAPTER EIGHT

NELL

Three consecutive days of twelve-hour shifts, nursing sick and dying patients, exhausted and disheartened Nell. The following Monday afternoon, she picked Booker up from the library and sped across the bridge toward Mount Pleasant. They were both tired and weary, and neither of them spoke until they arrived home. Booker entered the house ahead of her. "What the heck?" she heard him say. "Mom, I think we've been robbed."

Nell pushed him out of the way and plunked her bag down on the kitchen counter. Any love she still felt for Desmond turned to hate as she surveyed what remained of their home. "We haven't been robbed, son. Your father came to claim his things."

Desmond had taken the most valuable pieces from their collection of art and antiques—the heavy brass candlesticks from the mantel, rowing oars from above the french doors, and the most valuable paintings—and left them with glaring blank spaces on the walls and shelves.

A sympathetic friend from work who had used a divorce attorney several years ago had given the attorney's contact information to Nell. While she rummaged through the contents of her bag for the business card, Booker paced from room to room, reciting a commentary on every item his father had removed from the house.

Standing by the window staring out at the dock, he said, "I'm not surprised he took the *Miss Vivian*. He loves that boat more than he loves me. Do you think he left the skiff for me, or do you think he's planning to come back for it later?"

Nell sighed. "I have no idea, son."

He turned away from the window. "He took the painting of the farm in McClellanville," Booker said as he passed by the fireplace. "I loved that painting."

Without looking up from her purse, Nell said, "Me too, sweetheart. It was my favorite."

Booker stuck his head in Desmond's study. "He cleaned everything out of here, including the TV!" He returned to the kitchen and plopped down on a barstool. "What a jerk."

"Here it is," Nell said under her breath when she located the business card in her wallet.

She opened a bottle of pinot noir, poured herself a glass, and slid onto the barstool next to her son. She placed the business card on the counter in front of her and tapped out the number on the shattered screen of her cell phone.

"Who're you calling?" Booker asked.

"A divorce attorney that a friend from work told me about. I should've called her days ago." Nell reached Tabitha Fox's voice mail and left a detailed message, explaining the situation and requesting a return call at her earliest convenience.

"I'll have the locks changed first thing in the morning," she said to Booker when she ended the call.

"It's too late. He's already taken everything that's worth anything."

She couldn't argue with his logic. She took a gulp of wine instead. "What say we order pizza for dinner?"

His head shot up. "Really? Can we?"

Despite the long hours she worked at the hospital, Nell rarely consented to ordering takeout. She prided herself on providing her family a home-cooked meal nearly every single night and insisted they dine together at the table, sans cell phones. "As long as you place the order and pay the deliveryman when he gets here."

"Deal." Booker retrieved his computer from his backpack and opened it on the counter in front of him. "Is Tommy Tello's okay?"

"Anything's fine with me."

Booker's fingers flew across the keyboard as he accessed the website and reviewed the online menu for the Italian restaurant.

Nell didn't think Desmond capable of stooping to a level so low. Her soon-to-be ex-husband had done some rotten things during their married life, but stripping their home of their most valuable possessions, items they'd purchased with money from both their incomes, won the prize. Her heart had finally, mercifully, hardened toward Desmond. She felt liberated, ready to embrace her future, even if she wasn't quite ready to face the past.

An idea came to her, and she reached for Booker's computer.

"Hey, Mom. What're you doing? I'm not finished ordering yet."

"I just need to check something." She signed on to her bank's website and checked the available balance in their joint checking account. She signed off and slid the computer back toward her son. "I'm off tomorrow. If you can drag yourself away from the library, why don't we drive out to the Toyota place and see if the dealer's made any headway in finding you a 4Runner. We can test-drive a new model while we're there, to be certain that's what you want."

"Duh, Mom. I can totally drag myself away from the library for that."

~

With the breakup of her marriage, Nell had been thinking a lot about family in the past week. And seeing Lady in the parking garage had triggered a lot of memories, good ones as well as bad. She argued with her conscience for much of Tuesday until her conscience finally won out. There was no harm in going to see Willa. What threat did an old lady with cancer, a patient like the ones she tended every day, pose to Nell?

She went about her chores with heightened anticipation. Time had softened her toward Willa, and she found herself looking forward to reconnecting with her adopted mother. But how would she explain her relationship with the Bellemores to Booker after all the lies she'd told him about her upbringing? Perhaps she wouldn't be forced to confess the truth. Was that what she really wanted? She wasn't sure. She was tired of running from her past.

The divorce attorney returned her call in the late morning while the technician from the locksmith company was changing out her locks. Tabitha assured her that changing the locks was the right thing to do. "From now on, he'll need to seek permission to enter your home."

Nell opted not to tell the divorce attorney her plans for purchasing Booker's car for fear she might advise against it.

Tabitha sounded friendly but professional, a person Nell could confide in. She graciously agreed to meet on Nell's turf to accommodate her short lunch break. They set up a meeting for Thursday at noon in the hospital cafeteria.

She was waiting for Booker in front of the school when the final bell rang. "Orlando Holland, the Toyota salesman, has another appointment and can't meet with us until five," she explained when he got in the car. "I'm going to make a stop on the way since we have some extra time to kill."

She drove through the familiar streets of downtown Charleston and pulled up in front of the gray house on Water Street she'd once thought of as home.

"Who lives here?" Booker asked.

She considered how to respond. Lady and Willa were more than old friends. They were her adopted family. She'd have to save that conversation with her son for a more convenient time.

"An elderly woman I once knew who now has cancer." She turned off the car and opened her door. "This shouldn't take too long. Do you have some homework to occupy your time?"

"Sure," he said, unzipping his backpack at his feet. "I have to read three chapters for English. But hurry. I don't want to be late for our appointment at the Toyota place."

Nell got out of the car and approached the house. When the doorbell failed to ring, she banged on the knocker. She heard the pounding of feet on the stairs, and seconds later, Lady appeared at the door.

"I'm surprised you came," Lady said, slightly out of breath.

"I can't stay long. My son is waiting in the car."

Lady looked past her to her car. "You're welcome to invite him in. I'm sure Willa would like to meet him."

What about you, Lady? Would you like to meet my son? she thought but held her tongue. "Not today. He has homework. Maybe another time."

"That's probably for the best," Lady said. "Willa had a treatment today. She's not feeling a hundred percent."

"Why don't I come back another time, then?" Nell turned to leave, but Lady grabbed her by the arm. "No! Don't go. She'd never forgive me if I let you leave." Lady moved out of the way so Nell could enter the house.

"Okay, but only for a minute. I don't want to tire her out." Nell crossed the threshold and stepped back in time three decades. Little appeared to have changed in the house since she was last there. The white paint on the walls had yellowed, and the rugs were more threadbare, if that was even possible of the ancient Orientals. The same portrait of a regal-looking woman hung above the fireplace in the drawing room. *Who is that woman?* A distant relative on Willa's side of the family? Nell could never keep the woman's connection to the Bellemores straight. She doubted Lady knew who she was. Or if Willa even knew. Odd how people kept paintings of strangers in their home.

She followed Lady up the stairs and down the hall to Willa's room at the front of the house facing the street. The years fell away as Nell stood beside the bed of her adopted mother. The patches of gray hair left were pulled back in her ever-present braid, and those same penetrating blue eyes peered out from beneath saggy lids in a wrinkled face. Tears flooded those eyes when she saw Nell. There was no blame in them, only questions.

Willa's body tensed, and she reached for the kidney-shaped emesis basin. She heaved into the basin, but there was no vomit. Nell understood pain. She witnessed patients suffering every single day.

"On a scale of one to ten, how's your pain?" Nell asked.

"I don't have any pain. I just feel like I need to throw my toenails up." Willa heaved again. "As you can see, there's nothing left in my stomach to come out."

Nell went into the adjoining bathroom and soaked a washcloth with cold water. Returning to the bed, she pressed the cloth against the back of Willa's neck. "What kind of cancer is it?"

"Non–small cell," Lady answered, pulling up a seat on the opposite side of the bed. "Adenocarcinoma. She had the diseased portion surgically removed from her lung a month ago."

"Then the prognosis is good," Nell said from experience.

Willa's arthritic fingers gripped Nell's forearm. "I'm dying, Nell. I feel it in my bones. The good Lord is finally calling me home."

"She thinks she's dying," Lady said, massaging her temples. "The doctors say otherwise."

Nell lowered herself to the side of the bed. "Now, Miss Willa, don't go checking out on us just yet. You've got plenty to live for."

Willa managed a weak smile. "I do now that you're here. I can't tell you how happy I am to see you, my darling girl."

"And I'm happy to see you as well. It's been far too long." Nell's eyes met Lady's. "I don't remember if you said. Are you living here in the house?"

Lady nodded, but she didn't volunteer any additional information.

"How fortunate for you to have Lady with you," she said to Willa. "Do you have any grandchildren running around?" She was ashamed to admit she didn't know whether Lady had ever married, let alone had children.

"I'm divorced and have one child," Lady said. "A daughter, Regan. She's a senior in high school."

Nell's eyes grew wide. "At All Saints?"

Lady frowned. "You seem surprised. Have you forgotten that I went to school at All Saints?"

"Of course not," Nell said. "But unless there's more than one brilliant girl in the senior class named Regan, your daughter and my son, Booker, are friends. I assume they're friends anyway. I know they're in constant competition for the best grades."

"Such a small world," Lady said with a soft smile. "Regan talks about Booker all the time."

Willa's face lit up, and she pushed away the emesis basin. "How wonderful that your two children have become friends all on their own. And you're right. The competition between them is intense, as Regan says."

"I can't believe we haven't run into each other at school before now," Nell said. "In the carpool line at least. I'm embarrassed to say, I've never attended a parents' association meeting. They always seem to schedule them during the morning hours while I'm at work."

"Regan walks to school every day, which is why we've never seen each other in the carpool line," Lady said. "As for the parents' association, I've been to a few meetings. Two of them, if anyone's counting. And I can tell you, you're not missing much—all those mothers talking about their perfect children."

The animosity between them slipped away, and they fell into a relaxed conversation about senior year and college applications. Nell felt as though she was talking not to the young woman she'd grown to despise but the girl she'd loved like a sister. As it was with her patients who experienced intense physical pain, the mind, over time, had a way of erasing the bad and remembering only the good.

Nell found herself wondering about Lady's life. Why was she living with her mama? What had happened in her marriage that led to divorce? Did she have a career? It was too early in their reunion to ask such personal questions, and she sensed a reluctance in Lady to share details about her life. So she limited their conversation to safe topics like gardening and all the new restaurants opening in Charleston. She was content just to be in their presence, to witness the interaction between Willa and Lady. Their relationship had transitioned over the years. They were more like an old married couple than mother and daughter, picking at each other and finishing each other's sentences.

Nell had been there for thirty minutes when she heard murmured voices in the hall downstairs and stood to leave. "I should go. Booker is waiting for me in the car."

Willa reached for her hand. "Will you come back to see me?"

Nell smiled down at her. "I'd like that."

"When?" Willa pressed.

"I'd forgotten how determined you are," Nell said with a chuckle. "Saturday is my next day off. Does that work for you?"

"Saturday is lovely," Willa said. "You promise you'll come?"

She offered a firm nod. "I promise."

"And bring Booker with you?"

Nell worked hard to keep a straight face. That was a can of worms she wasn't yet ready to open. "We'll have to see about that." She patted Willa's hand. "You hang in there now, Miss Willa. You'll feel better once you get these treatments behind you. Think about how much fun you'll have regaining the weight you've lost. And if you're lucky, your hair will grow back curly."

Willa's hand flew to her head. "That would be a welcome relief. I know I should shave off this mess, but I can't bring myself to go to the beauty parlor. I can't bear having those women staring at me with pity."

Nell smiled at her. "In that case, I'll bring my clippers with me when I come on Saturday."

CHAPTER NINE

REGAN

Regan approached the Mercedes parked on the street in front of her house with curiosity. The only person she knew who drove a Mercedes was her father, and his graphite-gray sedan sported Illinois tags. She turned toward the house and then stopped in her path. Was that Booker in the passenger seat? She looked closer. The boy's face was partially hidden by the book he was reading, but she could tell from the shape of his head and curve of his neck that it was definitely Booker. What could he possibly be doing at her house?

She tapped on the car window. Startled at first, he shrank back, but then he recognized her and swung his car door open. "What're you doing here?"

"I live here," she said. "What're you doing here?"

He stuffed his book in his backpack and stepped out of the car onto the sidewalk. "You live in *that* house right there?" he asked, pointing at her house.

"Yes, Booker. What house do you think I'm talking about? You're parked right out in front of my house. Besides, you can't even see the neighbors' house through the bushes."

He craned his neck as he tried to see through the overgrown hedgerows on either side. "Oh. Right. My mother is visiting some old lady with cancer who lives in that house. I guess that would be your grandmother."

Regan nodded. "She's the only elderly woman on the street with cancer."

"That's an eerie coincidence, don't you think?"

She considered the possibilities before responding. "Maybe not. Your mother's a nurse. I bet they met in the hospital when Willa had her lung surgery last month."

"Except that Mom's patients all have kidney disease. Hmm . . . I love a good mystery," Booker said, rubbing his chin.

"In that case, Sherlock, why don't we go inside and find out how they know each other. I'm thirsty anyway. Do you want some lemonade?"

"Sure," he said, and followed her up the sidewalk, across the piazza, and into the house. He stopped short when they arrived at the kitchen. "Cool! A retro theme."

Regan slid her backpack off her shoulder and let it drop to the floor beside the door. "You're looking at the real deal, Booker, not a theme. My grandmother doesn't like change. She and my grandfather had this kitchen installed when they remodeled the house right after they were married in 1954."

Booker nodded his approval. "That's cool. A vintage kitchen. I bet these walls have seen some stuff."

Regan poured two glasses of lemonade from the pitcher in the refrigerator and handed one to Booker. "I'm sure they have."

Booker lifted the glass to his lips. "Do you think our mothers met somehow? Maybe through our school?"

"Maybe," Regan said, pressing the cool glass to her cheek. "But my mother's not involved with any of the parents' association stuff at school."

"Neither is mine. She's too busy at the hospital." Booker's eyebrows danced across his forehead as though he were solving a calculus problem. "I assume they're about the same age. My mom's fifty-three."

"Same as mine."

"Mine's originally from Charleston. What about yours?"

"Born and raised." Regan set her glass of lemonade down on the counter and removed the lid from a metal food tin. She offered Booker a cheese biscuit. "Want one?"

"Sure." He removed a biscuit from the tin and held the silver dollar–size biscuit, coated in powdered sugar with a pecan pressed in the center, close to his face for inspection. "It's not like a real biscuit."

"I know. It's intended for snacking, not to be served with a meal."

He stuffed the whole biscuit into his mouth at once. "This is good," he said, spitting out crumbs. "Did your mom make them?"

"Not hardly. My mom's a terrible cook. So is my grandmother." Regan nibbled at a biscuit. "I made them. I found the recipe card, labeled May May's Cheese Biscuits, stuck at the way back of the junk drawer. I think they're pretty good, if I say so myself, but Willa, my grandmother, claims mine aren't as good as May May's."

"Who's May May?" Booker asked, reaching for the cookie tin.

Regan shrugged. "Some housekeeper who used to work for them a long time ago."

"Maybe our mothers went to school together."

She laughed out loud. "I don't get it, Booker. Why do you care so much how they know each other?"

"Because my mom has a thing against white people. No offense, Regan, I'm sure she'd love you."

Regan's face grew warm. That surprised her about his mom since Booker was the most unprejudiced person she knew. Now her curiosity was piqued. "Surely your mom has white patients at the hospital."

"Of course. She's fine with them in a professional capacity. But all of her nurse friends are black."

"You know, come to think of it, my mother doesn't have any black friends that I can think of either." She heard footsteps on the stairs. "Why don't we just ask them how they know each other?"

Regan had often wondered about Booker's parents, the successful anesthesiologist and his nurse wife, but Mrs. Grady was nothing like what she'd expected. While Booker's pointy features matched his abrasive personality, his mother's face was soft and beautiful with unusual golden eyes.

Introductions were made around the room. "Whoa," Booker said when Regan's mother introduced herself as Lady Bellemore. "I've never met royalty before."

Nell nudged him with her elbow. "Lady is a nickname. Her given name is Adelaide."

Regan raised a brow at Booker. That was not something a casual acquaintance would know about Lady. Addie and Dell were the more popular nicknames for Adelaide.

Booker turned to his mother. "How is it the two of you know each other?"

Regan studied her mother's face as she waited for Mrs. Grady to respond. Lady wore her ever-present mask of cheerfulness to hide her sadness, but an unidentified emotion was etched in her frown lines and pinched lips. Was it discontent? Did she disapprove of Booker's mother for some reason?

"We knew each other when we were young, a lifetime ago. What time is it?" Mrs. Grady's golden eyes sought out the wall clock that was partially hidden by a rack of copper pots.

How is it she knows right where to find the clock? wondered Regan.

Mrs. Grady tugged on her son's elbow. "We should go. It's almost four o'clock."

Booker's body tensed. "We need to hurry." He drained the last of his lemonade and handed the glass to Regan. "Sorry to drink and run. We have a five o'clock appointment in West Ashley."

Whatever or whoever awaited Booker's attention in West Ashley was suddenly more important than their mothers' curious relationship. Regan and Lady walked their visitors to the door.

"See you tomorrow, Booker," Regan said.

He saluted her. "Sure thing. Thanks for the lemonade and cheese biscuits."

"Mom's counting on you for Saturday," Lady said to Nell. "She'll be disappointed if you don't come."

"I'll be here," Nell said in a cheerful voice.

"Why's she coming back on Saturday?" Regan asked as they watched Booker and his mother walk arm in arm to their car.

Lady closed the storm door. "She promised to visit Willa again."

"I don't understand any of this, Mom. Who is she to you?"

"Nell already explained that. We knew each other when we were young."

"I know what she said. Does that mean you were friends?"

Lady hesitated. "In a manner of speaking. Ironic, isn't it?"

"Hard to believe is more like it. You grew up in the seventies and eighties. At the risk of sounding like a racist, I can't see you being friends with too many—"

"Not all my friends came from privileged white families, Regan." Lady started off toward the kitchen. Over her shoulder, she said, "Your grandmother had a difficult day. Go up and check on her while I start dinner."

"Fine! Maybe she'll tell me what I wanna know," she mumbled to herself as she hustled up the stairs.

The stench of vomit burned Regan's nose when she entered her grandmother's room. "How're you feeling, Willa? Can I get you anything?"

Willa offered her a weak smile. "No, sweetheart. I'm okay for now. But you can sit and talk to me a spell."

"Do you mind if I open the doors?" Regan asked, one hand already on the doorknob. "It's stuffy in here."

"That'd be lovely, dear."

Regan threw open the french doors onto the piazza, letting in the cool salt-infused spring air.

Willa folded her arms on top of her comforter. "Now, tell me about your day."

She plopped down in the rocker beside her grandmother's bed. "So . . . you know my friend Booker, right? That guy in my class I'm always talking about who gets the same grades as me? Well, it turns out his mom and mine were friends growing up. But I'm guessing you already knew this. Seems like everyone knew it except Booker and me."

"Don't get sassy on me now, missy," Willa said, her face suddenly serious. "No one realized the connection between you and Booker until today. We haven't seen Nell in many years."

Regan fell back in her seat. "Why, though? That's what I'm asking. If Mom and Mrs. Grady were such good friends, why has it been so long since you've seen her? What's the big mystery?"

"Is that what they told you, that they were good friends?" Willa asked, picking a piece of lint off her blanket.

"Mrs. Grady said they knew each other when they were growing up, but she knew about Mom's nickname and exactly where to find the wall clock like she's been in this house many times before."

"Nell is a very private person, Regan. Our relationship with her is . . . well, it's difficult to explain. I'm not sure how much she's told Booker about us."

"He knows as much as I do. Nothing."

Her grandmother rolled her head away from Regan and stared out the window at the palmetto fronds rustling in the breeze. Several moments of silence passed before she spoke. "Nell's mother, Mavis, was our housekeeper. She had a stroke and died in my kitchen when Nell and Lady were only fourteen years old."

"Wait, what?" Regan sat straight up in her seat. "That's the saddest thing I've ever heard."

A faraway look settled on Willa's face. "I still remember the day. I was horrified when I arrived home from a garden club meeting to find paramedics loading poor Mavis into an ambulance in my driveway. Nell and I followed the ambulance to the hospital. Mavis was gone by the time we arrived. We were all heartbroken—Nell, Lady, me. Nell and Lady are the same age, only four months apart. Mavis and I raised our girls together like they were sisters." She let out a little laugh. "Although, truth be told, Mavis did most of the raising. She had more patience than me, a much better mother than I ever was. Not only was she my housekeeper, she was your mother's nanny and my best friend."

Willa set her blue eyes on Regan. "Nell had no other family—no father or grandparents or siblings—and no place to go. Lady begged for Nell to live with us. I was skeptical at first, but it didn't take long for me to realize it was the right thing to do. It's what Mavis would've done. The adoption was my idea. I wanted Nell to know how much I loved her and how committed I was to her."

"Hold on a minute." Regan leaned in close to Willa. "Are you saying you adopted Nell? Like she's part of our family?"

"That's exactly what I'm saying. Nell refused to change her name, though, and I went along with her on that. I understood she needed to retain some sort of connection to her mother. She seemed content with the arrangement. At least for a time."

Regan shook her head to clear it. "I'm so confused. If she's your adopted daughter, how come I never knew about her? Why doesn't she spend Thanksgiving or Christmas with us? Isn't that what families do?"

"Because something changed in Nell during the years following her mother's death. By the time she graduated from college, she wanted to move on with her life without us."

Regan furrowed her brow. "What changed?"

"That's the question I've been asking your mother for thirty-some-odd years. And I've yet to get a straight answer from her."

Regan jumped to her feet. "I'm gonna find out."

Willa's arm shot out, and she grabbed hold of Regan's hand with surprising strength. "No, Regan, stop! You'll only make things worse if you start poking around in their business. Nell came to see me today, and she promised to come back on Saturday. After all this time, we're finally talking again. If we bring up the past, we'll scare her off. Please, I beg you. This means so much to me."

Her grandmother's expression was one of desperation when only a minute ago, when she'd been speaking of Nell, her blue eyes had been alive and her face soft with love. Regan sank back down in her seat. She wouldn't be the one to take that away from her.

"You can't mention any of this to Booker," Willa said. "Let his mother tell him what she wants him to know."

Regan knew Booker would pester his mother until he got his answers, and Booker, in turn, would be all too eager to share his findings with Regan. She tried to put herself in Nell's shoes. She couldn't imagine being an orphan at the vulnerable age of fourteen. Even though she and her mother weren't that close, Regan would be crushed if something happened to Lady.

"All right, Willa. I'll let Booker figure this out on his own." She rose slowly. "I'm going to help Mom with dinner. Can I get you anything before I go?"

"No, thanks. But be a dear and close the door." Willa snuggled deeper beneath the covers. "It's chilly in here."

She closed the french doors, tucked the duvet cover around her grandmother, and kissed her forehead. "I'll bring your dinner on a tray when it's ready."

Regan found her mother in the kitchen with her hands in a bowl of ground beef, a half-full martini glass and an empty metal shaker on the counter beside her.

"Meatloaf?" Regan removed a paring knife from the knife block and began dicing an onion.

"Mm-hmm. How much did Willa tell you?"

"Enough." She wiped onion tears from her eyes with the back of her hand. "I can't imagine how hard it was for you when Mavis died."

"It was awful. I'd lost my father two years beforehand, but I wasn't that close to him. Losing Mavis was so much worse. Poor Nell was never the same. Even though we didn't part on the best of terms, seeing her here again in this house after all these years has brought back a lot of memories. I've never had another friend like Nell. I didn't realize just how much I'd missed her."

Tears that had nothing to do with onions glistened in her mother's eyes. Whatever happened between Nell and Lady was so painful it had kept the family apart for all those years despite their obvious love for one another. And they did love one another. She'd witnessed it on all three of their faces that afternoon.

CHAPTER TEN

LADY

Lady sat in the swing on the piazza after dinner, a copy of Pat Conroy's *The Prince of Tides* open beside her and a glass of wine in her hand. She could smell the low tide and hear the waves crashing against the seawall. The visit with Nell that afternoon had brought back bittersweet memories from a time in Lady's life when her bond with Nell had been the strongest. Before Mavis died. Before Daniel.

Draining the last of her wine, she set her glass down on the porch railing, rested her head against the back of the swing, and allowed her mind to drift back to another lifetime.

Lady's father died on an Indian summer day in early October of 1977. Lady was twelve years old at the time. His death had little impact on the everyday running of the household. He was a generous provider and wonderful entertainer when he chose to bestow his attention upon his wife and daughter. He was a man's man living in a man's world. He worked long hours as an investment banker and spent what little spare time he had playing golf and sailing his boat. Nevertheless, his absence created a void in their lives. With Thanksgiving and Christmas on the horizon, Lady and Willa had been brainstorming ways to change their holiday traditions and routines to lessen the impact of that absence. Willa had proposed a last-minute trip to New York, but all the hotels were booked, and she wasn't willing to fork over the money for the exorbitant airline tickets. Lady had suggested eating Thanksgiving dinner at one of the restaurants in town, but her mother insisted they have a home-cooked meal.

"I have the perfect solution," Willa announced at supper one night during the second week of November. "We won't be able to avoid the unavoidable. We're going to miss Patrick no matter where we eat. We'll have Thanksgiving here as usual, but this year, I'd like for you"—she locked eyes with Mavis—"and Nell to join us in the dining room."

Mavis shook her head with vehemence. "Oh no, Miss Willa. That ain't proper."

"I don't see why not. We eat supper together at this table every night. Anyway, since when do I care about being proper?"

Because her father had routinely left the house before dawn and rarely made it home in time for supper, Lady and Nell, from the time they were small children, had taken their meals with their mamas at the kitchen table.

"But Thanksgiving is different," Mavis countered. "Thanksgiving is family time."

"That's exactly my point. You and Nell *are* family." Willa turned her attention to Lady and Nell. "What do you girls think of the idea?"

"I like it," Nell said with a smile.

"I think you're right," Lady said. "It *is* the perfect solution. Having Nell and Mavis eat with us will help soften the blow of not having Daddy here." Thanksgiving and Christmas had been two of the few times she counted on her father being home. No matter what city they were in or who they dined with, she would still miss her father.

Willa grabbed Mavis's hand. "Please say yes, May May. It'll be fun. We'll make it a group effort. We'll spend the morning cooking in the kitchen, and when everything's ready, we'll enjoy our meal in the dining room. We'll dress casual. And no football allowed."

A reluctant smile spread across Mavis's face. "As long as you promise no football."

As Willa suggested, the foursome spent Thanksgiving morning in the kitchen with the small, grainy television tuned to the Macy's Thanksgiving Day Parade. They basted the turkey, mashed sweet potatoes, and baked two different kinds of pies—pecan and pumpkin. Just before two that afternoon, they gathered around a dining room table set with linens, crystal, and silver. Willa had just finished saying the blessing when the doorbell rang. Lady left the table and opened the door to their next-door neighbor, Mrs. Buckley. Lady had nicknamed her Bucktooth Betty because of her large and protruding front teeth.

"Lady, dear, may I borrow two eggs? I need them for the stuffing. Without thinking, I used all mine in the breakfast casserole this morning."

"Sure! I'll go get them for you."

Bucktooth Betty moved to follow Lady into the kitchen but stopped dead in her tracks when she saw Nell and Mavis seated at the dining room table with Willa.

"Oh my. I didn't mean to interrupt," she said, fidgeting with the string of pearls around her neck. "About those eggs—I just remembered I have another dozen in the basement refrigerator." She backed out of the room and fled the house as though its inhabitants were contagious with the Ebola virus.

"What a ridiculous woman," Willa said. "Sit back down, Lady. Your dinner's getting cold."

No one mentioned Bucktooth Betty's visit for the rest of the day, but the next afternoon, Lady and Nell were coming down from listening to music in Lady's room when they heard voices coming from the drawing room. Recognizing the visitor's voice as Bucktooth Betty's, they crouched out of sight at the top of the stairs and eavesdropped.

"I'm here to tell you, Willa, it's downright shameful the way you treat your help like they are members of your family. If you're not careful, you'll lose your friends. You'll never be invited to another party in this town again."

"For your information, Betty, my help *is* my family, not that it's any of your business. As for my social status, I have more friends in this town than you have weeds in your garden. And, honey, I'm here to tell *you* that you have a whole shit pot of weeds growing in your garden."

"Well . . . I never," Bucktooth Betty said and left the house in a huff.

Willa appeared at the bottom of the stairs. "The nerve of some people."

The girls giggled. Willa had known they were there the whole time.

Nell and Lady raced down the stairs, out the front door, and all the way to the seawall at the end of the street. They huddled together against the cool salty breeze.

"I hate for Miss Willa to lose her friends because of Mama and me," Nell said, her breath warm near Lady's ear. "You heard what Bucktooth Betty said. Miss Willa's never gonna get invited to another party again."

Lady looped her arm through Nell's. "Don't worry, Nell. That's not gonna happen. Mom's family has been part of Charleston society since before the Civil War. I know, because she's told me at least a thousand times. Bucktooth Betty doesn't know what she's talking about. She's from Minnesota or some such place where it's as cold as her heart."

"Wouldn't it be wonderful if we got to pick our families like we pick our friends?"

Lady paused, considering the idea. "If we live our lives according to Willa's rules, we can."

Nell stared out across the harbor, a faraway look in her eyes. "When I was little, I thought our mamas were sisters and you and I were cousins. Your daddy . . . well, I wasn't sure who he was. Their brother, I guess."

"That's funny," Lady said, laughing.

"Seriously, though, I thought that having different colored skin was like having different colored hair."

"I'm sure that's the way God intended it," Lady said. "Too bad old snotty pants Betty doesn't get it."

"Miss Willa has never been anything but kind to Mama and me."

"That's because she loves you. And Mavis is her best friend."

Nell shifted toward her. "That's my point, though. Old Bucktooth Betty would never be friends with her help."

"She might if Mavis was her maid. Your mama is a special person. Everyone who knows her loves her."

"Humph! Everyone but Bucktooth."

"Don't take it personally, Nell. Mrs. Buckley wasn't criticizing you and Mavis. She was attacking my mother."

They were quiet for a few minutes as they watched a flock of ducks fly by overhead. Several clusters of people were walking along the seawall, exercising after a day of feasting.

"Do you ever miss your father?" Lady asked.

Nell rolled her brown eyes. "That's a stupid question. How can I miss him when I never knew him?"

Lady nudged her. "You know what I mean. Do you want to meet him, to find out who he is and where he lives?" She'd asked Nell many times before about her father but had never gotten much of an answer.

Nell slumped her shoulders. "Not really. Mama refuses to talk about him. I get the impression he isn't a nice person. If I could meet anybody in my family, I'd like to meet my grandmother."

"Why's that?"

"Because grandmamas spoil their grandchildren. Like your grandmother spoiled you."

Lady smiled as she remembered her maternal grandmother. Granna had been a character, much like her daughter. Lady came from a long line of interesting and strong-minded women, a line that had reached a dead end when she was born.

Nell continued, "I love Mama so much, I'm curious about her parents, about her roots."

"Do you know what happened to your grandparents?"

Nell shook her head. "Except that they're both dead."

"I'm sorry, Nell." Lady rested her head on her best friend's shoulder.

"At least I have you. Forever," Nell said, and they recited their sacred pact in unison. "Together, forever. Let nothing or no one ever come between us." They sealed the pact with their secret handshake—fingers clasped together, thumbs and pointers forming the shape of a heart.

CHAPTER ELEVEN

BOOKER

Booker's head buzzed with excitement as he waited for his mom to come out of the dealership. He was getting a newer-model car than he'd expected with fewer miles than he'd hoped for, and he had to wait only one more day. The 4Runner was sweet, even if nautical blue wasn't his first choice in color.

Whatever had gotten into his mom lately, he approved of the assertive manner in which she'd handled the negotiation process. She seemed determined not to leave the dealership until they'd made a decision on a car. And Orlando Holland was all too happy to oblige, even if he had to stay late to close the deal.

"It could be tomorrow before I find what you're looking for, or it could take a month," Orlando had explained when they first arrived. "These things are hard to predict, Mrs. Grady."

His mother had cringed at the sound of her married name. She'd gone from loving his father to despising him in a day. "Please call me Nell. And next month won't work, Mr. Holland. We need a vehicle now. Can't we figure something out with one of these?" She spread her arms wide at the row of SUVs. "You're motivated to sell, and we're motivated to buy."

He chuckled. "All right, then. I'm sure we can work a deal on one of our demos. As long as you call me Orlando."

"I can do that," Nell said, bobbing her head with enthusiasm.

"Then let's go inside to my computer and check the inventory."

Orlando identified a 4Runner the dealership was willing to part with, and his mother talked him as far down on price as he could go. She instructed Booker to wait in the car while they discussed financing.

Booker was scanning radio stations thirty minutes later when she finally emerged from the building.

She tossed her bag into the back seat and fastened her seat belt. "We're all set to pick up your new wheels tomorrow evening after work."

"Thank you so much, Mama. I love you." Booker stretched across the center console and kissed her cheek. "I don't know how you made that happen so fast."

She smiled at him. "Sometimes, son, you have to strike while the iron is hot."

They talked about the car all the way back across town. "We need to make a quick stop at the Harris Teeter," she said as she exited Highway 17 toward the grocery store. "I didn't have time to go earlier today, and there's nothing at home to eat for dinner."

"Do you want me to cook steaks on the grill?" he asked as they entered the store.

"Steak sounds good. Why don't you go to the butcher counter while I get everything else on the list." She freed a cart from the line parked inside the door and headed off toward the produce section.

Booker had long since taught himself how to cook on the grill. Too many nights his mother would have the meat du jour all ready for the grill—steaks seasoned, hamburger patties made, baby back ribs rubbed—only to have his father fail to show for dinner. They would never have to wait for him again.

Booker knew which cuts were leaner and which had more flavor. After perusing the selections, he ordered two fillets from the butcher and waited for his mother at the checkout area.

Despite his elation over getting a new car, Booker couldn't stop thinking about Regan and her family as he scraped the grill rack with a wire brush. When his mom brought the steaks out to the patio, he said, "Tell me about Regan's family. How did you know each other back then, and why haven't you ever mentioned them before?"

She let out a sigh. "Can we please not talk about this right now?"

"Sorry, Mom, but you're not getting off that easy," he said as he forked the steaks onto the grill. "We can play it one of two ways. I can annoy you until you tell me what I want to know, or you can save us both the headache and come clean on your own."

"Fine. I'll tell you everything over dinner," she said, and returned to the kitchen to finish tossing the salad and warming the bread.

When he took the steaks inside, Booker was relieved to see his mom had set two places at the counter. He hated to ruin his good mood by having to stare at his father's empty seat.

Booker shoveled his food into his mouth, but his mother's plate remained untouched as she told him about her upbringing. She'd never known her father, which Booker already knew, and her mother had died when she was fourteen—also old information. But the news flash that her mother had worked as a maid for the Bellemores caused him to freeze in midchew. He set his fork down. This was not at all the story she'd repeated to him over the years whenever he'd asked about her family. "Go on," he said, deciding to save his questions for when she finished.

"My mother was their employee, but they treated us like family. Lady and I were only four months apart in age, more like sisters than friends. I was allowed to roam the house as though it were my own. I even napped every afternoon in Lady's room until we were too old to nap. Only at night, when we retreated to our tiny apartment at the rear of the house, was I reminded of my mother's position. Mr. Bellemore was a successful investment banker who worked long hours and was rarely home. Most of the time it was the four of us—Lady, Miss Willa, Mama, and me. We were like the modern-day version of lesbian mothers raising their children. That house was full of a special kind of love, a love that's difficult to explain." His mother's eyes glazed over, and her voice broke. A long minute passed before she continued. "When Mama passed away, Miss Willa asked me to live with them. A year later, she adopted me."

He balled up his napkin and tossed it onto his plate. "That's just great, Mom. We have this whole other family that I know nothing about. What does that make Regan, like my cousin or something?" He leaped to his feet and paced around the kitchen as he tried to process what she'd told him. He stopped on the other side of the counter facing her. "None of this makes any sense. Basically, you created a false background for yourself in everything you've told me about your family." He ticked off points on his fingers. "Your mother was a teacher. The principal of her school took you in after she died. You lost touch with the principal when he moved with his family to Arizona after you went away to college." He leaned across the counter to her. "If you had this big Kumbaya lovefest with the Bellemores, why did you lie about your upbringing?"

His mother, refusing to meet his eyes, stared down at her uneaten food. "It's complicated, son."

"It seems pretty simple to me. You were embarrassed to admit your family is white."

"The Bellemores aren't my family," Nell said.

"Yes, they are. If Miss Willa adopted you, she's your mother in the eyes of the law. What happened to you that made you hate white people?"

Her jaw dropped to her plate. "I don't hate white people. What on earth would make you say such a thing?"

"Because it's true. The anger is written all over your face whenever you're around a white person. You're standoffish, as though you don't trust them." He was on a roll, and he couldn't stop himself from saying things he'd wanted to say to her for years. "Something happened to you somewhere along the way that made you that way, and I want to know what it is. I'm not like you. Primarily because your prejudice has been such a turnoff for me. I don't judge people based on race, religion, or sexual orientation. In fact, I try not to judge people at all. I realize that everyone is born into different socioeconomic situations, and I admit it irritates me when people don't make the most of their God-given talents, but I don't hate them because of the color of their skin."

When Booker paused to catch his breath, his mother said, "Are you finished?"

He was just getting started, actually, but his mother's wounded expression prompted him to back off. "Just tell me the truth, Mom. I don't judge other people, and I won't judge you."

She shook her head. "I'm not sure I can. I've never told anyone. Not even Lady."

"Will you try? Talking about it might release some of the anger."

His mother stared intently at him, although Booker suspected she wasn't really seeing him. After a long minute, she pushed back from the counter and walked her plate over to the sink. She wrapped her steak in foil and placed it in the refrigerator. She removed a pint of mint chocolate chip ice cream from the freezer and two spoons from the silverware drawer. She handed him one of the spoons. "Let's go sit on the patio. It'll be easier for me to say what I have to say under the cover of darkness."

Outside on the patio, Booker lit the gas logs in the fire pit. They moved their lounge chairs close together to make sharing the ice cream easier.

"You're the last person I thought I'd ever tell my story to," his mother said. "But now that I think about it, you're just the right person to hear it. I was only a year younger than you are now when it happened. There's an important lesson for you to learn here, not only as my son but as a young man."

CHAPTER TWELVE

NELL

1981

Nell had never been disillusioned with her place in Lady's world when they were growing up. She was different from Lady's other friends. Her mother was the help. She attended a different school. She was of a different race. But neither Lady nor her friends ever treated her unkindly, at least not when they were young children. They included her in most of their activities. They rode their bikes to one another's houses, splashed in sprinklers on hot summer days, and played kick the can in their yards at night. There were times when she felt left out, when they went places Nell wasn't allowed to go, like sailing at the yacht club or dancing at cotillion. But they never intentionally hurt her feelings.

Smaller clusters of friends existed within their larger peer group. Mindy Bowen was the leader of their fearsome threesome. Nell and Lady had known Mindy since they were old enough to explore the neighborhood on their own. She lived around the corner with her parents and her older brother by eleven months, Hank, the rascal who was forever playing pranks on them. Mindy, a scrappy little thing with wicked green eyes, stood barely five feet tall and had a spirit as carefree as the mop of brown curls springing from her head. Because of her small size, she had to fight harder to protect herself against her brother. Although Mindy complained incessantly about Hank, Nell knew her friend secretly worshipped him.

Mindy and Nell started planning Lady's surprise party before Christmas, more than a month ahead of her sixteenth birthday in January of 1981. They enlisted Miss Willa's help in organizing refreshments and scheming a way to get Lady out of the house while they set up for the party. The calendar gods cooperated by arranging for Lady's birthday to fall on a Saturday. To occupy her time, Mindy took Lady to lunch at the Marina Variety Store Restaurant and to the afternoon matinée to see *9 to 5*, a movie starring Dolly Parton, which Nell was happy to miss. After loading up on junk food, soft drinks, and helium balloons at the grocery store, Willa and Nell stopped in at the bakery for the sheet cake and the sandwich shop for the party-size sub Willa had ordered.

They were unloading the car when Willa received a call from her friend Lynn Collier, inviting her to come for an impromptu dinner that evening.

"You're sweet to include me, Lynn, but we're throwing a surprise birthday party for Lady." Willa paused while Lynn argued her case. "In that case, how can I say no?"

"Say no to what?" Nell asked when Willa hung up the phone.

"To Lynn's cousin, the handsome widower she's been trying to set me up with for ages."

"But . . ." Nell stared at her, dumbfounded. "Are you seriously going to miss the party after we've worked so hard to make everything perfect?"

"I'll be here to greet everyone, and then I'll get out of your hair and let you kids do your thing. You don't need an old lady like me around anyway." Recognizing her concern, Willa patted Nell's cheek. "You worry too much, sweetheart. I'll be right down the street if you need me."

After unpacking the groceries, they donned their aprons and spent the next couple of hours in the kitchen. They made brownies and cookies and cocktail weenies. They popped enough popcorn to string ten Christmas trees and mixed up a large bowl of ranch dip for the vegetable tray. Nell made several batches of cheese biscuits using her mother's recipe. Miss Willa had hired and fired half a dozen maids since her mother had passed away. She'd finally given up trying to find someone suitable. "None of them measure up to your mama," she'd said, and divvied up the household duties between the three of them.

After they finished cooking, Willa and Nell moved to the den for the decorating. They tied a bouquet of balloons from the ceiling fan, draped pink crepe paper streamers from the fan to the edges of the ceiling, and hung a cardboard garland that read SWEET SIXTEEN from the doorway. They'd just finished lighting a fire in the fireplace, the last of the party preparations, and Nell was on her way upstairs to change, when Mindy and Lady returned home from the movies.

"I can't wait to tell Willa about this movie. She's gotta go see it. She'll love it." Lady started toward the kitchen, but Mindy grabbed her by the arm.

"Tell her over dinner," Mindy said, herding her up the stairs. "We need to hurry up and change."

They'd invented a birthday dinner at Poogan's Porch to throw Lady off the surprise.

Nell dashed up to her room to freshen up and change into her dress. Twenty minutes later, she was back downstairs waiting to greet the first guests. When she'd invited their friends to the party, Mindy had instructed them to come quietly around to the back door and dared them to breathe a word of the surprise to Lady. A group of twenty—boys dressed in khaki pants, button-downs, and penny loafers, and girls in Fair Isle sweaters and colored wide-wale corduroys—hurried up the driveway as their parents dropped them off at the curb. Nell took their presents from them and directed them to find a place to hide in the room. She dimmed the lights and managed to keep everyone quiet while they waited for the signal.

Willa's voice broke through the silence. "Fetch my coat for me, Lady. I think I left it in the den when I came in from the store. Check the closet. And hurry, else we'll lose our reservation."

On a mission to retrieve her mother's coat, Lady flipped the switch, and light flooded the den. Their friends shot out of their hiding places in a collective chorus of surprise. Much to Nell's delight, Lady seemed genuinely surprised. Her face glowed red as the crowd gathered around her to wish her a happy sweet sixteen. Miss Willa circled the room greeting each of their guests in turn before making her departure.

No sooner had she driven off than Mindy presented a bottle of tequila to the birthday girl. "Here's your present."

Lady stared at the bottle as if it were a live grenade. "Where'd you get that?"

"My cousin bought it for me," Mindy said, grinning as if she'd accomplished some great feat.

Todd, the star basketball player for Lady's school, punched the air with his fist. "Woo-hoo! Crank up the tunes. Let's get this party started." Mindy had put Nancy, their friend with the best taste in music, in charge of the stereo. She placed the recent hit single "Lady," by Kenny Rogers, on the turntable. Someone cleared the coffee table, and someone else slammed down two shot glasses, a shaker of salt, and a bowl of lemon wedges.

Nell had not been privy to this aspect of the party planning, although she wasn't surprised. A lot of their friends drank alcohol. They raided their parents' liquor cabinets every weekend. She'd sipped beer before with Lady at other parties but never hard liquor. Never Jose Cuervo tequila.

The crowd gathered around the table and chanted Lady's name over and over. Lady took a step closer to Nell. "I don't know about this," she whispered.

"I tried to convince Miss Willa not to leave the party unchaperoned," Nell said out of the corner of her mouth.

"Where'd she go anyway?"

"Down the street to the Colliers' house for dinner."

Lady shook her head. "Typical Willa. Close enough to come home if we need her but far enough away to give us some space."

"I'm not sure this is the kind of space she had in mind," Nell said.

"Come on, Lady." Mindy lifted the tequila bottle. "What are you waiting for?"

Lady looked at Nell and shrugged. "What the hell? You only turn sixteen once." She dropped to the knees of her kelly-green wide-wale corduroys.

Mindy filled the shot glasses with tequila. "Watch and learn." She removed a lemon wedge from the bowl and licked the skin she'd salted between her thumb and forefinger. She then kicked back the tequila and bit down on the lemon. "Now it's your turn."

With one last uncertain glance toward Nell, Lady licked the salt and gulped down the tequila, shivering as she sucked on the lemon.

Mindy sent an elbow to her ribs. "See! You did it."

More shot glasses appeared on the table, and Mindy filled each to the brim with tequila. She held a shot glass out to Nell.

Nell shook her head. "No thanks."

"Then the birthday girl will have to drink yours." She set the shot glass on the table in front of Lady, who repeated the process of licking the salt, drinking the tequila, and sucking the lemon.

When a group of late arrivals announced that it was snowing outside, the crowd flocked to the window in disbelief. Snow was a rare occurrence in Charleston. The atmosphere in the room turned festive, and the party kicked into high gear. Lynyrd Skynyrd blasted "What's Your Name" from the stereo speakers, and more liquor bottles, cigarettes, and twelve-packs of beer appeared. The roar of the crowd rose with the volume of the music as guests nibbled on food and mingled among themselves.

Nell was standing with Mindy and Lady, watching their friends get out of control, when Todd yelled, "Well I'll be damned. Look what the cat dragged in."

All eyes traveled to the door where Hank stood with a boy Nell had never seen, each of them sporting a twelve-pack of beer.

"I thought you only invited kids in our grade," Nell said to Mindy as though she wasn't happy to see Hank when she totally was. She was confused by her sudden attraction to a white boy, one she'd always thought of like a brother. She loved his innocent baby face that contradicted his mischievous personality.

"It's Hank," Mindy said. "I didn't think you'd mind if I invited my brother."

"More importantly, who's that with him?" Lady asked, rosy lips parted and blue eyes shining.

Hank called out, "Everyone, meet Daniel Sterling. He's a friend of mine from summer camp. His family just moved to Charleston from Atlanta."

"Lady Sterling," Lady said in a hoarse voice. "I could get used to the sound of that."

Their friends welcomed Daniel to Charleston as Hank led him through the crowded room toward the threesome.

"Happy birthday, Lady," Hank said, giving Lady a peck on the cheek. He ripped open the end of his twelve-pack and offered each of them a beer. "Daniel, you know my sister, Mindy. This is Lady. Today's her birthday. She's sweet sixteen."

Daniel bowed his handsome head to her. "Happy birthday, Lady."

"And this is Nell," said Hank as he turned toward her.

"Nell," Daniel repeated. "That's a nice name. Is it short for anything?"

"Just Nell." She stared at the floor to avoid his dark eyes that stared at her as though he was thinking improper things about her. His penetrating gaze made her feel uneasy.

Mindy leaned in close to her brother. "Alicia's here."

Hank's eyes followed hers to the auburn-haired beauty warming herself by the fire.

Nell's heart sank. *Why do guys always fall for the redheads?*

"Thanks, sis," Hank said, and worked his way through the crowd to Alicia's side.

As the night wore on, Nell kept one eye on Hank and Alicia and the other on Lady, who, after downing several more tequila shots, embarrassed herself by falling all over Daniel. She seemed oblivious to the fact that Daniel didn't appear the slightest bit interested in her. Nell cast quick glances at the wall clock. She was tempted to call Willa home from the Colliers' house, but she hated to embarrass Lady by having her mother break up the party.

A few minutes after nine, when a few of the guests left and others appeared bored, Daniel two-finger whistled to get everyone's attention. "I say we liven up this party. Who wants to play spin the bottle?"

"Spin the bottle is for babies," hollered an unidentified voice from the back of the room.

"Not the way I play." Daniel removed two joints from his shirt pocket and held them up for everyone to see.

"Forget spin the bottle. Let's play truth or dare." The boy with the unidentified voice stepped forward, and Nell saw that it was Ian Hill, one of the rowdier kids in their group.

Nell felt Daniel's eyes on her. "Truth or dare could work," he said. "What about you, Nell? Are you in?"

Across the room, she spotted Hank and Alicia sneaking up the back stairs to the apartment where Nell had once lived with her mother. She shrugged. "I guess."

Placing both joints between his lips, he lit them, inhaled deeply, and passed one to Mindy on his right and the other to Todd on his left. Nell declined when the joint was offered to her and was disappointed to see Lady squeeze the hand-rolled marijuana cigarette between her thumb and forefinger as she pressed it to her lips. First tequila shots and now pot. It was a night for firsts.

Daniel pushed back the sofa, and the group sat down on the floor in a circle. An empty beer bottle was spun to select turns. Players were forced to tell their dirty secrets. *Have you ever cheated on a test?* or *Do you masturbate?* Lady burst into an uncontrollable fit of laughter when asked if she'd ever french-kissed another girl. Nell wondered if her outburst was denial or admission of guilt. When players were brave enough to ask for a dare, they were made to perform a challenging task. Daniel choked down the whole platter of cheese biscuits Nell had made, and Mindy sprinted to the end of the snow-covered driveway in her bare feet. Nell was tempted to sneak away to her room, but she felt compelled to keep an eye on Lady, who was both drunk and stoned. Everyone had taken at least one turn by the time Nell was finally chosen.

"I dare you to make out with me in the closet," Daniel said with a sinister grin.

"I'll pass," Nell said.

"You can't pass. The game doesn't work that way." Daniel grabbed her wrist and pulled her to her feet. "Just one kiss. I promise."

She tried to wrench her wrist free, but his grip remained firm. As he dragged her away, Nell glanced back over her shoulder at Lady, eyes pleading with her best friend to save her. Lady glared back, her face contorted with jealousy. Why was Lady mad at her? She hadn't asked Daniel to choose her. She didn't *want* Daniel to choose her.

Mindy waved Nell on. "Don't be such a chicken, Nell. One little kiss won't hurt you. It's just a game."

Daniel opened the door, flipped the light switch, and gave Nell a gentle shove inside the walk-in closet. A hodgepodge of coats hung from a bar, suspended from wall to wall, in front of several rows of shelves that housed abandoned toys and old games—Clue, Monopoly, Scrabble.

Daniel spun her around to face him. His scent filled the tiny space—a mixture of alcohol, marijuana smoke, and sweat—and the evil glint in his dark eyes sent a surge of fear up her spine. Licking his lips, he said, "I've always wondered what brown sugar tastes like."

Pinning her against the wall, he pressed his mouth to hers and forced his tongue past her teeth. He tasted of cheese biscuits and beer, a mixture that made her want to gag. When she struggled to get free, he tightened his hold and crushed his body to hers. She felt his arousal as he rubbed himself against her. She tried to scream, but the sound was hollow inside his mouth. He bit down on her lip. "Shut up, bitch. You're only making it harder on yourself." He clamped one hand over her mouth while the other hand ripped open her blouse. He pulled her bra down and fingered her nipple, pinching it so hard it took her breath away. His mouth traveled down her neck, teeth biting and lips sucking her skin. He kneed her legs apart, grinding himself against her thigh. The motion got harder and quicker as he climaxed. He grunted, and his body grew still, but his hand remained clasped over her mouth. An excruciating minute passed before he lifted his head and stared down at her with utter disgust. "So now I know. Brown sugar tastes like shit. If you tell anyone what happened here tonight, I'll hunt you down and finish the job. Understand?"

She nodded, her brown eyes wide with fear.

He turned her loose, untucked his shirt to hide the damp spot on his pants, and fled the room.

She slid to the floor in a crumpled heap. She lay curled up, sobbing softly into her hands. The laughter in the other room had died down—everyone must have gone home—but the music continued. The thump thump thumping of "Another One Bites the Dust" vibrated the ancient wooden floorboards beside her head. In the distance, she heard the incessant sound of a dog barking and wished for someone to let the poor creature in out of the cold.

After what seemed like an eternity, someone tapped on the door. "Nell," Lady said in a soft voice. "Are you okay in there?"

"Go away and leave me alone," Nell shouted. It was way past time for Lady's help.

She scrambled to the back of the closet, away from the door, buried her face in an old beanbag chair, and bawled. She must have fallen asleep or passed out, because when she woke sometime later, the record player in the other room was skipping. She got to her feet, yanked Miss Willa's trench coat off the hanger, and slipped it on over her ripped clothing and bruised body. She cracked open the door and peeked outside. The room was empty. It appeared as though everyone had gone home. Someone had cleaned up—returned the food platters to the kitchen and thrown away all the beer cans and bottles. Only the lingering smell of marijuana smoke hinted at the party that had occurred there.

CHAPTER THIRTEEN

NELL

Long after she'd finished telling her story, Booker remained hunched over, knees on elbows, staring into the fire pit, his straight face conveying none of what was running through his mind. She'd found it easier to reveal the details of that night without his penetrating gaze on her, but now that he knew the whole sordid affair, she needed a sign from him—upturned lips or a slight nod or touch of his hand—to show that he still loved her.

There were things she couldn't tell Booker about the aftermath of that night. Things that had never crossed her lips. The baths and showers—three, four, sometimes five times a day, scrubbing her skin with Comet and a brush until it was raw and bleeding. The nightmares that tormented her where Daniel's face was close to hers, his breath reeking of marijuana, alcohol, and cheese biscuits, while blood dripped from his lips like a vampire's after he bit into her neck. And the paranoia. God, the paranoia that plagued her had been horrific. She knew how boys bragged about their sexual conquests and had no doubt that Daniel had blabbed to Hank, who, in turn, had told all their friends. She imagined the gossip mills spreading the rumors like wildfire all over town. Girls whispering in the hallways at school. Rooms that suddenly fell silent when she entered. Everyone talking about Nell, the slut, who'd let Daniel have his way with her.

Agonizing minutes passed before Booker finally shifted in his seat toward Nell. Flames from the fire lit up his face, but she couldn't interpret the emotion in his eyes. Was it pity? Or anger? Or disgust like she'd seen in Daniel Sterling's eyes on that snowy night so many years ago?

"So he raped you," Booker said, his voice flat and hard.

"Not technically, no. He assaulted me. I had bruises and bite marks up and down my neck. I wore turtlenecks for a week to cover them. I faked menstrual cramps to get out of dressing for gym class." Nell looked away. "His words were what hurt most of all. *Brown sugar tastes like shit.*"

"I don't get why Miss Willa left the party." Booker threw his hands up. "Like who leaves a bunch of teenagers alone without a grown-up around?"

Nell's mother would never have left the group unchaperoned. Of that much she was certain. But she felt inclined to defend Willa. "Times were different back then—different before mass shootings and terrorist attacks, gangs, and street violence made our world an unsafe place to live. Parents didn't feel the need to hover over their children like they do today. As kids, we were free to roam our neighborhoods from breakfast to supper. As young adults, because the drinking age was more lenient, parents were more relaxed about teenage consumption of alcohol."

Booker paused before responding, "I guess I can see that."

"You also have to understand Miss Willa's personality. Her love for Lady and me was never in question. She enjoyed our company. We had fun together, doing things and going places. But she couldn't be bothered with parenting. She was too busy being carefree." Nell lifted a finger. "Don't get me wrong. She made certain we understood proper etiquette, as if knowing how to conduct ourselves in any social setting was the key to a trouble-free and successful life. Lucky for me, my mother had already instilled in me the values she wanted me to have, based on her Christian beliefs. Lady learned enough from my mother to know the difference between right and wrong. But I think her priorities were misaligned from not having stronger parental guidance."

The lines in Booker's forehead deepened. "How so?"

"She was spoiled and self-absorbed and never made to work hard for anything. She dropped out of college, and it doesn't appear she's made much of herself. She's divorced, and at age fifty-three, she's still living at home with her mother."

"You're being judgmental again, Mom. You don't know what her life has been like. You gave up the chance to be a part of it when you divorced yourself from her family."

"Listen, Booker. I'm grateful for all Willa did for me, for supporting me financially and helping me get into college. But ours was a relationship of convenience. I needed a place to live, and Willa supported me to repay the debt of gratitude she felt she owed my mother." Nell's face softened, and her lips parted into a melancholic smile. "She and Mama were true best friends. May May, she called her. Nothing was the same for any of us after Mama died."

Booker sat up straight in his chair. "May May? As in May May's cheese biscuits, as in the cheese biscuits you made for the party that Daniel Sterling was forced to eat?"

Nell grimaced. "To this day, the thought of those cheese biscuits makes me sick to my stomach."

"Are you kidding me? They're amazing. Regan offered me some today. She found the recipe in the back of a drawer."

"I'd forgotten about that," Nell said, shaking her head and smiling. "A few weeks after Lady's birthday, Willa asked me to make a batch of cheese biscuits to take to a friend for Valentine's Day. I rarely denied Miss Willa anything she asked of me, but I couldn't bring myself to make those cheese biscuits for her. When she wasn't looking, I stuffed the recipe card in the back of a drawer. I'd been making those biscuits since I was a tiny girl, and I knew the recipe by heart, but I pretended I couldn't remember the ingredients."

"You lied, in other words."

"Why is everything so black and white with you, Booker?"

"Wow, Mom! Did you really just ask *me* that? I'm the king of gray. You, on the other hand, live in a black-and-white world. All black for the past thirty-seven years by your own choosing."

Tears blurred her vision, and her voice broke when she said, "I should never have told you any of this. I knew you wouldn't understand."

He slumped back against his seat. "I'm trying to understand, Mom. I'm just confused about some things."

"Then let's talk about it. What's confusing you?"

"I don't understand why you're so mad at Regan's mom . . . Lady, or whatever her name is. Is it because she didn't stop Daniel Sterling from taking you into the closet? She was drunk and stoned, the first time for both alcohol and weed according to you. And she had a crush on him, which means she would've been jealous that he picked you and not her. So she wasn't a great friend that night. But is that a good enough reason for you to shut her out of your life completely? Daniel Sterling is the one who rape—sorry, the one who assaulted you. Seems to me, you took your anger at him out on the whole Caucasian race."

She studied her son through the darkness. What a profound assessment from someone so young. She'd never felt comfortable telling anyone about the snowy night, not even her husband whom she'd been married to for twenty-eight years. Yet she'd made the spur-of-the-moment decision to tell her son. But was the decision made truly on impulse? Hadn't she known for some time that he would be the one she'd eventually confide in? As he'd grown into a young man, he'd developed a strong set of principles that Nell admired. Deep down, she'd known she could count on him to give her his unbiased opinion. He'd pronounced her guilty. *You took your anger at him out on the whole Caucasian race.* And she was prepared to accept this verdict, no matter how difficult it was to hear.

Booker had hit on the one point she'd been struggling with since about 1995, when the fog had cleared and she'd begun to suspect she'd made an error in judgment about Lady's role in the events of that night.

You took your anger at him out on the whole Caucasian race. She'd taken her anger out on Lady first, because she was the easiest target, and then, to a lesser extent, on Willa for not being at home to prevent the party from getting out of control. After that, her anger had expanded, little by little, to include everyone with white skin. She'd known it all these years, yet she'd had no control over her feelings.

Why didn't I ever seek therapy? she asked herself. The answer was simple and cut like a knife. *Pride.*

"Lady should've helped me. She knew I didn't want to go into that closet with Daniel Sterling," Nell said in her own defense, but her explanation sounded lame, even to her own ears.

"How did she know, though?" Booker asked. "Because you told her with your eyes? She looked to you to save her from taking the tequila shot, but did you?"

Nell shook her head. She couldn't defend herself, because he was right.

He lifted the spoon and stirred the soupy ice cream around in the carton. "Did you ever tell Lady what happened that night?"

Her cheeks burned. "No. I was too ashamed."

"Did you ever consider pressing charges?"

"Never. I was a black girl living in a white man's world. Getting Daniel in trouble would've been social suicide for me. I kept my mouth shut, worked hard in school, and bided my time until I went away to college and started a life of my own."

He hauled himself out of the lounge chair and moved to the edge of the patio. "I don't mean to sound cruel," he said with his back to her. "You're my mom and I love you. I'm so, so sorry for what happened to you. No man should ever assault a woman for any reason. But try to understand how I feel. For the past ten years, I've had to listen to you and Dad fight all the time—the insults and accusations. I would've given anything to have a sibling, someone I could talk to as I watched my father cheat on my mother and tear our family apart. And now I find out I have this whole other family. I'm disappointed and angry too, if I'm honest about it, that I've missed out on the chance to know your family."

"That's just it, though, Booker baby. The Bellemores aren't my family."

Turning around, he walked back toward her. "Are you sure about that?"

He stood, staring down at her, waiting for her answer. But she had none.

His voice was almost a whisper. "You realize Regan's last name is Sterling, don't you?"

She blinked her eyes hard. "What did you just say?"

"I said Regan's last name is Sterling. Whether that means her father is Daniel or not, I have no way of knowing."

Beads of sweat broke out across her brow despite the chill in the air. "You never told me her last name. I've only ever heard you call her Regan. Until this afternoon, I didn't know if she was black, white, Asian, or Hispanic."

"Because you never asked," Booker said in a sad voice.

The truth hurt. She'd been so uninvolved in her son's life. The grueling hours she worked as a nurse consumed so much time. And then, on her days off, she had errands to run, a house to keep, groceries to buy. A failing marriage to nurture.

Was it possible that Lady had married Daniel Sterling? "It has to be a coincidence. Surely she would never have married him." Nell shook her head as she dismissed the unthinkable.

"I wouldn't be so sure."

"Lady told me today that she's divorced. I wonder if Dan—if her ex-husband still lives in Charleston."

"That much I know," Booker said. "Her father is some big lawyer. He lives in Chicago with his new wife."

CHAPTER FOURTEEN

BOOKER

Booker went to bed confused by his emotions and woke up mad as hell. He felt the anger deep in his core. No human with a heart could have done what Daniel Sterling had done to his mother. The man was vicious and cold-blooded. Booker understood that these kinds of assaults happened all the time. Daily headline news offered proof—women emerging from the woodwork accusing public figures of sexual harassment and abuse. But this kind of violence had never hit close to his home. He'd been such a fool, a complete idiot, to treat everyone as equals, to give everyone the benefit of the doubt until proven guilty. Maybe he should be a criminal attorney instead of a doctor. He would get great satisfaction in putting sick and twisted men behind bars where they belonged.

Wow, he thought as he dragged himself out of bed. *This has been some week. First Mom and Dad are getting divorced, and now this.*

He avoided his mother's questioning eyes as he picked at his sunny-side up eggs—happy eggs, as his mother called them. She'd always fixed him happy eggs as a child when he was feeling blue. But happy eggs couldn't touch his mood that morning. Any more than the thought of picking up his 4Runner that afternoon could diminish his simmering anger.

Regan was waiting for him at his locker when he arrived at school. "So? Did you find out anything about our mothers?"

He busied himself with transferring his textbooks from his backpack to his locker. He had no idea what to say to her. There was always a chance that Daniel Sterling wasn't her father but an uncle or a distant cousin. Booker needed more time to determine the best way to tell her what he had learned.

"Trust me, Regan. You don't want to know. Sorry. I have to get to class now." He slammed the locker door and turned away from her.

The repulsive vision in his mind's eye of Daniel Sterling's assault on his mom prevented him from concentrating during classes that morning. He still had no clue what to tell Regan, and as the clock approached the noon hour, his dread over having to go to the cafeteria for lunch escalated. He was relieved to be called to the headmaster's office after third period. Well, almost.

"Am I in trouble?" he asked the headmaster when he entered his office.

Terrence Long was years past retirement age, but he loved his job too much to quit. His students appreciated his sense of humor and respected him for the strict but fair manner in which he ruled the school.

Mr. Long chuckled. "Did you do something wrong?"

Booker shrugged. "Not that I know of."

Long motioned Booker to the seat across the desk from him. "Have a seat, Mr. Grady. You're not in trouble."

He lowered himself to the edge of the chair. Booker, unlike a few of his classmates who had a propensity toward trouble, had never been inside Mr. Long's inner sanctum. An avid outdoorsman, the headmaster had lined his walls with photographs of his biggest catches and kills. One particular photograph captured an image of him standing beside a marlin that hung bill down from the scales and was three times his size. Someday Booker aimed to catch a fish like that.

The headmaster steepled his fingers. "With only a couple of months left in your high school career, I thought this would be a good time for us to discuss the next phase of your academic career. I understand from Mrs. Holmes you're upset about being wait-listed at Harvard."

Booker thought about all the times he'd been in the guidance counselor's office in the past week—at least once a day—enlisting her support in helping him get off the wait list.

"Yes, sir. I was hoping for acceptance. But I refuse to give up. I've spoken to the head of admissions at Harvard and emailed all the professors I met when I visited last fall."

"That's the fighting spirit I like to see in my students. I'm here to assist you in every way. I made a few inquiries of my own."

Booker tensed. "You did?"

Long's eyes filled with pity. "I'll be honest with you, son. Getting into Harvard is always a challenge, but the competition is even stiffer than usual this year. My source doesn't hold out much hope of you getting off the wait list before May first."

Booker choked back tears.

Mr. Long continued, "However, he has promised to reevaluate your application again when your final transcript becomes available." He flipped open a file in front of him. "Your midterm grades are strong, although I see a little room for improvement in AP Chemistry." He closed the file and rested his hands on top. "You're looking at a long wait, and I would definitely pay the deposit for your second choice of schools, but getting off the wait list for Harvard isn't out of the realm of possibilities."

"Ugh!" Booker exclaimed as he ran his hands through his cropped hair.

"It's way too early to get discouraged, Booker. Stay focused, and keep working hard. I had a student once who got off the wait list for his dream college as he was moving into the dorm of his second choice. If you decide to wait it out, make sure your parents buy tuition insurance."

"Adding valedictorian to my résumé might help. When will you make that decision?"

Tilting his head to the side, Long studied Booker's face as if trying to decide what to tell him. "You are one of the best students this school has ever seen. But so is Regan. In cases such as these, when two students' grades are essentially tied, some schools have selected two valedictorians. I know of a school in Florida who once reported ten valedictorians. But that goes against everything I believe in. I promote healthy competition here at All Saints. You should know that about me by now. The race for valedictorian is close. As of this minute, Regan is a fraction of a stride ahead of you. But all that could change. You still have plenty of time."

Booker's heart began to race, and he experienced a sudden tightness in his chest. He was too young to have a heart attack. Or was he?

The headmaster continued, "As I said, you have the full support of my office and staff. Anything you need, do not hesitate to ask."

"Yes, sir." He squirmed in his seat, casting a glance toward the door.

"The race is far from over, Booker. We have thirty-seven more school days until you cross the finish line. However, if Regan beats you out, you can hold your head high. Considering the number of top performers in your class this year, being second best is pretty darn good in my opinion."

"Salutatorians don't get accepted to Harvard," Booker mumbled.

"I beg to differ, young man. Plenty of students who are neither valedictorian nor salutatorian get accepted at Harvard."

"Not this student." Based on the statistical information he'd studied online, Booker suspected he didn't stand a chance without the valedictorian title. He felt dizzy when he stood to leave, and sweat trickled down his back as he waited for the headmaster to excuse him.

Mr. Long rose from his desk and walked him to the door. "Let me know how I can help."

"Thank you, sir." Finding it increasingly difficult to breathe, Booker hurried out of the office and down the hall to the nearest exit in search of fresh air.

A light drizzle had driven students inside from the patio where they typically gathered after lunch. Booker moved to the edge of the patio and stared out over the deserted basketball courts as he tried to steady his breath. He felt a tingling sensation in his arms and hands. Was he having a stroke? Should he call himself an ambulance?

He heard the door bang shut and footsteps on the concrete behind him. "There you are. I've been looking all over for you."

Booker turned to face Regan, and for the first time ever, he resented her. His longtime study partner and friend, who'd encouraged him to strive for excellence, had become a threat. They were no longer competing to be top of their class. The stakes had increased. She was single-handedly responsible for him not going to Harvard.

"If I didn't know better, I'd think you were avoiding me," Regan said. "I'm dying to know what you found out about our moms."

His nostrils flared as a surge of anger pulsed through his body. She'd already been accepted at the college of her dreams. She had nothing better to do than play Nancy Drew. But he'd already solved the mystery.

"What's your father's name, Regan?"

She squished her eyebrows together. "Daniel Sterling. Why?"

Booker wasn't surprised. Somehow, he'd known Daniel Sterling was her father.

She gripped her backpack to her chest. "What does my father have to do with anything?"

"Because I discovered why our mothers had their falling out. *Your* father raped *my* mother on *your* mother's sixteenth birthday."

Emotions crossed her face in quick succession—confusion, then denial, followed by pain. Good! He wanted her to hurt as much as he was hurting. He didn't feel the slightest bit guilty for bending the truth. In his mind, what her father had done to his mother was rape.

"I don't believe you."

"Then ask your mother." He brushed past her, leaving her standing alone in the drizzle on the terrace.

Inside the building, he turned left and hustled down the hall. He was no stranger to the nurse's office. He suffered from seasonal allergies. When the pollen counts were exceptionally high and his daily over-the-counter medicine wasn't doing its job, he'd stop in to see Nurse Carol for a Benadryl.

He burst into her office. "We need to call an ambulance. I'm having a heart attack."

She looked up from her lunch, a plastic container of leftover spaghetti that stunk up the room. "What are your symptoms?" she asked, pushing aside the spaghetti and wiping her mouth.

"Pain in my chest. Shortness of breath."

The nurse reached for his wrist and felt his pulse. "Your heart is racing." She motioned to the examination bed next to her. "Sit down, close your eyes, and tell me about your favorite summertime activity."

"Wait, what? I'm having a heart attack, and you want to talk about fishing?"

"Trust me on this." With her fingers still pressed against his wrist, she pulled him down to the bed. "Try to clear your mind and tell me about your favorite fishing hole."

He was unsure of the nurse's objective, but he did as he was told. With his eyes closed, he described the secret spot where he took his boat at low tide and the doormat-size flounder he'd caught there last summer. After a few minutes, his heart rate slowed, and the pain in his chest eased up.

"Feel better?" she asked when he opened his eyes again.

He nodded. "So I'm not having a heart attack?"

"Not a heart attack, Booker. A panic attack. Have you ever experienced anxiety before?"

Anxiety? "Nope. Never." Which was surprising, when he thought about it, considering his level of intensity.

"I get students in here every day with similar symptoms, especially seniors. You kids are under an enormous amount of stress with application deadlines and college decisions."

While the symptoms of his panic attack had subsided, the doom and gloom remained. He mentally listed all the things that had gone wrong in his life during the past week. His parents had separated and were getting a divorce. He'd been wait-listed with little hope of getting into Harvard. He was losing the race for valedictorian. He'd found out his mother was assaulted as a teenager by his best friend's father. Worst of all, the most recent addition to his list, was the cruel way he'd broken the news to said best friend about the assault.

"It might help if you talked to the counselor," Nurse Carol said. "I can call and see if she's available."

He didn't need to talk about his problems with a shrink. He needed to pull up his grade in chemistry. "No thanks." He jumped to his feet. "I need to see a teacher about a grade."

CHAPTER FIFTEEN

REGAN

Regan waited until Booker was out of sight before rushing inside to the restroom. Elbowing her way through the group of girls primping in front of the mirror, Regan locked herself in a stall, dropped to her knees, and vomited her lunch into the toilet.

There was a tap on the stall door, and her friend Janie said in a soft voice, "Regan, sweetie, are you all right in there?"

Regan swallowed a wave of nausea. "I'm fine. I think I ate something that made me sick."

"Should I get the nurse?"

"No, but thanks. I'll have the office call my mom."

"Okay, then. If you're sure."

Regan waited until the restroom was empty before emerging from the stall. She rinsed her mouth out and splashed cold water on her face. She stared at her reflection in the mirror—pale skin, red-rimmed eyes, and trembling lips. Was what Booker said true?

She walked to the headmaster's office with her head lowered and eyes on the ground so as to avoid eye contact with anyone in the hall. "I'm sick and need to go home," she said to Mrs. Redmond, the gray-haired receptionist. "Will you please call my mom for permission?"

Mrs. Redmond peered at her over cat-eye glasses. "Do you need to see the nurse?"

"I just threw up in the restroom. I'm pretty sure that means I'm sick."

The receptionist pushed back from her desk, away from Regan, as though she might be contagious. *Nausea over discovering your father is a rapist isn't catching,* Regan thought.

Mrs. Redmond lifted the receiver from its cradle and tapped the buttons on the phone as Regan called out the number. She greeted Regan's mother and explained the situation. "Just a minute. I'll ask her." The receptionist held the receiver away from her face. "It's raining out. Would you like your mother to come pick you up?"

"I'll walk. I need the fresh air," Regan said, and left the office before either woman could object.

The drizzle had increased to a steady rain, and she darted from one awning to the next as she headed down the street toward home. Deep down, Regan knew Booker had been telling the truth. Her father was not a warm-and-fuzzy kind of guy. Even during the good years of her parents' marriage, she'd never seen him show affection toward her mother, not even a peck on the cheek in parting. As a young child, when she'd latched on to his leg, begging for him to pick her up, he'd patted her on the head and gently pushed her away as one might an irritating puppy. It was more than that, though. Plenty of men and women had trouble showing their emotions. Something was off about her father, something lurking in his dark eyes and the firm set of his thin lips that rarely parted into a smile.

She'd always been more than a little afraid of him. Once, when she was nine, her mother had taken Regan to watch him deliver closing remarks in a murder case. He'd struck an imposing figure—tall and handsome in a tailored suit, addressing the jurors in a commanding voice. She carried his genes in her DNA. Did that mean she was capable of harming another human being? She'd never felt aggression toward anyone, except her mother for drinking too much and wasting her life, but that was more annoyance than anger.

Regan passed over Broad Street into the residential section, and when it began to pour, she ran for shelter in the doorway of a friend's house two blocks from home. She removed her phone from her backpack and called her father's cell phone. When her call went to voice mail, she hung up without leaving a message. She tapped on the contact information for his office.

"May I speak to Daniel Sterling?" Regan asked after the receptionist recited the long list of partners who made up her father's law firm.

"Who may I say is calling?" the nasal voice responded.

"Regan. I'm his daughter."

"Just a minute," she said and placed Regan on hold.

Classical music filled the line for two minutes before the receptionist returned. "I'm sorry. He's in a meeting and can't be disturbed. Would you like to leave a message?"

"Can't you put me through to his voice mail?"

"I'm sorry, miss. Daniel Sterling doesn't do voice mail. If you'll give me your name and number, I'll pass it along to his administrative assistant."

Did I not just tell you I was his daughter?

"Never mind," she said and ended the call. The receptionist had placed her on hold for two minutes. Clearly, her father wasn't interested in speaking with her.

Regan hadn't seen her father in two years, despite the custody agreement that stipulated monthly visits. He never initiated a phone conversation with her, and on the rare occasion she reached out to him, it took him several days to call her back. His new wife, the home-wrecking slut who'd broken up her parents' marriage, sent her birthday and Christmas presents—expensive gifts that proved how little she knew about her husband's daughter. What did a seventeen-year-old girl who wore uniforms to school every day need with a pair of Jimmy Choo black velvet booties with four-inch spiked heels? Regan displayed the booties on a shelf in the bookcase in her room as a reminder of the type of person she did not want to become.

She returned her phone to her backpack and zipped it up. Oblivious to the lightning cracking in the distance and the heavy rain flooding the streets, she trudged toward home in her soggy tennis shoes.

Her mother was waiting for her on the piazza. "Thank the Lord! I've been worried sick. I was about to get in the car and come looking for you. Why on earth would you walk home from school in weather like this?"

"It's fine, Mom." Regan tugged off her wet tennis shoes and left them on the wooden porch floor.

Lady followed Regan inside. "Mrs. Redmond said you're sick. Do you have menstrual cramps?"

Regan rolled her eyes. Why, whenever something was wrong, did her mother always assume it had to do with her period? "I threw up at school."

"Oh." Lady took a step back, pressing her fingers to her lips.

"Chill, Mom. I'm not contagious." She left her backpack in the front hall and went upstairs. She peeled off her sodden clothes, slipped into her bathrobe, and wrapped a towel around her dripping hair. She crossed the hall to her room and climbed into bed. Even the warmth from the down comforter couldn't stop her body from shivering and teeth from chattering.

Her mother appeared in the doorway. "Can I get you anything? Perhaps a cup of hot tea."

She drew the comforter tight under her chin. "You can turn up the heat. It's freezing in here."

"It's April. We haven't had the heat on since February." Lady removed a crocheted blanket from the back of the love seat beside the bed and draped it over her. "You know how your grandmother is about the electrical bill."

Willa insisted they keep the thermostat set on sixty-six in the winter and seventy-eight in the summer.

"I don't care what month it is. Willa has lung cancer. This is one time you should veto her. She could catch pneumonia in this house."

"You've been out in the rain. You'll warm up in a minute." Lady sat down on the edge of the bed. "Tell me what's bothering you, sweetheart. You're not usually so snippy."

Regan caught a whiff of cigarettes and vodka. How many martinis had her mother consumed for lunch? Or had she been drinking since breakfast?

"You want to know what's wrong, Mom? I'll tell you what's wrong." She struggled to sit up in bed. "Booker's mother told him what happened at your sixteenth birthday party. It would've been nice if I'd heard it from you and not from him."

Lady's body grew still. "Heard what?"

"That my father raped his mother." Regan watched her mother's face for her response.

Lady gasped and brought a shaking hand to her forehead. "I knew something bad had happened to Nell that night. I tried to get her to confide in me, but she never would."

"Booker's mother trusted him with the truth. I think you owe me that much."

"I suppose you're right," Lady said in a resigned tone of voice. "Let me fix you some tea first, to help you warm up."

Her mother got up and left the room before Regan could stop her. She didn't want tea. She wanted the truth. Lady returned ten minutes later with a mug of tea in one hand and a tumbler with clear liquid and ice in the other. Vodka on the rocks. The martini pregame was over. Barely two o'clock and the party was in full swing. A number of comments came to mind, but Regan held her tongue. This was one time she wouldn't begrudge her mother her alcohol, if liquid courage was what it took for Lady to tell her what she so desperately needed to know.

Her mother set the tea down on the nightstand and moved the gooseneck rocker closer to the bed. She rested her head against the back of the rocker and closed her eyes. "It all started on a snowy night in January of 1981."

CHAPTER SIXTEEN

LADY

1981

Lady fell hard for Daniel Sterling the first moment she laid eyes on him. She found him strikingly handsome with his thin face, dark wavy hair, and dimpled chin. His authoritative presence, the way he manipulated situations to his advantage, captivated her. He was so different from the boys she knew, so much more advanced—far more man than boy, actually. But she lacked experience in hitting on men, and her attempt at getting his attention proved disastrous.

She'd avoided the party scene until then. Never had much to drink, aside from a couple of beers consumed at friends' houses over the past few months.

"Lighten up a little, Lady," Mindy said as she poured the first tequila shot. "Getting drunk on your sixteenth birthday is a rite of passage."

She drank several more tequila shots and, after Daniel arrived, three or four beers on top of that. The alcohol washed away her inhibitions and made it easier for her to flirt with him. At least that's what she believed at the time. She didn't realize until the next day how drunk she'd gotten and what a fool she'd made of herself. When Daniel brought out the marijuana, she eagerly partook in the hopes of impressing him.

Why not? she thought. *It's your birthday. Live a little.* But she was unprepared for the effects of the pot. She was paranoid at first, her butt glued to the floor where she sat cross-legged during the game of truth or dare, afraid to move for fear of toppling over. Then she broke into hysterics when asked if she'd ever french-kissed another girl.

She didn't find it funny, however, when Daniel chose Nell, and not her, to make out with him in the closet. She shot Nell the death stare as he dragged her off. For the first time in her life, Lady resented her best friend.

While the game continued, Lady crawled across the floor and onto the sofa, where she fell into a semiconscious state. She was vaguely aware of movement around her. Mindy ordering everyone to help clean up. The shuffling of feet and dragging of furniture as the room was restored to its preparty state. The incessant barking of a dog in the distance. Murmured goodbyes as guests retrieved their coats from the hooks in the back hallway. Blasts of cold air from the opening and closing of the back door as her friends exited the house.

Sometime after the last person left, Lady was lying on her back and staring at the ceiling, trying to piece together the events of the evening, when a disheveled Daniel emerged from the closet. She rolled off the sofa to her feet and crossed the room to him.

"Everyone's gone home," she said, her arms spread wide at the empty room.

He nodded. "I can see that."

"Where's Nell?"

He gestured at the closet and, with a self-satisfied smirk on his lips, said, "Give her a minute to get herself together. She's basking in the afterglow, if you know what I mean."

Lady's face flushed warm. Had Nell done more than just kiss this handsome stranger?

"I'd better get going," he said, his eyes on the door.

"Oh. Right," Lady said, and stepped out of his way.

He shrugged on his coat. "Happy birthday, Lady." He leaned down and brushed his lips against her cheek.

She touched the wet spot on her face. "Thanks."

She watched him go. Like a child, he threw his head back and stuck his tongue out to the snowflakes as he sauntered down the driveway.

Returning to the den, Lady stood outside the closet with her ear pressed to the door. She heard the muffled sound of crying. *Why is Nell crying? Did she consent to something she now regrets?*

She called out to her, "Nell, are you okay in there?"

"Go away and leave me alone!" she answered.

As a sense of dread settled over Lady, she left the closet and paced around the room, biting her fingernails as she considered what to do. She tried to recall how much Nell had drunk. She remembered her holding a can of beer but noticed she'd passed on the joint and tequila shots. Had she gotten caught up in a moment of drunken lust and let Daniel take advantage of her? Surely he hadn't forced himself on her. He didn't seem the type. She was tempted to call her mother home from the Colliers' but thought better of it. She didn't want her mother to see her intoxicated, and if Nell had, in fact, done something she wished she hadn't, getting Willa involved would only embarrass her more.

She went to the kitchen and finished tidying up. When all the party platters were stored away, she plopped down at the table and watched the seconds click off the wall clock. It was eleven thirty, her head was throbbing, and her mother was still not home when she heard footsteps in the back hallway. Nell, with her eyes glued to the floor and Willa's trench coat wrapped tight around her body, padded through the kitchen.

Lady waited several more minutes before deciding to turn in as well. She would not beg Nell to tell her what'd happened with Daniel if Nell didn't want her to know. She'd never asked for a birthday party. She hated surprises. She'd been content with the original plan of going to the movies and out to dinner with her mother and two best friends.

Now her life was ruined. She'd gotten drunk and high and made a fool of herself in front of a guy she'd been attracted to.

Lady lay awake for hours. It was well past twelve thirty, well after the faint sobs in the room next door subsided, when she heard her mother's car pull in the driveway and her footsteps on the piazza. She finally drifted off, and when she woke a few minutes after eleven the following morning, the snow had melted. She retrieved her slippers from under the bed and her robe from her closet. She knocked on Nell's door, and when no one answered, she peeked inside. The room was empty. Her bed was made and her draperies open. She found her mother in the kitchen drinking coffee and reading the Sunday *Post and Courier*.

"Why didn't you wake me for church?" Lady asked as she filled a glass with orange juice.

"Services were canceled because of the snow," Willa said without looking up from the paper.

"But the snow's melted."

Willa shrugged. "I know. It's ridiculous."

Lady retrieved the box of Special K from the pantry. "Where's Nell?"

"At church. Her services weren't canceled."

"Oh. I guess her preacher has a four-wheel drive."

She wasn't surprised that Nell had gone to church. She rarely missed a Sunday. But her worry mounted when Nell missed Sunday brunch, a sacred time for Willa and the girls. When she called midafternoon to say she was at a friend's house working on a project and would not be home for supper, Lady knew she was lying. She'd spotted her book bag upstairs in her bedroom earlier that morning.

During the days and weeks that followed, Nell avoided Lady at every turn. She left before breakfast and returned home after supper. She couldn't gauge the emotions simmering beneath the surface of Nell's steely demeanor. Was she afraid or sad? Clearly, she was angry at Lady. But why? What had she done at the party that was so wrong?

Lady grew increasingly worried that Nell might be pregnant and was relieved to see a tampon wrapper in the bathroom trash can one morning in early February.

"Tell me what's bothering you," Lady said when they met in the hallway outside the bathroom late one night. "Are you sick or something? You've been taking an awful lot of showers lately."

"Mind your own business, Lady."

"Have I done something wrong?"

Nell set her golden eyes on Lady. "If you don't know, I shouldn't have to tell you." She started toward her room, but Lady grabbed her by the arm.

"That's the problem. I don't know." Lady lowered her voice so her mother couldn't hear. "I had too much to drink that night. I don't remember most of what happened."

"Then that's your problem," Nell said and closed the door in her face.

Over time, Lady grew angry at Nell in turn. She viewed Nell's unwillingness to confide in her as a betrayal of their relationship. Did their friendship mean so little to Nell that she couldn't be bothered to address whatever was wrong? Even if Nell never forgave her, Lady deserved a chance to apologize for whatever she'd done to make her so angry. The animosity between them festered, and by the time summer rolled around, their home had become a silent battlefield.

Willa demanded to know what had caused the rift between the girls. Lady couldn't tell her what she didn't know, and Nell refused to talk. Willa assumed Lady was at fault and tried to make it up to Nell by lavishing her with gifts and praise. The praise was well deserved. Nell's grades had steadily improved since her mother's passing, and with the extra time she'd been spending in the library, she made dean's list that spring semester. During the following two years, their junior and senior years in high school, Nell's fury fueled her drive to succeed while Lady's anger sapped what little ambition she possessed. Willa helped Nell secure a partial-ride scholarship to study nursing at Spelman College, but on the flip side, she had to pull strings to get Lady into Converse College, her alma mater, because her grades were so poor.

With both of them away at college, between the distance and lack of communication, the divide became too great for any bridge, no matter how tall or long or strong, to bring them back together.

CHAPTER SEVENTEEN

LADY

When Lady opened her eyes after finishing her story, she saw that Regan had fallen asleep, her tea untouched on the nightstand beside her.

Lady drained the rest of her vodka and stared down at her ice cubes. The roots of her alcoholism traced back to those first tequila shots on her sixteenth birthday. During the ensuing months, she'd gotten into the habit of taking nips from whichever of her mother's liquor bottles was the fullest at any given time. She preferred vodka, but she wasn't picky. The alcohol made the pain of her rift with Nell more tolerable. That summer, with Nell no longer number three in their threesome, she and Mindy grew closer. Desperate to escape the gloom that had settled over their house, she spent the summer with Mindy at her parents' beach cottage on Sullivan's Island. They had some wild times together during those long hot months. They drank to excess, experimented with drugs, and lost their virginities to suntanned surfer boys they hoped they'd never see again. That marked the beginning of her thirty-seven-year stumble down the path of life, her only direction an arrow pointing her toward the nearest vodka bottle.

She'd made a few detours toward sobriety along the way. The year she married Daniel, when her mother treated her like a princess and Daniel treated her like his queen. During her pregnancy and the first years of Regan's life, when the joy she experienced holding her child was the only high she craved. When Daniel called her a drunken lush after she'd gotten smashed at her forty-fifth birthday dinner and she'd given up booze in hopes of saving her marriage. That last bout of sobriety had lasted a year, until Daniel left her for his secretary and she'd been forced to move back in with her mother. Would she be stuck in this drunken haze of a life if she'd worked harder to make something of herself?

She glanced up from her drink and saw Regan staring at her.

"Why'd you marry him?" she asked, her lovely blue eyes glistening with tears and her sweet voice tinged with blame.

"Because I loved him. At least I thought I did when he asked me. And because I was twenty-nine years old and desperate to be married and have children like the rest of my friends."

Regan rolled over on her back and flung her arm across her face. "That's not what I'm asking, Mom, and you know it. Why did you marry a rapist?"

Lady set her empty glass down on the nightstand. "Haven't you been listening, sweetheart? Until this afternoon, I never knew what happened to Nell that night. The idea that Daniel might have mistreated her in some way crossed my mind for about a second, but I quickly dismissed it. Nell and I were as close as friends can be. We'd shared our deepest, darkest secrets since we were old enough to keep secrets. I had convinced myself that she would have told me if he'd raped her." Lady hung her head. "I truly thought she'd had consensual sex with him, regretted it afterward, and was acting out of shame."

"Did you ever talk to Dad . . ." Regan paused, her face contorted in pain. "To Daniel about that night?"

"Of course I did." Lady remembered the conversation well. On their fifth date, the night Daniel had professed his love for her on the bench swing on the piazza, she'd jokingly asked why he'd picked Nell and not her to make out with him that night.

"Geez, Lady, that was more than a decade ago. We were teenagers playing a silly game. Why does it even matter now?"

"Because Nell changed after that night, and I've always wondered what happened between you two."

"Who is this Nell person to you anyway?"

"Nobody anymore. We used to be friends." By that time, six years had passed since Nell's college graduation when she'd banished Willa and Lady from her life. Instead of pressing him for more details about that night, she'd snuggled back up to him on the swing. "She's in my past. You're my future."

Regan brought her back to the present. "Well, what'd he say?"

"He claimed he didn't remember."

"Isn't that convenient?" Regan mumbled.

"Perhaps, but maybe he honestly didn't remember. After the night of my birthday, I didn't see Daniel again until his cousin's wedding the year before we married. He didn't remember me when we were reintroduced. He'd been away at boarding school, then college, then law school. He was working in Richmond, Virginia, at the time."

"What kind of monster rapes someone and doesn't remember it?" Regan asked.

Lady sighed. "I don't know, honey. He was such a gentleman when we first started dating, and we were madly in love. He never gave me any reason to suspect that he might have mistreated Nell. At least not back then."

"What do you mean, *at least not back then*? Are you saying that he mistreated you later?"

Lady debated how much to say. Regan would see right through her if she lied. "Toward the end of our marriage, he pushed me around a few times." She decided to leave it at that. When her daughter was feeling less vulnerable, she would have a long talk with her about abusive men.

"Am I like him?" Regan asked in a small voice.

Lady moved from the rocker to the side of the bed. "Not at all, my darling. You are pure goodness. You have been since the day you were born. The light shines from within you. If you ever doubt that, look in the mirror."

Regan turned on her side, placing her back to Lady. "If you don't mind, I'd like to be alone."

"Okay, sweetheart. Let's talk more when you've had a chance to process everything."

Lady picked up the empty glass and full cup of tea and left the room. She peeked in on her mother, who was sleeping peacefully, on her way downstairs. She filled her glass with ice and vodka and took her pack of cigarettes outside to the piazza. She lit a cigarette and inhaled.

Was it possible that Daniel had actually raped Nell? While her gut told her it was true, Lady had experienced so much uncertainty about that night that she needed to hear it directly from Nell, not secondhand from her teenage son. *And what must Nell think of me for marrying a rapist?*

Willa had insisted on sending Nell an invitation to Lady's wedding. For the sake of avoiding an argument, Lady had agreed to invite Nell, but on the way to the post office, she'd removed Nell's invitation from the stack and torn it up. She'd felt no obligation to invite Nell to her wedding. In the six years since her graduation, Nell had neither visited them nor answered any of Willa's numerous calls or letters. In her own words at graduation, Nell had made it clear she wanted to move on with her life without Willa and Lady Bellemore.

Not until Daniel's palm smacked her cheek for the first time was Lady able to identify with what Nell had experienced in the closet that night. But to this day, she still didn't understand why Nell had held Lady responsible. Fine, if she wanted to take her anger at Daniel out on Lady. But why hadn't she reported him to the police? Or at least told Willa? Their mother would've known how to handle the situation. Think of the heartache she could've spared not only Lady but all the other women Daniel had probably mistreated along the way. And Lady felt certain there'd been plenty.

She had been married to Daniel for seventeen years when he hit her for the first time. She'd been needling him about some insignificant household matter and pushed him too far. She'd been too stunned to react and dismissed it as an isolated incident. No harm done aside from a handprint on her cheek. And he'd been ever so remorseful, bringing her flowers and chocolates home from work every day for a week.

A month later, however, he'd gone postal on her when she'd confronted him about the pink lipstick on the collar of his white starched button-down shirt. She'd been waiting for him at the top of the stairs when he'd come home late from work for the fourth night in a row. "Who is she, Daniel?"

"You don't know her."

Lady's eyebrows shot up to her hairline. "*I don't know her?* You're not even going to defend yourself, hotshot criminal attorney that you are?"

"What's the point, Lady? You and I both know this marriage is over."

"So now our marriage is over? We've had a few bumps in the road, Daniel, but divorce never entered my mind." He tried to turn away from her, but she grabbed him by the elbow. "You can't drop a bomb like that and just walk away."

"Let go of me!" He raised a hand to strike her, and when she used a nearby side chair to shield herself from him, he threw her and the chair down the stairs.

He started down the stairs after her, and she scrambled up, limping through the dining room to the kitchen on a broken ankle. She snatched the cordless phone off the wall, locked herself in the pantry, and called 911. She talked to the operator while waiting for the police to arrive.

After she gave her statement, Daniel pulled the two policemen aside. He handed each of them his business card with the name of his law firm printed across the front. "I'm sorry, Officers. This is embarrassing. My wife's had too much to drink tonight. She tripped over the chair in the upstairs hall and fell down the stairs. I was in the bedroom when it happened."

Both officers' eyes traveled from the broken chair on the floor to Lady, who was sitting on the bottom step, icing her ankle.

"I thought I smelled alcohol on her," the younger of the two officers said.

"She gets delusional sometimes when she drinks." Daniel twirled his finger near his head as if to say his wife was nuts. "I'll tuck her into bed, and she'll be fine in the morning."

"All right, then. Make sure she gets that ankle looked at." With a final glance toward Lady, the older officer slipped his notepad back in his shirt pocket. "Call us if you need us."

Just like that, her husband had manipulated the situation to make her look like the guilty party. Naturally, the policemen believed a successful attorney over a drunken housewife.

After the policemen left, Lady called a taxi to take her to the emergency room. She returned home, her ankle set, just after midnight. She slept in the guest room with the door locked, and the next day, she kicked him out of the house and changed the locks. Lady gave herself a high five. That was one of the few take-charge moves she'd made in her life. She found out a week later when he called to say he was moving with his new secretary to Chicago that he'd been planning to leave her for some time. He'd been offered a position with one of the top criminal defense firms in the nation, a career move that had been in the works for months without her knowledge.

Lady called Daniel's secretary the next day to warn her. "I think you should know that he's abusive. He pushed me down the stairs and broke my ankle."

She'd met Sheila the previous December at the firm's Christmas party. She was everything Lady was not—young and blonde with a toned body and gigantic breasts.

Sheila laughed, a high-pitched cackle that made Lady shiver. "Puh-lease. Your pathetic attempt to get your husband back isn't going to work."

Lady's knuckles turned white as she gripped the phone. "I don't want him back! You can have him. You deserve each other."

Lady couldn't have cared less what happened to Sheila. She'd called out of a sense of obligation. No woman should be mistreated by a man. If only Nell had had the courage to do the same, Lady wouldn't have married Daniel. But then she wouldn't have Regan, and her sweet daughter was worth all the pain and suffering she'd endured.

~

For the rest of the afternoon, Lady sipped vodka and chain-smoked cigarettes while watching the storm system move through. She was more than a little tipsy when she went inside to fix dinner around six o'clock. She browned hamburger meat in an iron skillet on the gas stove and dumped in a jar of store-bought spaghetti sauce. While she watched the sauce simmer, she pinched off pieces of a french baguette and stuffed them into her mouth to soak up some of the alcohol. The sweet fragrance of Carolina jasmine drifted in through the open window over the sink, reminding Lady that springtime was upon them. The season of rebirth usually made her feel alive, but all she wanted to do was curl up and die.

When everything was ready, she made a tray for her mother and took it upstairs.

Feeling wretched after her last chemo treatment, Willa pushed the tray away. "I can't eat a bite. I just want to sleep."

"Then let's get you ready for bed." Lady helped her mother to the toilet and into a clean gown before tucking her back into bed.

"You stink, Lady," Willa said when her daughter leaned down to kiss her forehead. "You drink entirely too much. No man wants a drunk for a wife."

Lady ignored her mother's comment. She'd start worrying when her mother stopped criticizing.

"Your dinner tray's on the nightstand if you get hungry. Ring your bell if you need me." She'd found a sterling silver bell, engraved with CHRISTMAS 1965, the year Lady was born, at the back of the breakfront in the dining room. The bell had saved Lady from having to run up and down the steps to check on her mother during these past few weeks when she'd been so ill after her chemo treatments.

Turning off the overhead light, she left her mother's door ajar and went down the hall to Regan's room. She knocked lightly on the door. "Regan, honey. Dinner's ready."

Her daughter's voice sounded faraway and muffled as though coming from beneath the covers. "I'm not hungry."

"How 'bout I make a tray for you?"

"I said, I'm not hungry." At the sound of her daughter's angry tone, Lady stepped back from the door. Regan had never snapped at her before.

"Good night, then," she said and returned to the kitchen.

She toyed with her spaghetti with one hand while holding her glass of vodka with the other. She'd never felt so lost and alone. Regan would leave for college in the fall, and the reality that Willa wouldn't live forever was beginning to hit home. Lady had few friends, no career, zero romantic prospects. What would she do with the rest of her life?

After she'd dropped out of college but before she'd married Daniel and become a stay-at-home wife and mother, Lady, with Willa's help, had secured a position as an administrative assistant for an executive at Charleston's First National Bank. Lady had excelled at managing her boss's life, much better than she'd ever managed her own. Considering her twenty-five-year absence from the workforce, no one in their right mind would hire her now, no matter how efficient her organizational skills.

She gripped the neck of the Tito's bottle. Vodka was the one thing she could count on. Her constant companion. Her past, her present, her future.

CHAPTER EIGHTEEN

REGAN

Regan woke up in the worst mood ever. She considered faking sick for school. She felt nauseated, although she suspected the icky feeling in her stomach had more to do with hunger than sickness. She hadn't eaten since lunch yesterday, and she'd vomited that up in the bathroom at school. Her attendance record was exemplary. Didn't she deserve a mental health day every now and then? She'd missed her afternoon classes the day before and had done no homework. Her teachers would be lenient this once, but missing another day of school meant getting further behind.

By the time she convinced herself to go to school, she was running late and didn't have time to shower. She rolled out of bed and changed into her uniform, which was still damp from her walk home in the rain the day before. She was all thumbs as she tried to braid her hair. Frustrated, she removed a pair of scissors from her top dresser drawer and sawed off the bottom four inches of her hair. "It's only hair. It'll grow," she said to herself at the sight of her ragged hairline in the mirror. She raked her straggly locks back, secured them with an elastic band, and left the room.

Her mother's bloodshot eyes popped out of their sockets when she saw Regan's spiky ponytail. "What happened to your hair?"

"It was time for a trim."

Lady planted her hands on her hips. "I could've scheduled you an appointment at a salon."

"Too late now." Regan's mouth watered at the sight of two poached eggs and applewood-smoked bacon awaiting her at the kitchen table. "I don't have time to eat." She grabbed a banana from the bowl of fruit on the counter and her backpack from the bottom of the stairs and fled the house.

Regan panicked in first period when her calculus teacher ordered them to clear their desks and handed out stapled sheets of paper. She'd forgotten all about the scheduled test. Should she ask the teacher for more time to study? Surely Mrs. Becker would understand. After all, she'd gone home sick from school the day before. But when she reviewed the material on the front page, she thought, *I know this stuff*, and elected to go ahead and take the test. A mistake, she realized by the third page.

She suffered through, and when she finished, brain fried, she handed the test to Mrs. Becker and bolted from the room.

A group of her classmates gathered by their lockers after class. "Was it me, or was that test ridiculously hard?" Janie asked.

"I doubt I got any of the problems right," Wes said, hanging his head. "It's spring semester of our senior year. I thought teachers were supposed to give us a break."

Janie nudged Regan with her elbow. "How'd you do?"

She shook her head. "Same."

Booker joined their group. "What about you, dude?" Wes asked. "What'd you think of that test?"

Booker shrugged. "It was hard, but I did all right, I guess."

A collective moan escaped the group. "There goes any hope for a curve," Wes said.

Regan's day proceeded downhill from there.

Her government and politics teacher reluctantly granted her an extension on the paper that was due that day with a stern warning.

"You're in the homestretch, Regan," Mr. Gill said in an abrasive voice. "Don't start slacking off now."

Staring at him, she thought, *Seriously? I ask for one extension in my four-year high school career and you make me feel like a criminal.* But she held her tongue and hurried out of the room.

When her French lit teacher called on her to recite the passage they were required to memorize for homework, she was forced to admit in front of the whole class that she wasn't prepared. Then, as if all of that wasn't enough, in chemistry lab, with Booker breathing down her neck scrutinizing her every move, she clumsily knocked over a beaker and nearly caught the lab on fire.

Booker caught up with her on the way to the library after school. "Regan, wait!" He ran ahead of her and stopped her in her path. "About yesterday. When I said your father raped my mother, that wasn't exactly the truth. He got rough with her, but he never actually . . . well, you know."

Regan glared at him. "Are you saying you lied?"

"I prefer to think of it as stretching the truth." His lips spread wide into his stupid grin, the one he used when he was trying to make her laugh.

"Either you lied yesterday or you're lying today. Which is it, Booker? You know what? Never mind. I don't want to hear it. It won't make me feel any better either way." She pushed him out of her way and continued on her path to the library.

She bypassed the table where she usually studied with Booker and found a cubicle in a remote corner of the second floor. She removed her books from her backpack and set them on the desk, but thoughts of her father prevented her from focusing on her schoolwork. Had he raped Nell or not? Did it really matter? He'd gotten rough with her, and that was bad enough. He was cruel and inhumane. He'd pushed her mother around, his own wife. Maybe he'd pushed Regan around too. Surely she wouldn't forget something like that. Or would she? The brain was an amazing organ, capable of repressing memories that were too difficult to process.

Two hours ticked off the clock before she was able to focus on her homework. But even then, she wasn't on top of her game. Her government paper was only mediocre, and she struggled with the calculus problems that usually came so easy for her.

It was almost eight o'clock when she left the library. She arrived home to find her mother reeking of booze and cigarettes, while sitting at the table with two untouched dinner plates in front of her.

Regan sat down opposite her and forked off a bite of cold Salisbury steak. Her eyes narrowed as she studied her mother's face. Her forehead was wrinkled and her lips pursed in concern. "What's wrong?"

"It's your grandmother. This last treatment has hit her hard. She's having a rough go of it."

"I'll go up and see her."

When Regan moved to get up, her mother grabbed her arm and pulled her back down. "Don't disturb her now. She's settled in for the night. I'm hoping the worst is behind her and tomorrow will be a better day."

"She's not going to die, is she?" Regan asked, her blue eyes wide with alarm.

Lady gave her head a solemn shake. "I don't know, sweetheart. I certainly hope not. Your grandmother's a fighter, but she needs our prayers right now."

Regan cast an anxious glance toward the stairs. "Should we call somebody or take her to the hospital?"

"I've spoken to her doctor's nurses several times today. We're doing all we can for her for now." Lady eyed Regan's plate. "You need to eat. I can't have you getting sick on me too. Are you feeling better today?"

Regan hunched over her plate. "I guess."

The subject of her father hung in the air between them as they ate dinner, but Regan and her mother were too exhausted and worried about Willa to talk about Daniel. After helping Lady with the dishes, Regan poured herself a glass of milk and trudged up the stairs. Despite her mother's warning not to bother her grandmother, she peeked in on her anyway. Willa was fast asleep with her mouth wide open. She tucked her blanket tighter around her and left the room. Avoiding the sight of her ruined hair in the bathroom mirror down the hall, Regan took a long hot shower and fell into bed.

She woke the following morning to a silent house with no aroma of coffee wafting up from the kitchen. When she went downstairs, dressed and ready for school, she was alarmed to find the newspaper still on the piazza and the kitchen dark and empty. No matter how drunk her mother had gotten the night before, she always woke in time to make breakfast for Regan before school. She flew back upstairs and was relieved to find Lady asleep on the love seat beside Willa's bed, her neck bent at an awkward angle and a string of drool hanging from her lower lip. She considered waking her mother but thought better of it. They'd obviously had a difficult night.

With a heavy heart, Regan grabbed a protein bar from the pantry and ate it on her walk to school. When her teacher handed out the graded calculus test, her eyes blurred with tears as she stared down at the D written in red marker with a note for Regan to see the teacher after class.

Regan waited for the classroom to empty before approaching her desk. "What happened?" Mrs. Becker asked. "Your homework grades for this section were excellent as always."

"I went home from school sick on Wednesday and didn't feel like studying that night. I thought I understood the material well enough to take the test."

"You should've told me, Regan. I would've given you more time to prepare."

Tears spilled from her eyelids and slid down her cheeks.

Mrs. Becker held a tissue box out to her. "Oh, honey." She rounded her desk and gave Regan a half hug. "Is everything okay at home?"

She nodded, not trusting her voice to tell Mrs. Becker that her grandmother had cancer and might die.

Mrs. Becker walked her to the door. "Don't worry about this test. You know I drop the lowest grade. You'll be fine."

Her father was a rapist and her beloved Willa might die. Regan didn't think she'd ever be fine again, but she nodded just the same.

She struggled to pay attention in her classes for the rest of the day. She felt like she was losing her edge, and she couldn't let that happen, not with Willa counting on her to be valedictorian.

She requested a hall pass during fifth period and was relieved to find the bathroom empty. "Get a grip on yourself, Regan," she said to her reflection in the mirror. "Forget about your father. Daniel Sterling is a virtual stranger to you. He moved to Chicago with that slut wife of his when you were ten, and you've seen him exactly three times since. Your last visit was more than two years ago. He doesn't care about you. He never calls you, and when you manage to get him on the phone, you have nothing to say to each other because you have nothing in common with him."

Regan turned on the faucet and splashed water on her face. Drying her face with a paper towel, she said, "You've worked too darn hard for too long to let a low-life woman beater get in the way of you accomplishing your goals. If he comes to your graduation, which is a big *if*, you can confront him then about Booker's allegations. Until then, forget him."

She balled up the paper towel and tossed it into the trash can on the way out of the bathroom. With her head held high, she marched back to her fifth-period class.

Regan rarely stayed after school on Friday afternoons unless she was working on a big project. When the final bell rang at three o'clock, she rushed home to check on Willa. She found her mother in the same spot beside Willa's bed where she'd left her that morning.

Regan tiptoed into the room. "How is she?"

"About the same." Lady stood and stretched. "She doesn't appear to be in any pain. She's taken a few sips of water, but other than that, she's been sleeping all day."

"Have you been sitting by her bed this whole time?"

"Pretty much. I took a quick shower and ate a sandwich. I don't want to leave her alone. I'm afraid she'll wake up and try to get out of bed. I'm worried she's too weak to even ring the bell."

"I'll sit with her for a while," Regan offered. "Why don't you go lie down or take a walk?"

"Do you mind?" Lady asked. "I could use some fresh air."

Regan let her backpack slide down her arm to the floor. "I don't mind at all. I have plenty of homework I can do."

~

For the rest of the evening and all through the night, Regan and Lady took turns sitting with Willa. Late morning the following day, Lady had gone to the grocery store and Regan was working on an assignment for her government class when she felt Willa's eyes on her.

"What have you done to your beautiful hair?" Willa asked in a hoarse voice.

Regan ran her hand down her short ponytail. "It was getting on my nerves, so I cut it all off."

Willa lifted her fingers to her balding head. "I know what you mean about it getting on your nerves. Nell promised to do the same with what's left of my hair." Her eyes fluttered shut and then opened wide again. "What's today?"

Regan closed her government book and stuffed it in the backpack at her feet. "Saturday, why?"

"Nell's coming today." She glanced at the clock on her bedside table. "Good heavens, it's almost noon already." She lifted back the covers to reveal her bony legs. "You need to help me get ready."

"No way, Willa. Mom says you're too weak to get up." Regan took the covers from her grandmother and tucked them tight around her. "You'll have to wait until she gets back from the store."

"Then bring me my hairbrush and cosmetics bag from the bathroom and my bed jacket from the closet, the blue silky one with the ruffled collar."

Regan did as she was told, even though she doubted Nell would show up. She held the hand mirror in front of her grandmother's face while she smeared on makeup and brushed her thinning hair.

"This won't do at all," Willa said when she brushed a clump of gray hair free of her head. "Fetch one of my scarves out of the top drawer of my dresser."

"That's a great idea, Willa. Just what I need to cover my bad haircut."

Regan selected a floral scarf for her grandmother and one with geometric shapes for herself. They giggled as they covered their heads with the scarves, tying them off at the bases of their necks.

"Let's take a selfie." Holding her phone up in front of them, Regan leaned in close to her grandmother while she snapped the pic.

"Did Nell say what time she's coming?" Willa asked.

"Not that I know of." Regan spotted *Pride and Prejudice* on the nightstand. "Why don't I read to you while we wait."

Her grandmother adored Jane Austen. She'd read all her novels multiple times. Willa settled back against the pillows and closed her eyes to listen. Regan had finished a chapter and was just starting the next when they heard a car pull in the driveway, followed by footsteps on the piazza and the storm door banging shut.

"There's my Nell. I knew she'd come," Willa said, propping herself up against the headboard.

Even if Nell had once lived there, Regan doubted she would enter the house without knocking first.

Willa watched the doorway with anticipation, but when Lady appeared a few minutes later, her face fell in disappointment. "Oh. It's you."

"Nice to see you too, Willa." Lady crossed the room to the bed. "You're looking perky."

"Of course I'm perky. Nell's coming to visit me today."

Regan and her mother exchanged a look. Lady was as skeptical as Regan about Nell's visit.

"Don't get your hopes up too high, in case she doesn't come," Lady said. "Nell has a demanding career. There's always a chance she'll get tied up at the hospital."

"Humph." Willa crossed her arms over her chest. "If Nell said she'd come, she'll come."

"If you say so." Lady plumped up a pillow behind Willa's back. "Let's get some food in you so you'll have the energy to visit with her when she gets here."

Regan's heart went out to her mother. Lady had remained steadfast to Willa all these years despite Willa's obvious favoritism toward Nell.

Lady placed a hand atop her mother's silk-clad head. "I like your kerchiefs, girls. It's a good look for both of you."

Regan smiled. "Thanks, Mom." She got to her feet. "I'll bring in the groceries for you."

"And I'll fix our brunch," Lady said, following her from the room.

Lady prepared a large platter of scrambled eggs, cinnamon baked apples, hash browns, and biscuits, which they ate at the table on the second-floor piazza off Willa's room. They spent the afternoon playing card games and listening to Kristin Hannah's latest release on audiobook via Regan's portable speaker. Willa remained cheerful all throughout the long hours, but by dinnertime, when there was still no sign of Nell and the sun fell below the horizon, her spirits plummeted.

CHAPTER NINETEEN

NELL

Nell sat at the kitchen counter drinking coffee and staring at the Saturday newspaper. She'd read the same headline twenty times. CHARLESTON'S TRAFFIC CONGESTION PROBLEMS WORSEN. "Tell me something I don't know," she said, letting the paper drop to the counter.

The things Booker had said on the patio the other night had haunted her for days. Daniel Sterling had been the one who'd assaulted her, but she'd taken her anger at him out on white people in general. With the exception of her patients, of course. She prided herself on treating each of them the same. If she'd gotten help back then, she would've lived a more fulfilled life, would've felt like a whole person instead of this broken resemblance of one.

She left the counter with her coffee and sauntered around the room, considering the bare spots on the walls in the sitting area where the prized pieces of her art collection had once hung. This house had never been much of a home, merely a place to park their possessions. Truth be told, between their complicated work schedules and Booker's extra-curricular activities, they'd rarely spent much time there. Desmond's family's farm in McClellanville held her fondest memories. She and Desmond had spent their first Christmas together at the farm and every major holiday since then. Being in the marshlands with moss-draped trees and salt-infused air restored a sense of peace in her. And she felt comfortable, like she could truly be herself, around his parents, who were always welcoming and never judgmental.

~

Nell remembered meeting Desmond in an elevator at eleven o'clock at night at the end of her first shift as a student nurse at Emory University Hospital. Alone in the elevator, an awkward silence had fallen between them as they rode down from the sixth floor. Tall with broad shoulders, he towered over her, and while she felt his eyes on her and smelled his woodsy cologne, she didn't dare look up. When the elevator doors opened on the dark and deserted ground floor of the parking garage, he motioned for her to exit the cart. She hesitated. Acres of empty rows separated her from her car.

"May I walk you to your car?" he'd asked.

She risked a quick glance at him. The twinkle in his eyes and dimples at the corners of his lips assured her she had nothing to worry about.

"Sure." She raised her arm, her tote bag dangling from the crook in her elbow, and pointed at her car. "I'm right over there."

They'd learned the essentials about each other—name, school, field of study—by the time they'd crossed the parking deck to her car, and a whole lot more when he took her to dinner the next evening.

By the end of the following month, October of Nell's senior year at Spelman, she and Desmond had committed to a serious relationship. To her relief, he did not make fun of her for being a virgin. He was patient and gentle with her as he introduced her to the art of expressing and receiving sexual pleasure. They shared many things in common, including an appreciation for ethnic foods, old movies, and all things southern. And they were equally committed to excellence in their careers, to saving lives and making the sick healthy again.

When Desmond invited her to spend Christmas with his family on their farm in McClellanville, she'd eagerly accepted. She didn't feel the least bit nervous during the drive to South Carolina on Christmas Eve. By that time, after four years of visiting the homes of her friends' families for all the major holidays, plus some minor holidays as well, she considered herself the quintessential houseguest. She knew which wines and flowers to take as hostess gifts and how to buy small but meaningful presents for birthdays and Christmases.

She fell in love with the Gradys at first sight—Donald with his wire-rimmed spectacles on the tip of his nose and cardigan sweaters reeking of mothballs, and Ada with a crop of silver hair and long graceful limbs like her son—as well as their home, the restored farmhouse with sweeping views of coastal marshes.

In all the homes she'd visited for Christmases past, the process of exchanging gifts differed depending on the household. Some families lavished one another with elaborately wrapped expensive presents while others had only a few packages under the tree. As was the case in the Grady home.

They exchanged gifts after a simple supper of oyster stew, ham biscuits, and Waldorf salad before going to the midnight candlelight Christmas Eve service at their Episcopal church. As they were enjoying a brandy by the fire after church, Nell's mind traveled back to the lovely Christmases she'd shared with her mama in their tiny apartment at the rear of the Bellemores' home. The gifts had been things they'd both treasured—a hand-knitted sweater for Nell and lavender body lotion for her mama.

The following morning, Nell gathered with the Gradys in the kitchen, where they nibbled on Danishes and sausage rolls, with everyone pitching in at one point or another to help prepare the noonday Christmas feast—oven-roasted stuffed turkey, collard greens, and cornbread, with pecan pie for dessert.

After the dishes were put away, Nell and Desmond went out to the hammock at water's edge and snuggled together under a wool blanket.

"I'm glad my parents retired here from Alabama five years ago," Desmond said, inhaling the crisp salty air. "But I would've loved to have lived on the water as a boy."

She nestled in close to him, resting her head on his chest. "What child wouldn't thrive in a place like this?"

"I miss my family, all my aunts and uncles and cousins, in Alabama, but I want to raise my family on the water. Near a major medical center, of course. Would you ever consider moving back to Charleston?"

"I'd move anywhere to be with you," she said. *As long as it's nowhere near Water Street.*

"I can see us working at MUSC and living in a big house with a dock full of boats. I'll teach our son to fish, and on the weekends, we'll pack picnic lunches and go exploring in our boat."

"Sounds perfect to me." She kissed the tip of his chin. "When can we move?"

He chuckled. "I have to finish my residency first. But it'll happen soon enough."

And that was fine with Nell too. The more time and distance she put between herself and the Bellemores, the better off she'd be.

"Yoo-hoo!" Ada called from the house. "I hate to see you go, but you two need to get on the road. I've already packed turkey sandwiches and a thermos of coffee for your drive. You'll get back at midnight as it is."

In the driveway a short time later, when she leaned in to kiss Nell's cheek, Ada whispered, "I can see he cares about you. It's written all over his face. And I know you're good for him, because I'm an excellent judge of character."

Nell felt an unexpected lump in her throat as they drove off toward Atlanta. Desmond's wasn't the big rambunctious family she'd always thought she wanted, but they were good folk, as her mother used to say.

Donald was every bit the gentleman she'd imagined her father-in-law would be, and Ada was the type of woman she could one day love like her own mama. For the first time ever, she felt as though her life was taking the right direction.

~

When they'd met for lunch on Thursday, the divorce attorney advised Nell to sell the house and divide the equity. She'd told Tabitha she'd think about it, and while the idea of making a fresh start appealed to her, giving up the last remaining piece of her former life terrified her. Besides, this was the only home Booker had ever known, and she had qualms about making such an important decision without consulting him first. Ultimately, though, the decision was hers. He would leave for school soon, and she'd be alone in a house that held few good memories for her.

Booker shuffled into the kitchen in his slippers and pajamas, rubbing sleep from his eyes. "Morning," he mumbled as he popped a K-cup into the Keurig and pressed "Brew."

"Since when do you drink coffee?" Nell asked.

"Since I have a ton of work to do today, and I'm trying to get off the wait list for Harvard, and Regan is ahead of me for valedictorian."

Her son had not been himself for days. He'd shown ample appreciation to Nell for buying him a car—kissing and hugging her repeatedly and saying thank you at least a thousand times. But his delight had been short-lived. Nell was no stranger to stress. She saw it every day in her patients—coping with pain, recovering from surgery, accepting difficult diagnoses—and their families, who were struggling to juggle their lives while taking care of a loved one in an extended hospital stay. Booker had always been driven, but he'd always been able to manage the pressure. The past few nights, he'd come home from the library tightly wound and short-tempered. She hated to see him so worked up. Considering all his angst in the face of his parents' divorce and the Harvard wait list, she regretted having added to his burden by telling him about Daniel.

Nell got up and went to him. "Son." She touched his arm. "Don't do this to yourself. Would it be the end of the world if you didn't get into Harvard?"

He yanked his arm away. "Yes, Mom. It would be the end of the world." He dumped three heaping spoonfuls of sugar into his cup and then added cream until his beverage was the color of a vanilla latte. He lifted the mug to his lips and slurped.

"Can you even taste the coffee through all that sugar?" she asked with a hint of a smile on her lips.

"I'm not interested in tasting the coffee. I'm drinking it for the caffeine."

"Go easy, baby. Too much caffeine can have a negative impact on the body."

"I'm aware. I don't have time for a lecture from Nurse Nell today. I need to get to the library." He gulped down his coffee as though his life depended on it.

She moved to the stove. "At least eat some breakfast before you go. I made oatmeal."

He started out of the room. "I'm not hungry."

"Maybe not now, but you will be around ten o'clock. Then you'll have to take a break from studying to get food."

Booker turned around. "Fine. I'll eat some oatmeal."

He sat down at the counter while she ladled the hot cereal into a bowl. She added a dab of butter, sprinkled raisins and cinnamon sugar on top, and set the bowl in front of him. "I was hoping we could go to dinner and catch a movie tonight. Unless you've made plans with your friends."

"I'll be in the library all day." He noticed her dejection and added, "But I could probably meet you somewhere for a late dinner."

"Great! Tell me where you'd like to go, and I'll make the reservation."

"Hmm, let's see." He devoured heaping spoonfuls of oatmeal while he thought about it. "Why don't I text you when I'm leaving the library and we can meet at Taco Boy for a quick dinner. That way I can study some more when I get home."

"You're going to burn out, son."

He waved a dismissive hand in the air. "I'm in the homestretch, Mom. You don't need to worry about me. I can last a few more weeks. What're you doing today?"

"Well . . ." She stood, looking down on him from across the counter. "I'm supposed to visit Willa, but I don't know how I can face Lady knowing she may have married Daniel Sterling."

For the past two nights, Nell had stayed up past midnight searching the internet for information about Daniel Sterling. Although she found out little about his personal life, she learned of a Daniel Sterling in Chicago, a successful criminal attorney with a firm bearing his name. Thirty-seven years had passed since she'd last seen Daniel. While the image of the teenage Daniel was still as fresh in her mind as it'd been the night of Lady's birthday party, it was difficult to say whether the man with salt-and-pepper hair on the firm's website was the same Daniel Sterling.

Booker looked up from his oatmeal. "Oh, she married Daniel Sterling all right."

Nell's jaw dropped. "How do you know?"

"I asked Regan, and she confirmed that her father's name is Daniel. I'm sorry, Mom. I accidentally told Regan about her father."

"You told Regan *what* about her father?" Her eyes narrowed in confusion and then grew wide. "Please tell me you didn't tell her about Daniel assaulting me?"

He lowered his gaze. "Except that I may have used the word *rape*."

She slammed her coffee mug down on the counter. "Why would you do such a thing, Booker? I told you that's not what happened."

"I know, Mom. I was having a bad day. I'd just found out that Regan was beating me for valedictorian." Booker planted his face in his palms. "I wish I could take it back. I didn't mean to hurt her."

When she'd confided in her son about that night, she'd never meant for him to tell anyone. Least of all the Bellemores. Regan was an innocent party. The last thing she wanted was for Regan to get hurt. "Poor Regan. How did she respond?"

"She went home sick that afternoon. I tried to explain everything to her the next day, but she wouldn't listen. She's not speaking to me at the moment."

Nell considered the potential fallout from his disclosure. Regan would've told Lady, who would've told Willa. Now everyone knew the secret she'd worked so hard to hide for thirty-seven years. Oddly, instead of being angry or worried, releasing the burden she'd been bearing for decades was liberating. Which was exactly what Desmond had tried to tell her.

She could no longer ignore the suspicion that had been gnawing at her since learning Lady may have married Daniel Sterling. If he had assaulted Nell in the closet that night, a stranger he'd only just met, to what extent had he mistreated his wife?

Nell went to the Keurig and brewed herself another cup of coffee. "This isn't your problem to worry about, Booker. This is my mess, and I never should've dragged you into it. The last thing I wanted to do was interfere in your friendship with Regan."

Booker scraped the last of his oatmeal onto his spoon and licked it. "I'm not too worried about it. Regan's not the type to stay mad for long." He pushed back from the counter and walked his bowl to the sink. "I need to get going."

He dashed upstairs to his room and returned five minutes later. He paused in the kitchen long enough to stuff his shirttail in his jeans, tie the laces on his running shoes, and grab a handful of protein bars from the pantry.

"Protein bars are no substitute for a proper lunch," Nell said as she walked him to his car. "There are plenty of places you can grab a quick bite to eat. It'd do you good to take a break and get some fresh air. I'm seriously worried about how much you've been studying lately."

"I'll be fine, Mom." He opened his car door and climbed in. "I'll text you tonight before I leave the library."

As Booker was driving out of the driveway, he passed his father coming in. Desmond slowed and rolled down his window. Booker finger-waved at him and kept on going. Nell observed them and then watched as her soon-to-be ex-husband pulled to a screeching halt in front of her. His door swung open, and his long legs appeared.

"What the hell, Nell? I thought we agreed to wait until graduation to buy him a car." He towered over her. There was something sexy as hell about a handsome doctor wearing scrubs.

She glared at him. "What's the big deal, Des? Graduation is less than two months away."

His arm shot out, and he pointed down the road where Booker had just driven in his new car. "You can't use my money to pay cash for a car without consulting me first."

She planted her hands on her hips. "Like you consulted me when you took *our* most valuable pieces of art out of the house? I used *our* money to buy Booker's car. I contribute *my* salary to *our* joint account."

"The money's not the issue," he said with a heavy sigh. "The issue is the timing. Did you think for a second that maybe I wanted to participate in the purchase of his first car?"

"No more than you ever considered what a hardship carpooling has been for me all these years with my long hours at the hospital. You were the one who insisted he go to a private school downtown. Yet you never once drove him to school or Boy Scouts, swimming lessons, or any of the numerous other activities Booker has been involved in over the years."

"You never asked me to drive him, Nell."

"Ha. I asked you a gazillion times. You were always too busy. Like when I had that horrible flu his fifth-grade year, I had to drag myself out of the house in my bathrobe to go pick him up." She turned on her heel and headed toward the house.

"Wait a minute, Nell. I'm sorry I got angry. Can't we make nice for a minute? I was hoping we could work things out amicably since this divorce is what we both want."

She spun back around to face him. "Did you just say what I think you said?"

"What part?"

"That part about the divorce being what we both want."

"Well isn't it?" Desmond peered at her over the top of his Ray-Ban aviators.

"Only because I refuse to put up with your extramarital affairs any longer. You're truly delusional, Desmond. Have your attorney call mine."

She went inside and slammed the door, leaning against it until his car rumbled out of the driveway. She returned to the safety of her kitchen and placed her coffee in the microwave to reheat. She'd been crazy to marry him in the first place and a fool to believe him when he promised to change. He'd never cheated on her before they were married. Of that much she was certain. But he was easy prey to the pretty nursing students who fell all over him. The sooner she could finalize her divorce, the sooner she could get him out of her life and move on. She had a lot of making up of lost time to do.

As she was removing her coffee from the microwave, she noticed a missed call and voice mail on her phone. She listened to the message from the on-duty charge nurse at the hospital. The stomach flu was circulating among the nursing staff, and they were desperate for her to fill in. She immediately texted back that she was on her way. Immersing herself in her work won hands down over spending the day at home alone.

CHAPTER TWENTY

LADY

Willa's health declined throughout the day on Sunday. Lady attributed the deterioration to Nell not showing up for her promised visit on Saturday. Her mother seemed to have given up on life. The hope that had been so apparent on her face not twenty-four hours prior had vanished. She refused to eat or even brush her teeth. She even rejected Regan's offer to read *Pride and Prejudice* to her. Regan's face grew more concerned with each passing hour, and even though Willa slept for much of the afternoon, she never left her grandmother's side.

Lady finally banished Regan from Willa's room around eight o'clock that night. "Go to bed, sweetheart. We've had an exhausting weekend. You need to get a good night's sleep so you'll be fresh for school tomorrow."

Regan reluctantly dragged herself off to bed.

Lady kept vigil, dozing off and on in the gooseneck rocker beside her mother's bed. As the night wore on, her mother's breathing grew more labored and her skin warmer to the touch, but she was too out of it to hold the thermometer under her tongue. Lady rummaged through the hall linen closet for the ear thermometer she'd had for Regan as a child. Her temperature continued to climb, reaching 104 as the first rays of daylight streamed through the windows.

Lady, not wanting to alarm her daughter, waited for Regan to leave for school before calling the doctor's office. She was on hold for only a brief moment before a nurse picked up the call. Lady identified herself and explained the situation.

"Call an ambulance right away," the nurse said. "Have them take her to the emergency room at MUSC. I'll let them know you're coming."

Lady was waiting on the piazza when the ambulance arrived ten minutes later.

"This way." She held the door open for them. "First room on the left at the top of the stairs."

The crew of three maneuvered the stretcher through the door and up the stairs to Willa's room. Lady stood out of the way as the EMTs worked on her mother. One of them reported Willa's vitals into her Bluetooth headset while another secured an oxygen mask to her face and the third prepared the stretcher for transport. On the count of three, they lifted Willa's frail body onto the stretcher and tightly fastened bands around her legs and torso. Lady trailed them out of the house the same way they'd come in less than five minutes earlier.

"You're welcome to ride with us to the hospital," the only female EMT said to Lady as they loaded Willa into the back of the ambulance. "But she's in good hands with us, and you may want your car later."

"That's a good point," Lady said. "I'll follow you there."

She grabbed her car keys and handbag and hurried out to Willa's car. A car accident on Calhoun Street, causing traffic backups throughout the downtown area, made the going slow. Lady turned on the hazard lights and kept her eyes glued to the ambulance's back bumper as they navigated across town to the hospital. She parked in a handicapped spot near the ambulance. She couldn't take the chance of losing her mother by going to the parking deck. With a whole row of empty handicapped spots, she figured God would forgive her this once.

She followed the gurney through the maze of emergency room hallways and into a vacant cubicle. The EMTs shifted Willa from the stretcher to a hospital bed. Once they left the room, nurses swarmed the cubicle, crowding around her mother's bed. One of the nurses stood at a computer monitor, barking orders, while the others inserted an IV, drew blood, and hooked up monitors. Lady stood in the corner paralyzed with fear, her handbag clutched to her chest. Seconds clicked off the wall clock. Twenty minutes had passed before Lady stopped one of the nurses, on her way out of the cubicle, for information. "Excuse me. Can you tell me what's happening? Is my mother going to be okay?"

"We're assessing her now. The doctor will be in to talk to you soon," she said and scurried off.

Another fifteen minutes passed before a doctor entered the cubicle. He was so young, Lady wondered if he knew how to use the stethoscope dangling around his neck. While he listened to Willa's chest, his eyes traveled the room. When he nodded his head in acknowledgment of her, Lady nodded back. Moving over to the computer, he rubbed his chin with one hand as he clicked and scrolled with the other. Finally, he turned away from the computer and addressed the nurses, issuing instructions Lady didn't understand.

He approached Lady. "I gather you're a family member."

Lady held out her hand. "I'm Lady Bellemore, her daughter." When his face scrunched up in confusion, as so often happened when she met strangers, she explained, "Lady is a nickname for Adelaide."

"Adelaide," he repeated, pronouncing her name slowly as if testing the sound on his lips. "A southern name for a lady."

It was Lady's turn to look confused.

"My wife is expecting," he explained. "We're researching names. After all, doesn't every man want his daughter to grow up to become a lady?"

She noticed the wedding band on his ring finger. He was handsome in a rugged way with a scruffy beard and dark wavy hair in need of a trim. His warm brown eyes and soft-spoken tone suggested a gentle manner. "Names can be deceiving, Dr. . . . ."

"Atkins. Resident pulmonologist." He held his hand out to shake. "I've spoken with your mother's oncologist, Dr. Olson, regarding her case. I'm afraid she has pneumonia. The cancer has compromised her immune system, which makes her condition difficult to treat. She's a very sick woman."

Lady's heart raced, her eyes brimmed with tears, and her tone was barely audible when she asked, "Is she gonna die?"

"Not if we can help it. We'll hit her hard with intravenous antibiotics and hope for the best. We'll have to admit her, of course. We're waiting for a room now. Hopefully it won't be too much longer."

Lady wished she knew what questions to ask. She understood so little about medicine. "How long will it take for the antibiotics to work?"

"At least a couple of days, *if* the antibiotics work. I don't mean to alarm you, but if there is anyone you need to call, you should go ahead and call them."

Lady's jaw went slack, and her immediate thought was of Nell. The years washed away, and suddenly she was fourteen again, desperately in need of her best friend, her adopted sister.

She felt a hand on her bare arm. "Are you all right, Ms. Bellemore?"

"So you think she's going to die?"

"I don't like to make predictions. In cases like these, I think it's better to say what needs to be said now than regret not having the opportunity later."

Lady suddenly found it difficult to breathe. "I understand. Please excuse me. I need to call my daughter." Brushing past the doctor, she exited the cubicle and staggered down the hall a short distance before collapsing against the wall.

In the cubicle across the hall, an elderly man with an oxygen mask strapped to his face cried out in pain. Lady was wondering if she should go for help when she noticed a nurse in blue scrubs coming her way, her rubber-soled shoes squeaking against the linoleum floor as she rushed to the man's aid. Lady inched down the wall until she could no longer see inside the cubicle.

She rummaged through her handbag for her cell phone. She stared at the screen, unsure of the best way to get in touch with her daughter. She couldn't very well text Regan to tell her that Willa was dying and she needed to hightail it over to MUSC to say goodbye. She worried that if she called her and Regan had forgotten to put her phone on silent, she would disturb the class and make the teacher angry. Besides, Lady needed a moment to collect herself before she spoke to her daughter. If she broke down on the phone, she would scare Regan.

Lady searched her contacts for the school's number. She identified herself to Mrs. Redmond, the office assistant, when she answered on the second ring. "I need to get a message to my daughter as soon as she's free from class. It's a matter of some urgency," Lady said, and explained the situation to the assistant.

"I understand, and I'm terribly sorry about your mother," Mrs. Redmond said in a sincere tone. "I'll personally deliver the message to her when class is over in ten minutes."

Lady breathed a sigh of relief. "Thank you. And please have her call me as soon as possible."

Twenty minutes later, she was standing outside her mother's cubicle, gripping her phone, when Regan called in hysterics. "Oh God, Mom! She's not dead, is she? Please tell me Willa's not dead!"

"No, sweetheart. She's not dead. But she's very sick. Take an Uber to the hospital. I'll text you the address."

With the paltry alimony Daniel gave her, Lady didn't have the money to buy a car for herself, let alone one for Regan. Living in the heart of a walking city like Charleston, they got along fine by sharing Willa's old Buick Riviera.

"Excuse me," she said to a white-coated female doctor passing by. "What's the address for this building?" She waved her phone at the doctor. "I need to text it to my daughter."

"You're in the emergency department at Ashley River Tower. Have her google the address."

"Thanks," Lady said absently as she texted Regan the name of the building.

Ashley River Tower. Isn't this the building where Nell works? She'd been so focused on following the ambulance, she'd failed to notice where they were going. Lady glanced up at the ceiling, wondering if Nell was on duty on one of the upper floors and whether she should get in touch with her. She quickly dismissed the idea. If Nell was concerned about Willa's health, she would not have broken her promise to visit her on Saturday. She hoped Willa didn't land on Nell's floor. She couldn't remember if Nell had mentioned her specialty.

Lady returned to her mother's cubicle, where a nurse informed her that a room had become available. She directed Lady to a bank of elevators. "We'll take your mother up in a separate elevator and meet you on the fourth floor. Room 1426."

Lady sent Regan another text. Willa's been assigned a room. Meet you by the elevators on the fourth floor.

On the way up, Lady studied the faces of the men and women in the elevator—family members of patients who wore grim faces. The doors opened and deposited Lady on the fourth floor. She stared out of the bank of windows across the Ashley River. The sun shone bright in a cloudless periwinkle sky. Perfect weather for outdoor activities. She remembered the day her father had extended a rare invitation to take Lady and Nell sailing. The girls were about ten at the time. With Nell sitting close to Lady and her father at the helm, they'd glided across the harbor, giant sails flapping in the wind. It seemed like just yesterday, yet it had been so long ago. She'd let time slip away from her, not days or months but decades.

CHAPTER TWENTY-ONE

BOOKER

Booker's stress escalated with each passing day. Although he hadn't experienced another full-fledged panic attack, the symptoms were ever present, threatening to strike at any given moment. At night, he woke covered in sweat from the same stress dreams in which he showed up for class without his homework assignment or unprepared to take a test. While Booker was holed up in the library, his friends were out partying every night, enjoying their last months together before they ventured off into the world. A part of him yearned to join them, to forget about Harvard and pick one of the schools that had invited him to be part of their student body. He reminded himself repeatedly that these last two months were mere blips on his radar, that partying with his friends could not compare to having a degree from Harvard. He was trying as hard as he could but felt his chances of getting off the wait list slipping further from his grasp as Regan continued to finish one step ahead of him at every turn.

Regan was still angry at him, which added a whole different layer of stress. He desperately wanted to talk to her about her father and his mother, but she refused to respond to his texts or answer his calls. He sensed something was very wrong in her life, something that had nothing to do with him. Something with her grandmother maybe. He'd questioned her friends, but none of them seemed to know what was troubling her either.

Booker's concern for Regan mounted when he saw Mrs. Redmond pulling her aside after third period on Monday. He lingered at his locker while he eavesdropped on their conversation. Stringing tidbits of overheard conversation together, he deduced that Regan's grandmother had been admitted to the hospital that morning.

When he saw Regan making a beeline for the front entrance, he caught up with her. "Regan, wait."

"Not now, Booker," she said over her shoulder as she burst through the double doors.

He lengthened his stride to keep up with her. "I overheard your conversation with Mrs. Redmond. Is your grandmother okay?"

"I'm not sure. I'm on my way to the hospital now, not that it's any of your business."

"Why don't you let me drive you?"

She glanced at him and then did a double take. "Since when do you have a car?"

"Since last week. Mom decided to give me my graduation present early, her way of getting back at my dad for leaving her."

Regan stopped walking. "Wait, what? I didn't know your parents got separated. When did that happen?"

He shrugged. "A couple of weeks ago."

Her face softened. "That sucks, Booker. I'm really sorry."

"It's been a long time coming," Booker said. "I would've told you about it if you'd returned any of my calls or texts. I'm sorry about the other day and the way I handled the situation. It was insensitive of me."

"I can't talk about this right now. My Uber's gonna be here in a minute." She turned away from him and continued to the end of the sidewalk.

He joined her on the curb. "The thing is, Regan, whatever happened between my mother and your family has nothing to do with us. We were friends long before we knew about their past."

She shifted her backpack from one arm to the other. "That's just it, though. Their relationship is no longer in the past. Their lives have collided again, and the impact from that collision affects you and me. Your mother broke her promise to visit my grandmother on Saturday. And because of that broken promise, my grandmother might die."

Booker thought back to Saturday. His mother had mentioned a visit with Willa, but when he'd met her at Taco Boy that night for dinner, she'd been dressed in scrubs and on her way home from a shift at the hospital. "I think you're being overdramatic. What does my mother's broken promise have to do with your grandmother's health?"

"If you'd seen her, Booker, you'd know what I'm talking about. Willa was so excited for your mother's visit. She put on makeup and fixed her hair. She waited eagerly all day long for her to come. Not only did your mom not show up, she didn't bother to call either." Regan's voice broke, and her eyes glistened with unshed tears.

At that moment, as she stood there looking so vulnerable, Booker realized how much he loved Regan. Not love, as in romance. He wasn't into white girls. But he cared about her more than he'd ever cared about any of his other friends, and it made him sad to see her hurting so.

"I vaguely remember Mom mentioning something about visiting Willa on Saturday, but I was so wrapped up in worrying about studying, I wasn't really listening. I know she went to work, so I'm not sure what happened. She should've called Willa to explain, though. I know she's been having problems with her phone. Maybe she didn't realize how important her visit was to your grandmother."

"I'm pretty sure she knew," Regan said in an unsteady voice. "And there's no excuse for breaking a dying woman's heart."

A silver Toyota sedan with an Uber decal on the back passenger-side window pulled to the curb in front of them. Regan climbed in the back seat and slammed the door.

When the car started off, Booker ran alongside it, knocking on the window and yelling, "Stop!"

The driver slammed on the brakes, and Regan cracked her window. "I'm in a hurry, Booker. What do you want?"

"Promise you'll call me if you need anything. Or if you just want to talk."

With a curt nod, she closed the window.

Booker watched the car speed away from the curb before turning back toward the building. He felt the weight of the world on his shoulders and considered cutting classes for the rest of the day. But he couldn't afford to get slack now. He had to last for only two more months.

Class was already underway when he got to fourth period.

"You're late, Mr. Grady," his chemistry teacher said when Booker interrupted his lecture on his way into class.

"I'm sorry, sir. I was talking to Regan. Her grandmother was rushed to the hospital this morning. She's upset, and I was trying to make her feel better."

"Oh." Mr. Shaffer's eyes narrowed. "I'm sorry to hear that." He motioned Booker to his desk. "Please have a seat."

Booker's mind began to race as soon as he sat down at his desk. Unlike his dad, his mother was not one to break promises. Then again, he'd learned a lot about his mother in recent days that surprised him. Was Willa going to die? Could Nell somehow be responsible for her decline in health? Regan clearly blamed his mother, but did she blame him too? Why had he called her father a rapist? His heart began to palpitate, and sweat trickled down his back. *Breathe deeply and think positive,* he told himself. He'd researched panic attacks on the internet and learned certain techniques to ward them off when he felt them coming on. Thus far, he hadn't needed to use them. Taking deep breaths, he reminded himself that he was only having a panic attack, not a heart attack, and that he wasn't dying.

He removed his phone from his pocket, and under the cover of his desk, he typed out a text to his mother. **Regan's grandmother was taken to the hospital this morning. She may be dying. Thought you should know.** He opened his chemistry book and tried to focus, but thoughts of Regan and Willa and Nell kept intruding on his concentration.

He'd read enough online to understand that fear was the source of his panic attacks. But what was he so afraid of? He was disappointed, for sure. Disappointed in his father for too many reasons to count, and his mother . . . well, he wasn't exactly sure why he was so disappointed in her. Perhaps that she wasn't the strong moral woman of high values he'd always thought her to be. That she was human, capable of making mistakes. That she'd banished Willa Bellemore from her life when Willa had done so much for her. That she was guilty of bias. He admitted that sounded harsh, but wasn't it true? Mostly, though, he was disappointed in himself for not being smart enough for Harvard, not working hard enough to secure the position of valedictorian, for being soft when he should've stood strong. Booker was afraid of failure. And he was failing in every aspect of his life.

He thought maybe he should see a doctor about his anxiety, but he was too young to start medicating himself to relieve stress. If he couldn't stand the pressure in his small high school in Charleston, South Carolina, he'd never survive the pressure cooker at Harvard or out in the cutthroat world.

There was no place for emotions in the real world. He had a choice. He could be a nice guy. Or he could be successful. But a man couldn't be both. Nice had gotten him nowhere. Certainly not into Harvard. Regan's father, a man who assaulted women, was one of the top criminal attorneys in the country. And his own father, a womanizer who repeatedly cheated on his wife, was considered one of Charleston's best anesthesiologists. Not that Booker condoned their abusive and immoral behavior. That wasn't the point. The point was, he needed to toughen up. Stop being a mama's boy. Stop letting his emotions show. Better not to have any feelings at all. He'd made a fool of himself just now chasing after Regan, begging for her forgiveness. He didn't blame her for rolling the window up in his face. He'd freaked her out by blubbering like an idiot. *Promise you'll call me if you need anything. Or if you just want to talk.* Who said stuff like that? Not his friends. Most of them were jerks. He saw the way they treated their girlfriends. Certainly not like a gentleman should.

How did that saying go? Nice guys finish last? That's it, Book! No more Mr. Nice Guy.

He cleared his mind and turned his attention to the chemistry lecture.

CHAPTER TWENTY-TWO

REGAN

The elevator doors parted, and Regan stepped out, into her mother's arms. "I can't believe this is happening," she sobbed.

"Nothing's happening yet, sweetheart." Lady cupped her head as she held her close. "I didn't mean to scare you. I just thought you'd want to be here."

Regan sniffled as she pulled away. "I'm glad you called me. Where is she? I want to see her."

"They just brought her up from the ER. I haven't been to her room yet. I was waiting for you."

They walked arm in arm down the corridor until they found room 1426. A team of four nurses surrounded the bed, but Regan managed to catch a glimpse of her grandmother's face, pale with rosy splotches on her cheeks. Fresh tears began to well, and Regan bit down on her lower lip to stop it from quivering. Her mother took her by the hand and led her to the other side of the bed, over by the window and out of the way of the activity.

Regan couldn't tear her eyes away from her grandmother's frail body. Even from a distance, she could see a thin film of perspiration covering Willa's face. "Is she in a coma?"

She'd intended the question for her mother, but a pretty nurse, who couldn't have been much older than Regan, offered her a sympathetic smile. "Not a coma. She's somewhat responsive. She's in a state of delirium caused by the fever and her illness."

Regan relaxed a little. "So she knows we're here?"

"To some extent." An older nurse spoke to Regan as she injected a clear liquid into the IV tube. "Many of my patients, after recovering from their illnesses, have reported they were aware of the goings-on around them while in similar states."

She removed the needle, tossed the syringe into a biohazard disposal container, and moved to the whiteboard on the wall. "I'm Linda, and I'll be Mrs. Bellemore's nurse for the rest of the day." She scrawled her name across the board in black marker. "And this is my nurse technician, Lisa." She nodded at the pretty nurse. "If you need anything, press this call button." She pointed to a red button on the side of the bed. "There's also a call button here"—she held up a remote control that was attached to the bed—"as well as the controls for the TV."

Regan doubted her grandmother would be watching any TV.

"You should talk to her," Lisa said as she squirted hand sanitizer on her hands. "The sound of your voices will comfort her."

As she watched the nurse technician leave the room, Regan admired her long silky black ponytail.

She waited until the nurses were gone before inching closer to Willa. "What do I say? I don't know how to tell her goodbye."

Lady joined her daughter bedside. "It's premature for goodbyes. Let's focus on the positive. Tell her how much she's loved, and encourage her to keep fighting."

Regan pressed her fingertips against Willa's flushed cheeks. "If her skin is so hot, why is she shivering?"

"That's the fever." Searching through the room's wardrobe, Lady located a stack of thin cotton blankets and spread them over Willa's body.

"We should read to her," Regan said. "I bet she'd like that."

"I should've thought to bring *Pride and Prejudice*. I left the house so quickly, I didn't have time to pack a bag. I'll run home later and grab some of her things." Lady started toward the door. "I saw a bookcase in the lobby near the elevator when we came in. I'll see if I can find a novel she would approve of."

Regan pulled the recliner close to the bed. "We're here for you, Willa. Just let us know if you need anything."

Lady returned with a paperback copy of Jeannette Walls's *The Glass Castle*. "I hope you don't mind a memoir. There's not a whole lot to choose from, mostly cowboy romances, mysteries, and Harry Potter."

"This is fine," Regan said, and thought, *Just what we need, more family dysfunction.*

Regan read for more than an hour, until her voice was hoarse and her mouth dry. She closed the book and held it out to her mother. "Would you like to read for a while?"

Lady glanced down at the book and up at the wall clock. "Let's take a break. I can't believe it's past one already. No wonder my stomach is growling. There's a cafeteria downstairs. Why don't you go grab a sandwich. I'll stay with Willa until you get back, and then I'll go."

Regan shook her head. "You go ahead." She was anxious to have some time alone with her grandmother. "I have a protein bar if I get hungry," she said, patting her backpack on the floor beside her.

"You need to eat more than a protein bar, honey."

"I'm fine, Mom, really. But you can bring me a bottled water."

Standing, Lady removed her purse from the floor beside the bed. "All right, then." She tucked the thin white covers tight around Willa. "I won't be long. Call or text me if you need me."

Regan waited for Lady to leave before reaching for her grandmother's hand. "You can't go dying on me now, Willa. You have to get better so you can come to my graduation. I'm working hard to keep my grades up. My adviser thinks I'll be named valedictorian. I want you to be proud of me."

She moved to the edge of her seat and leaned in close to Willa, elbows planted on knees. "There are so many things I need your help with. For starters, you have to go shopping with me for my dorm room." She cupped her hand over her mouth and lowered her voice. "You and I both know Mom has terrible taste." She lowered her hand. "I've met some girls on the UNC Facebook page for accepted students. Several of them have asked me to room with them. How do I go about picking a roommate? They all seem so nice. Several are from North Carolina. But the girl I really like is from New Orleans. We have a lot in common, as much as I can tell from Facebook.

"There's a girl in my class at All Saints who's on the wait list for UNC. She asked me to room with her, but based on her grades, I doubt she'll get in. She's too much of a partyer for me, and I'd prefer to live with someone I don't already know anyway. How do I say no without hurting her feelings? I need you to wake up, Willa, so you can help me figure these things out."

Regan shifted from the lounge chair to the edge of the bed. "My friends were talking this morning before school. Over the weekend, they all got asked to the prom. I don't wanna go. Well . . . not really, but sorta. I mean, it's my senior prom. I'll always regret it if I don't go. At least that's what you told me. See, you need to get better so you can convince me to go. I'm sure no one will ask me. There's this one boy in my class, Arthur Broadbottom. He's super shy." She giggled. "I would be too if I had a name like that. But he's cute in a little boy kind of way with his big blue eyes and white-blond hair. I thought about asking him. But what would I wear? Mom would pick out some slinky long gown with sequins and heels so high I'd embarrass myself by falling on the dance floor. Remember that god-awful dress she made me wear to cotillion that time, the one with the big pink flowers all over it? Ugh. I can't go to prom if you're not around to help me get ready." She swatted at her ponytail. "And what would I do about this hair?"

Regan sighed. "What I really need, though, is to talk to you about my dad. Booker claims Dad acted inappropriately toward his mother on the night of Mom's sixteenth birthday party. Mom has told me her side of the story, but I'd like to hear yours. And Dad won't return my calls. I don't know what to think or who to believe or what to say to Booker. I'm sorry, Willa, for dumping this on you when you're so sick."

Willa ran her tongue across her dry, cracked lips and uttered something Regan couldn't make out.

"What's that?" She lowered her head close to her grandmother's lips. "Are you trying to say something?"

"Nell," Willa muttered in a voice so soft Regan could barely hear. "What about Nell?"

Someone coughed behind her, and Regan looked up to see Lady in the doorway. She wondered how long her mother had been standing there and how much she'd heard.

"Willa and I were having a little heart-to-heart talk—one-sided, of course." Regan shifted back to the lounge chair. "Did you get some lunch?"

"Yes. There's a Subway down there if you're interested. And I brought you this." She handed Regan a bottle of water and a white chocolate macadamia nut cookie.

"Thanks, Mom," Regan said, breaking off a small piece of the cookie.

Lady went to the window and looked out over the MUSC campus. "So what were you telling Willa in your one-sided heart-to-heart talk?"

"Nothing important. But she tried to talk just now. Maybe she's getting better."

"It'll take a few days at least. And that's provided she doesn't have any complications. You should go back to school. I know you've missed most of the day, but if you leave now, you can probably make your last class."

"I don't know, Mom. I'd hate to leave her. I want to be here when she wakes up. And what if something happens?" Her voice broke, and she couldn't continue.

Her mother lifted Regan's backpack off the floor and handed it to her. "I'll stay right here by her side. Keep your phone on silent. If I need you, I'll text you."

"You're right. I should probably go. I'm already behind in school from missing that day last week." She slung her backpack over her shoulder and moved to the end of the bed. "Willa and I have an understanding. Don't we, Willa?" She pinched her grandmother's big toe through the blanket. "You're counting on me to be valedictorian, and I'm counting on you to get well."

CHAPTER TWENTY-THREE

NELL

A disgruntled patient, a finicky old man with no family support, kept Nell on her toes all day at the hospital. By seven o'clock, she was ready to turn her shift over to the night nurse. When she collected her things from the break room, she noticed her phone was dead. She'd charged the battery the night before and barely used it during the day. She'd been expecting the damaged screen to eventually cause it to die.

Nell tossed the phone back in her bag. She would stop in at the Apple Store on her way home. She slipped on her windbreaker and headed down the hall. Booker having his own transportation was making her life so much less complicated. She should've insisted Desmond buy him a car when he got his license.

Nell experienced a sense of déjà vu—and not in a good way—when she spotted Lady in the crowded elevator. No one spoke on the ride down except two of her coworkers who were discussing the most recent episode of *This Is Us*. She stared at Lady with a questioning gaze, but Lady kept her eyes glued to the back of the woman's head in front of her.

What was she doing at the hospital? Had she come to confront Nell for failing to show up for her visit with Willa on Saturday?

The elevator emptied at the first floor, the floor that housed the connector to the parking garage. When Lady stayed behind in the elevator, Nell stepped back inside.

"What are you doing here, Lady?" Nell asked as they rode down to the ground floor.

Lady refused to meet her eyes. "I'm here with Willa. She was admitted to the hospital earlier with pneumonia."

"How did that happen?"

"You're the nurse, Nell. Why don't you tell me?" The doors parted, and Lady fled the elevator.

Nell followed on her heels. "Of course I know how a person gets pneumonia, Lady. I'm just surprised is all. For a woman fighting lung cancer, she seemed in reasonably good health when I saw her."

Lady kept walking. "That was almost a week ago. The last chemo treatment was hard on her. And she was crushed when you broke your promise to visit on Saturday."

Nell increased her stride to keep up with Lady as they crossed the lobby. "Are you blaming me?"

"I'm not blaming you for her cancer. Even you don't have that much power. But I blame you for a lot of other things."

When they reached the exit doors, Nell, pointing at the ceiling, said, "You know the entrance to the parking deck is on the next floor up."

"I know how to get to the parking deck. I've been there, remember? The night Willa sent me to tell you about her cancer. What a mistake that was," Lady said, and burst through the exit doors.

As she hustled to keep up with Lady, Nell thought back to that night in the parking deck. How surprised she'd been to see Lady after so many years. And saddened to learn Willa had cancer. Nothing had been the same since that night, the same night Desmond had come home reeking of perfume and she'd told him she wanted a divorce. One day shy of two weeks and so much had happened. *Is it possible I could have changed so much in such a short amount of time?*

Lady arrived at a beat-up old Buick sedan of some extinct model and spun around to face Nell. "I warned Willa that bringing you back into our lives was a mistake. We would've been better off if I'd lied and told her I couldn't find you. She hasn't been the same since you kicked us out of your life. Neither of us has, if you want to know the truth. You don't get to call the shots anymore, Nell. Something happened the night of my sixteenth birthday that changed you. And I want to know what it was."

Nell glanced around the parking lot. A crew of EMTs, unloading a patient from an ambulance, was within earshot. "This is not the time or the place to discuss this."

"You're right about that," Lady said, her hands balled into fists at her sides. "The time to discuss it was the night it happened. Or sometime during the days or weeks afterward. I asked you repeatedly back then. I begged you to tell me what'd happened in the closet that night with Daniel. You wouldn't talk to me, your then best friend, yet you confided in your son, who told my daughter, who now thinks her father is a rapist. Tell me, Nell. I have a right to know the truth. I *deserve* to know the truth. Did he rape you?"

Nell studied Lady's face, flushed now with anger. The years—and, Nell suspected, too much time with the bottle—had not served Lady well. But she saw traces of the girl who had been the best friend she'd ever known beneath the puffiness, wrinkles, and broken capillaries.

"All right." As she collapsed against the car, the years fell away, and Nell was back in the closet with Daniel.

"Technically, he didn't rape me. We didn't have sex, if that's what you want to know. But he assaulted me. He left bite marks and bruises all over my body." She squeezed her eyes shut, trying unsuccessfully to block out the memory of Daniel's malicious grin, his lip curled in disgust. *Brown sugar tastes like shit.* "And he said things to me, things I can't bring myself to repeat. He robbed me of my innocence and my dignity. Nothing was ever the same for me after that." She opened her eyes. "Now I have a question for you, Lady. Why'd you marry him after what he did to me?"

Her head jerked back. "After what he did to you?" she said, her voice raised. "I had no idea what he did to you, because you never told me what he did to you."

Nell's mouth dropped open. "What did you think happened, then?"

"I honestly thought the two of you had consensual sex, that you agreed to do something you were later ashamed of. I considered every possibility on the planet for about a minute. But I dismissed every single one of them. You want to know why? Because I believed in my heart that you would've told me if he'd mistreated you. You and I'd shared all our secrets since we were tiny little girls. How was I supposed to know you were keeping the biggest one of all from me?"

Nell looked away, unable to meet Lady's wounded gaze. "You're right. We knew everything there was to know about each other. There were plenty of things we never said, things that never needed saying because, somehow, we just knew. Like we were telepathic or something. I just assumed you knew this too."

"Well, you assumed wrong. And your assumptions altered the courses of all our lives. You walked away from Willa and me. We considered ourselves your family, and you shut the door on us. After all my mother had done for you." Lady pointed at the hospital building. "That woman loves you, Nell, more than she ever loved me." Her voice broke, and tears streamed down her cheeks. "God knows why after the way you've treated her."

Nell's chin quivered. "You said yourself that something changed in me that night. The truth is, that change began two years beforehand when I lost my mother. I didn't understand the impact her death had on me until years later. I *am* grateful for everything Willa did for me. Without her, I would've been forced into foster care. Instead, I lived a privileged lifestyle in a loving home. But I was proud of my mama, and I was proud of who I was. *She* was my link to your world. When she died, I felt like I no longer belonged. I felt like a misfit. Things that were once so right suddenly seemed so wrong. And the incident with Daniel, terribly wrong in itself, exacerbated the feelings I'd been struggling with for two years. It was all too much for me. And even now, after all this time, it's difficult to explain."

"Then save it. Because I don't care anymore." Swiping at her tears, Lady nudged Nell out of the way so she could open the car door. "I'm in a hurry. I need to grab some of Willa's things from home and get back as soon as possible. I don't want to leave her alone for too long."

"I'd be happy to go sit with her until you get back."

"No! You've done enough damage already." Lady slid behind the steering wheel and started the engine. "I mean it, Nell. Mama is too weak to ride on your emotional roller coaster. I want you to stay away from her. And from me."

CHAPTER TWENTY-FOUR

NELL

1981

During the immediate aftermath of the assault, Nell wore turtlenecks to cover her bruises and a stony expression to hide the pain she felt inside. She trudged through the days, forcing herself out of bed in the mornings after nights of tormented sleep. She saw Daniel everywhere, in the faces of the men she passed on the sidewalks and the boys in her class at school. At night, when she was alone in bed, his hateful words to her at the party echoed throughout her room.

Willa and her teachers noticed and expressed their concern for her uncharacteristically sullen mood. But the real change happened deep within her and was more gradual. Throughout the spring and summer months of that year, she experienced a cataclysmic shift in her perspective on life where everything she had once held dear suddenly seemed meaningless and insincere. Dinners at home were torturous affairs. One, in particular, stood out from all the rest.

It was a warm evening in late May, a week before school let out for the summer. Taking advantage of the pleasant weather, Willa had set the table on the piazza. She'd called the girls to supper, and Nell was on her way out the front door to the porch when their maid, Bernice, motioned her to the kitchen.

"Help me with these plates, girl. My arthritis is acting up something terrible."

Nell cringed but did as she was told. She didn't mind being asked to help out. She helped out around the house all the time. It was Bernice's derogatory use of the word *girl* that made her angry.

Willa had long since given up on finding a suitable housekeeper when, in March, one had unexpectedly fallen into her lap. Out of the blue, the neighbors down the street had moved to Texas, leaving their beloved Bernice without a job. Willa felt compelled to help the Steeles by offering Bernice a job. At first, things appeared to be working out well with Bernice. Willa and Lady had grown fond of her and were disappointed when Bernice announced she was moving to Savannah, Georgia, in June to live with her daughter. Nell, on the other hand, wished Bernice a speedy farewell. Bernice had made it clear through subtle innuendos how much she disapproved of Nell's presence in the Bellemores' home.

Nell forgot about Bernice once she'd taken her seat at the table on the piazza. She refused to let that old battle-ax spoil her good mood, a rare feeling those days. The sweet scent of honeysuckle filled the evening air, reminding her that summer was not far off. As a child, she'd longed for summer evenings when she and Lady were allowed to stay outside after dark to catch fireflies.

Nell felt overdressed in a skirt and blouse next to Willa, who was still wearing her gardening clothes and sun hat, with dirt caked beneath her fingernails, and Lady, who appeared on the piazza in her new bikini, four triangles of white crocheted cloth attached by strings with the tag still hanging out of the bottoms.

Willa's eyeballs popped at the sight of Lady's bikini. "That swimsuit is vulgar. March yourself back upstairs and change into proper attire."

Lady stomped her foot and went inside to change.

"And return that swimsuit to the store tomorrow," Willa called after her.

Lady was back in a flash wearing a terry cloth cover-up over her bikini. Nell could smell the alcohol on Lady's breath despite the mint gum she was smacking. Five out of the past seven nights, Lady had shown up intoxicated for dinner, and Nell found it disturbing that Willa didn't seem to notice. Who knew where Lady got the alcohol or where she went to drink it? Nell suspected she'd been cutting classes. She certainly hadn't been studying. At least not that Nell had observed. Willa would hit the roof when Lady's grades came.

They held hands as they blessed their food—liver and onions, Nell's least favorite dish. Bernice's cooking was almost as bad as Willa's. Almost.

Lady removed the gum from her mouth and stuck it to the side of her plate. "So . . . ," she started as she sliced off a sliver of liver. "Mindy's parents asked me to spend the summer with them on Sullivan's Island."

"The whole summer?" Willa asked with raised eyebrows. "I don't think so."

Lady let out an exaggerated sigh. "Why not?"

"Because that is too much of an imposition on the Bowens."

"It's not, actually. They practically begged me. Mr. Bowen is hiring us to work in his sandwich shop during the day, and the next-door neighbors want us to babysit their twin four-year-olds when they go out at night. Come on, Mama, please," Lady said in that whiny voice that grated Nell's nerves.

"You may visit them for a week, possibly two. That's a gracious plenty." Willa turned away from her daughter and set her eyes on Nell. "And what're your plans for the summer?"

She shrugged. "I'm planning to earn as much money as possible for college. I've interviewed for several jobs. I'm waiting to hear back from them."

"Good for you! How admirable of you to want to save money for college."

"That's just great!" Lady dropped her fork on her plate with a clatter. "Let me get this straight. Nell's admirable for getting a job, but I have an opportunity to work at the beach, and you won't let me because I didn't offer to help pay for college. I'll give you every dime I earn if you let me go. I don't want to be stuck in Charleston this summer, sitting around this house all day watching Nell sulk."

Willa cut her eyes at her daughter. "Watch your tone, missy."

Lady mimicked her mother. "Watch your tone, missy."

Willa's face beamed red. "I'm tired of your attitude, Lady Bellemore."

Lady balled up her napkin and tossed it on her plate. "And I'm tired of you putting Nell on a pedestal, when she's not your daughter and I am."

"You're both my daughters, Lady."

Lady rolled her eyes. "Yeah, right."

"You may be excused." Willa nodded her head at Lady, a signal for her to leave the table. "And take your plate to the kitchen."

Lady pushed back from the table. "I don't care what you say, Willa. I'm spending the summer on Sullivan's with the Bowens. They're nicer to me than you are." She stormed off the porch, nearly colliding with Bernice, who'd been eavesdropping from inside the doorway.

Bernice appeared flustered. "Oh goodness. Excuse me, Mrs. Bellemore. I came to see if you need anything." Bernice moved toward Lady's plate, but Willa motioned her away. "We'll worry about that later, Bernice."

Bernice hustled back inside.

"Now that that's out of the way, we can eat our supper in peace," Willa said. "I'm sorry, Nell. I don't know what's gotten into Lady lately."

Nell stared down at her plate, the liver and onions blurred by tears. "It's fine."

"No, it's not fine. Nothing has been fine around here for months. Lady's delivery needs some work, but her message was loud and clear. And I happen to concur. I sense that something is desperately wrong in your world. But I can't help you if I don't know what it is."

Nell cast her eyes down and silently debated whether to confide in her adopted mother, finally deciding against it. Lady had made it clear that Nell's presence in their lives was causing problems in her relationship with her mama. She had only two more years of high school, and then she'd be off to college.

"Nothing's wrong, Miss Willa. May I please be excused? I'm not hungry." Without waiting for an answer, she gathered her plate and Lady's and took them inside.

Bernice was waiting for her in the kitchen, a self-satisfied smirk on her lips. "Miss Lady's right, ya know? It's not fitting for a black girl to live in a white woman's house. You're not a member of this family no matter how much you think you is. I knew your mama well. This ain't what she would've wanted for you."

Nell elbowed Bernice out of the way of the sink. "Funny thing, Bernice," she said as she rinsed the dinner plates, "I never heard my mama mention your name once."

"See there! That hoity-toity attitude of yours ain't gonna get you nowhere. Time you learned your place in life. Your place is right here in this kitchen."

"That's where you're wrong, Bernice." Nell stored the plates in the drying rack and turned to face the old woman. "God gave me a good brain, and I plan to use it. I'm gonna make something of myself. I'm gonna rise above all this." She held her arms wide. "That's what my mama wanted for me. You know how I know? Because she told me so a thousand times."

Nell grabbed her book bag and raced upstairs to her room. She spent the rest of the night studying for an algebra test, doing her best to block out the sound of Lady's loud music vibrating the wall between their rooms. For the first time since Lady's birthday party, she didn't cry herself to sleep that night. Nell had been fooling herself to think she belonged in this house. Daniel and now Bernice had put her in her place. Their words had been a wake-up call, not a reminder of who she was but of who she wanted to become.

~

After a series of nasty arguments, Willa finally relented and allowed Lady to spend the summer on Sullivan's Island with Mindy. Nell was thrilled to see them go. She needed space without Lady hovering over her, her scrutinizing gaze always watching her.

Nell spent her nights that summer babysitting for children of members of her church and her days candy-striping at Roper Hospital. She volunteered with a girl from her school whom she'd known but had never considered a friend. Like Nell, Angie aspired to be a nurse. In their free time, when they weren't researching nursing programs at the public library, they were exploring the many wonderful cultural opportunities the city had to offer. Nell and Lady shared a history, one that was not of their choosing but of their circumstances. But Nell's friendship with Angie was based on the many things they had in common. Nell had always kept her school and home lives separate. She'd never considered inviting any of her black friends from school to her house. Not only was it too complicated to explain why she lived with a white family, she was also embarrassed by their wealth when most of her schoolmates were underprivileged. But on a sweltering afternoon in early August, when Nell and Angie were strolling along the seawall and found themselves at the end of her street, she invited Angie to come over for a glass of sweet tea.

"Wow! You live here? Your parents must be rich," Angie said, marveling at the house as they walked up the sidewalk to the back door.

"Not my real parents." Nell held the door open for her friend. "Come on in. We'll get some tea and I'll explain."

Because the inside of the house was ten degrees hotter than outside, they took their tea to the piazza where overhead fans offered relief from the heat while Nell told Angie about her mother dying and how she'd come to be adopted by the Bellemores.

"You're fortunate to have a wonderful family to take care of you, but I can see how it might feel weird," Angie said.

"And getting weirder by the minute." As the afternoon wore on, Nell confided in Angie about her growing resentment toward her situation. "It's hard to live in a white girl's world, Angie. Is it wrong of me to want out?"

"Not at all," Angie said. "But look at the bright side. You only have two more years of high school to endure. And you don't have to worry about paying for college."

"That's very true." Nell doubted she would've had the chance to even go to college if her mother were still alive. "Thanks for listening and for being so understanding."

"You can tell me anything. That's what friends are for."

Nell had never felt comfortable confiding her innermost feelings to any of her other friends. Even Lady. Especially Lady. When they were children, Lady and Nell had told each other everything, but that sharing of secrets had changed over the years. As with most things in their relationship, Lady had to be in control, the center of attention. Now Lady did most of the talking and Nell the listening.

Nell's stomach was growling for dinner when Willa arrived home from lounging beside the pool at the yacht club a few minutes later.

The girls stood to greet her. "Willa, I'd like you to meet my friend Angie."

Willa extended her hand to Angie, but she didn't meet her gaze, let alone make idle conversation like she did with Lady's friends.

"Do you mind if Angie stays for dinner?" Nell asked Willa. "I was thinking about making BLTs."

Willa's face beamed red. "Not tonight, sweetheart. I'm awfully tired. Let's wait and do it another time."

"I totally understand." Angie snatched her bag up off the table. "My parents are expecting me at home for dinner anyway."

"I'll see you tomorrow, then, Angie." Nell walked her friend to the edge of the porch and watched her scurry down the sidewalk to the street. She waited until Angie was out of sight before spinning on her heel to face Willa. "That was rude. You never treat Lady's friends like that."

"I didn't mean to be rude, honey. I'm sorry if I came across that way. This heat has me all outta sorts." Willa waved her hand in front of her face, fanning herself. "We'll invite your friend over for dinner later in the week when we have more time to prepare."

As much as she preached equality, Willa was the last person Nell thought would be unwelcoming to any of her friends, regardless of race. Willa never mentioned having Angie to dinner again, but as the summer came to an end, she began to drop subtle hints encouraging Nell to socialize more with her other friends, the white girls she and Lady had grown up with. The girls who, she was beginning to realize, were never her friends.

CHAPTER TWENTY-FIVE

LADY

Lady's hands trembled as she struggled to light a cigarette on her way out of the hospital parking lot just after her encounter with Nell. Their confrontation had brought back all the anger, hurt, and sorrow from long ago. As if she weren't worried enough about her mother's health, terrified, in fact, that she might lose her. She felt horrible about what had happened to Nell on her sixteenth birthday. How scared and alone she must have felt. If only she'd confided in Willa, she would've gotten her some help. But then things would've turned out differently, and Lady wouldn't have Regan. And Lady refused to feel guilty about that.

Taking a right-hand turn onto Halsey Boulevard, she merged onto Lockwood and punched the gas pedal. She craved a drink in a very bad way.

Regan had called an hour ago to check on Willa. "How is she?"

"About the same. She's mumbling and moaning, but she hasn't said anything intelligible. Her fever's still pretty high, though."

"I can come stay with her tonight if you need me," Regan had offered.

"Thanks, sweetheart, but you're where you need to be. I'm fine to stay here. You finish your studying, and then get some supper and a good night's sleep."

"I may spend the night with Janie if that's all right with you. I don't really want to sleep at home alone."

"That's fine with me," Lady had said. "I will feel better with you at the Jensens'. Tell Janie hello, and we'll talk in the morning."

Regan had already come and gone by the time Lady arrived home. She packed a suitcase for her mother and an overnight bag for herself. She stopped in the kitchen on her way out and filled her flask with vodka. To take the edge off, she took a swill from the bottle before screwing the lid back on and slipping it into her purse.

She drove slower on her return to the hospital. She contemplated grabbing some snacks from the convenience store and then decided that booze was the only sustenance she needed. At that time of night, she had no trouble locating a parking place near the elevators in the garage.

Her mother's condition remained the same, but the nurses had changed shifts, and the night nurse named Crystal, a woman with jet-black hair and eyes as dark, whose abrupt manner intimidated Lady, was finishing her assessment.

Lady set Willa's suitcase in the corner out of the way and waited for Crystal to leave the room before removing some of the items she'd brought from home. She smeared Vaseline across her mother's cracked lips and massaged cream into her dry hands. She opened *Pride and Prejudice* to the dog-eared page and settled into the lounge chair beside the bed to read. After forty-five minutes, her thirst got the best of her and she retrieved her flask from her purse. She made up the sofa with the blanket and pillow she'd brought from home. Propping herself against the pillow, she stared out the window at the twinkling lights of downtown Charleston, allowing herself to relax after a harrowing day.

Her mind turned back to her showdown with Nell in the parking lot. Unleashing her wrath on her old friend had released decades of pent-up emotions. She'd stood up to Nell with a strength she hadn't known she possessed, and through that strength, she'd gained confidence. She patted herself on the back. *Well done, Lady.*

She brought the flask to her lips and, thinking better of it, withdrew it without taking a sip. Vodka was not what she wanted. Nor what she needed. What she no longer craved. She untangled herself from the blanket and crossed the room to the bathroom, setting the flask on the edge of the sink. She splashed cold water on her face and dried it with a scratchy brown paper towel. She took a good hard look at herself in the mirror for the first time in years. And didn't like what she saw.

You don't have any control of whether your mama lives or dies, Lady Bellemore, but you have control over you, she whispered to her reflection. *You control your health, at least to some extent. You control your weight, what you eat and drink.* She unscrewed the lid on the flask and poured the vodka down the drain. *You control your wardrobe and skin care. You control how you spend your days. You control your future. You're only fifty-three years old, a youngster compared to your eighty-one-year-old mama. You could live twenty or thirty more years. But you've got to make some changes. Take back control of your life. Stop going through the motions of life and live.*

Dropping the empty flask in her purse on the way back to the sofa, she stretched out and made herself as comfortable as possible on the stiff cushions. For the next few hours, she dozed off and on, acutely aware of nurses coming in and out of the room to check vitals and reposition Willa when her blood oxygen dropped. The hall finally grew quiet, and Lady fell into a deep sleep. She had a nightmare about her sixteenth birthday, a surreal and twisted account of the party where Daniel raped Nell and a baby girl named Regan with Booker's face was born nine months later.

Lady woke around daybreak to the shrill of alarms and a team of nurses swarming the room. She rushed to her mother's bedside. "What's happening?"

"That's what we're trying to figure out," Crystal said, elbowing Lady out of the way.

Lady rounded the bed to the other side and inserted herself between two kinder-looking nurses.

"Her fever has spiked," the nurse on the right said. "The antibiotics don't appear to be working."

Fear gripped Lady's chest. "What does that mean?"

"That means we try some new antibiotics," the nurse on her left said. "We've paged the doctor on call. He'll be here shortly."

Lady returned to the sofa and sat down, burying her face in her hands. *Please don't die, Mama. I need you here with me. You're the strongest person I know. Show me that strength now.*

As she watched the nurses work, her mind drifted back to her nightmare. She remembered most of it in vivid detail, but there was something important about her dream she couldn't recall. She sensed that this thing, whatever it was, was vital to her reaching a resolution in her relationship with Nell.

As the conversation between the nurses grew urgent, Lady regretted her decision to pour her vodka down the drain. While giving up the booze was the right choice for her, she questioned her strength to see it through.

Unable to bear it any longer, she ran out of the room and down the hall to the chapel she'd noticed during her comings and goings. A row of wooden benches, three deep, was arranged in front of a small table that served as an altar, holding a vase of fresh flowers and a guest book. Relieved to find the tiny room empty, she sat down on the front bench and bowed her head in prayer. She prayed with every emotion she possessed, like she hadn't prayed in years. She turned her anguish over to God, asking him to grant the doctors the knowledge and skills to save her mother's life.

When she lifted her head again, she was surprised to find an elderly black woman sitting beside her. She'd been too lost in her prayers to notice she'd entered the chapel.

"Someone you love in trouble?" the woman asked.

Lady stared at her brown eyes, dark skin, and full lips. She wasn't in the habit of confiding in strangers, but something about this woman seemed vaguely familiar. "My mother," Lady answered in a soft voice.

"Cancer?" A dimple near the right side of the woman's mouth gave the impression she was smiling despite her serious expression.

Lady nodded. "Lung cancer. She has pneumonia. I'm not sure she'll make it."

"I'm sorry to hear that," she said, folding her arthritic hands in her lap. "Does she know you love her?"

Lady thought this an odd question, and it bothered her that she wasn't sure of the answer. "I think so."

"Now is not the time for uncertainties. Your mama needs to feel your strength."

Lady fought to keep her voice steady. "That's the problem. I'm not strong." The strength she'd experienced only hours ago had vanished.

The woman raised a penciled eyebrow. "According to whom—you?"

Lady nodded. "And my mother. She's never actually said it, but I know she thinks it."

The woman shifted on the bench, angling her body toward Lady. "Do you have children of your own?"

"Yes," Lady said. "I have a seventeen-year-old daughter."

"Are you proud of her?"

Lady squirmed, uncomfortable under her piercing gaze. "Of course I'm proud of her. She's my daughter."

"Just as, I'm sure, your mother is proud of you."

There was so much about Regan for Lady to be proud of. She was intelligent, ambitious, good hearted, and good natured. What was there about Lady for Willa to be proud of? Alcoholic. Unemployed. Divorced.

The woman continued, "You've come to the right place if you're looking for strength. Ask Jesus to walk at your side, and he will hold your hand through whatever lies ahead."

Lady had come to the chapel to beg God to save her mother's life. Sure, she wanted more time with Willa, but if she was honest with herself, she was terrified of being alone. According to this woman, she'd approached the situation all wrong. Whether her mother lived or died, having faith in the Lord would give her the strength to persevere—*through whatever lies ahead.* Did that include the arduous months of detox and the challenges of starting a new life? Lady thought that was asking too much for someone who had so little faith in herself, let alone in the Lord. She'd once considered herself a devout Christian. She'd gone to church nearly every Sunday of her youth, but her faith had waned over the years with each hard knock life had given her.

She stared down at her lap, afraid to meet the woman's eyes for fear she might discover her a fraud. When she looked up again some minutes later, the woman had departed the chapel as quietly as she'd come in.

CHAPTER TWENTY-SIX

NELL

Nell stole away from her floor during lunchtime on Tuesday to visit Willa. Throughout the night and the long hours of the morning, she'd pondered all Lady had said to her in the parking lot the day before. And she realized just how much pain the choices she'd made all those years ago had caused the only real family she'd ever known.

Exiting the elevator on the fourth floor, she walked toward Willa's room, bracing herself for another confrontation with Lady. But Willa was alone in her room, a tiny frail woman fighting for her life. Nell approached the bed. The monitors showed a rapid heart rate and elevated blood pressure, signs that she was still running a fever.

"Hey there, Miss Willa. It's me, Nell. I'm so sorry you're having such a tough time. Your family . . . Lady and Regan are counting on you to get better. I have some things I need to get off my chest. I'd rather talk to you when you get better." *On second thought, what if I don't get another chance?* Nell took Willa's hand in hers. "Oh heck, I might as well say them now, since you can probably hear me."

She took a deep breath to steady her voice. "I'm sorry for breaking my promise to visit on Saturday. I had to work at the last minute, but I have no excuse for not calling to let you know I wouldn't be coming. This is years . . . no, decades overdue, but I came here to apologize for cutting you out of my life. You didn't deserve to be treated that way. You were a generous and loving mother to me, and I slammed the door in your face."

Nell stared out the window as she gathered her thoughts.

"I'd like to explain, if I may." She sat down gently on the bed. "You see, those years were difficult. Mama's death was hard on me . . . and then . . . after the way Daniel treated me . . . Well, I was determined to make it on my own. I convinced myself that I didn't need you in my life. I allowed foolish things, like the color of our skin, to cloud my judgment."

Nell readjusted Willa's finger pulse oximeter and watched her oxygen saturation level increase. "There, now that's better."

Nell continued, "When I was growing up, our home was like a hippie commune of mothers and daughters living together as sisters." Nell snickered. "Except for poor Mr. Bellemore. I can only imagine how he felt being surrounded by so many women. No wonder he spent so much time on his boat. He was a good sport about it, though. He never seemed to resent our presence in your lives."

She traced the outline of Willa's thin leg beneath the blanket. "Thanks to you, Miss Willa, Mama and I had a good life. You were a second mother to me from the day I was born, my adopted mother long before you signed the papers.

"You need to get well so that I can make up for all the heartache I've caused you. I've deprived all of us the opportunity to be a family. I've deprived my son the chance to know his grandmother. And Regan and Booker the chance to be cousins. But it's not too late. You just need to get better.

"I'm having some trouble in my life, Miss Willa. My husband has left me for another woman. Breaking up after twenty-eight years of marriage is difficult, even if it's for the best. I could use some of your comforting words right about now. I always valued your advice. For the life of me, I don't know why I never told you about Daniel. I guess I was scared that you'd stop loving me. Maybe—"

Lady stormed into the room. "What do you think you're doing?"

Nell jerked her head around. "Geez, Lady. You shouldn't sneak up on a person like that. You scared me."

"I thought I told you to stay away from us."

Lady, who'd obviously been at the hospital all night, was still wearing the same rumpled khakis and faded long-sleeve T-shirt from the day before. Nell, having worked the overnight shift many times, doubted she'd gotten much sleep from the constant interruptions.

Lady dropped her purse on the desk beside the TV. "You can't just swoop in at the eleventh hour expecting her to forgive you. Not after the way you treated her."

Nell sprang to her feet. "Were you eavesdropping on me?"

"So what if I was? I need to know what you said to her so that I can do damage control if and when she wakes up. We were living a quiet existence until you came back into our lives. You've caused this family enough pain to last a lifetime." Lady strode across the room to the door. "Now please leave," she said, gripping the knob.

"You're not without fault here, Lady. You were jealous of the way Willa treated me, and you acted like a spoiled brat. Come to think of it, not only did you act like a spoiled brat, you *were* a spoiled brat. Your mother granted you anything your little heart desired. And you couldn't stand it when you had to share her with me."

"Why you—" The sounding of alarms interrupted Lady midsentence. She turned to the monitors. "What is it? What's going on?"

"She's going into cardiac arrest." Nell rushed to the door and yelled down the hall, "Code Blue! Stat!"

Nurses crowded into the room with a redheaded female doctor on their heels. Nell pulled Lady out of the way, and they hovered near the doorway as the medical staff prepared to defibrillate the patient. She noticed Lady sucking on a fistful of her T-shirt, like she used to suck on her favorite ratty blanket as a child. Out of habit, she tugged on Lady's arm. "Stop sucking your shirt, Lady."

Lady smacked Nell's hand away. "Don't you dare touch me," she said in a voice loud enough to get everyone's attention.

Glancing over her shoulder, the doctor suspiciously eyed Nell's scrubs and ordered her to clear the room. Nell dragged Lady out into the hall and stood near the doorway, listening to the commotion inside until Willa was out of danger.

Nell turned toward Lady. "Sounds like her heart is back in rhythm. You should go be with her."

Lady's blue eyes were wide with fear, and a sheen of sweat covered her face. Nell knew little about Lady's present-day life. Or her life for the past thirty-plus years. Based on her temperament of late, in the parking lot the day before and in the room just now, Nell suspected her old friend might be unstable.

Worried the redheaded doctor might question why she was harassing a family member, Nell started moving toward the elevator to avoid further contact. She wouldn't put it past Lady to file a complaint, and she'd worked too hard to let Lady ruin her career.

"Wait! You can't leave now!" Lady said, hustling along beside her. "We need you here."

"I have to get back to my floor, Lady. My lunch break is almost over."

Lady tossed her hands in the air. "Fine! Walk away. That's what you always do anyway."

Nell glanced at her watch. "Look, Lady, my patients will come searching for me if I'm not back soon. And since my presence is obviously a source of agitation and discomfort for you, I see no point in staying. Miss Willa's in good hands. The staff will get you anything you need."

She stepped to the nearby elevator and punched the up button. Removing her new phone from her pocket, she accessed her apps, created a new contact, and typed in Lady's name. "What's your number?" Lady mumbled her number, and Nell entered it into the phone. She tapped out a text—This is Nell—and pressed send. "Now you have my number. Call me if there is anything I can do, either in a professional capacity or if you just want me to sit with Willa while you grab a bite to eat. I can usually get away, as long you give me a few minutes' notice."

"We've gotten along fine all these years without you. Somehow I think we'll survive." Lady spun on her heel and stormed off down the hall.

Nell gaped at her retreating back. A minute ago, she was begging her to stay. Same old Lady, never could make up her mind.

CHAPTER TWENTY-SEVEN

WILLA

Willa woke with a start from a dream she couldn't recall. She slipped on her robe and trudged down the stairs to the kitchen where Mavis waited with tea for her at the table.

She lowered herself to the chair next to her old friend. "I'm feeling my age these days, May May. How is it you continue to look so young when my bones ache, my skin sags, and my hearing's so bad I can't hear myself think?"

Mavis's lips parted in a smile as she lifted her fingers to her cheek. "Must be my night cream."

Willa's mouth dropped open. "You actually spoke to me! After decades of one-sided conversations, you're talking to me again?"

She laughed. "Just this once."

Willa relished the sound of Mavis's laughter in her kitchen. She eyed her grandmother's Limoges tea service and a plate of cheese biscuits. "I see you brought out the good china and made cheese biscuits. What's so special about tonight?"

"We used to make all our important decisions over a proper cup of tea. Remember?"

"I'm confused, though. What decision are we making tonight?"

"Hold your horses. We'll get to that in a minute." Mavis poured two cups of tea, adding a spoonful of sugar to one and a drop of cream to the other. "First, have one of these." She passed her the plate of cheese biscuits.

Willa took a cheese biscuit and bit it in half. "These are divine. They're fluffier than usual. What'd you do different?"

"Must be the altitude." As Mavis spread her arms wide over her head, the walls of the kitchen vanished, and the linoleum floor dropped out from beneath them, leaving them surrounded on all sides by deep-blue sky.

Willa gripped the edge of the table. "What on earth?"

"Earth's down there," Mavis said, lowering her gaze.

Willa craned her neck to see patches of land and bodies of water thousands of miles beneath them. "I don't understand, May May. What's happening?"

Mavis stroked Willa's arm. "No need to be afraid, Miss Willa. You're not alone." She slid the teapot between them and opened the lid. "Look inside."

Willa peered down inside the pot. What she saw took her breath away. "That's me! In a hospital bed! Am I dying?"

"That's for you to decide."

She gulped back fear. "Since when does one have a say over whether they live or die?"

Mavis lifted a plump shoulder. "Happens sometimes. You've been sending us mixed signals. You told me yourself, you're ready to join the afterworld, yet we're getting vibes that you're nervous about leaving your loved ones. I'm here to help you decide if your mission on earth is complete."

"How do I make a monumental decision like that?"

"The same way you make any decision—by looking at it from every angle." She nodded at the teapot. "Have a peek."

An image of Regan at Willa's bedside suddenly appeared inside the teapot. "That's my granddaughter. But I can't hear what she's saying."

"Oops. I forgot to turn the volume up." Mavis snapped her fingers, and Regan's sad voice filled the air.

Willa white-knuckled the collar of her bathrobe as she listened to Regan pouring her heart out to her.

"You're an important part of her life," Mavis said. "She'll miss you if you die."

"Perhaps I'm too important to her. Is it possible my relationship with Regan has come between my granddaughter and her mother?"

"You tell me. It ain't my job to answer the questions, Miss Willa. I'm merely here to listen."

Willa returned her attention to the teapot, where Lady had taken center stage. Despite her tired and bedraggled appearance, it was obvious her daughter was taking excellent care of Willa.

"What's this?" Willa asked when she saw Lady emptying a flask in the bathroom sink. "She's pouring out her booze. Does this mean she's ready to quit drinking?"

Mavis held a finger to her lips. "Shh! Listen."

The hospital room faded away, and a small chapel of sorts came into view. "You've come to the right place if you're looking for strength," an elderly black woman was saying to Lady. "Ask Jesus to walk at your side, and he will hold your hand through whatever lies ahead."

Willa looked up from the teapot to study Mavis's face. She had the same slight dimple on the right side of her mouth as the woman in the pot. "Is that you?"

"Deep down inside, Lady is ready to clean up her act, Miss Willa. But she has a difficult road ahead."

"I love my daughter with all my heart, but I'm not sure she has it in her to quit."

Mavis's jaw tightened. "One thing's for sure—she can't do it alone."

"You don't know, May May. You haven't been around for thirty-nine years. My expectations regarding my daughter are low for a reason. She's disappointed me one too many times."

"Let me give you a little heavenly advice, Miss Willa. Your low expectations are your problem, and you need to fix them. If you don't believe in her, Miss Lady will sense it."

"I'm sure she already does."

Willa looked back inside the teapot. This time Nell was at her bedside, pleading with her not to die. Willa gasped, and her hand flew to her mouth. "Oh no! Poor Nell. Her husband left her for another woman." Willa listened with brow furrowed and head cocked to the side. "She apologized for shutting me out of her life. Do you think she means it?"

"My Nell made some bad decisions in her life, but I believe she's ready to own up to them."

"She mentioned Daniel. I didn't realize the two of them even knew each other."

"There's a lot you don't understand about the past, Miss Willa. It's up to you how much you want to know."

Mavis closed the lid on the pot and topped off their cups with tea. When she set the teapot down again, Willa lifted the lid. "What happened to them? They disappeared."

"Assuming they were ever there in the first place," Mavis said with a glint in her eye as she sipped her tea.

"This dream or hallucination"—Willa held her arms out wide—"whatever this thing is, is getting weirder by the minute."

Mavis winked at her. "Welcome to heaven."

Willa's eyebrows shot up. "Is that where I am, in heaven? What happened to me deciding whether I want to live or die?"

"Oh. Sorry. That's a phrase we use up here like you earthly beings say *Welcome to the real world.*" She turned her bulky body to face Willa. "Before you decide whether you want to live or die, you must first experience a little slice of heaven." She took hold of Willa's hands. "Now close your eyes and try to relax."

Closing her eyes, Willa allowed the tension to drain from her body. Soft music filled the air, and a calm she could only describe as serenity came over her. She experienced no worries or desires or hunger or pain. She simply existed, floating high above the earth on her own cloud. The peace was so consuming she couldn't bring herself to open her eyes again.

Some minutes later, she heard Mavis's soft voice near her ear. "Nice, ain't it?"

"Hmm-mm. I've never felt this kind of contentment before."

Mavis clapped her hands, and Willa snapped out of her dreamlike state.

"Tell me something," Mavis said. "What exactly were you after when you asked Lady to find Nell?"

Tension returned to Willa's body. "I wanted to see her one last time."

"Come now, Miss Willa. You can't lie to an angel."

"I'm not lying to you, May May. I just don't know how to answer your question, because I'm uncertain of my motives. I was looking for closure, I guess. And I wanted to apologize to Nell for letting her down."

"What're you talking about? You did more for my child than any woman could ever ask of another."

"That's not true, and you know it. You would've done the same for Lady."

Mavis looked away. "Except that I didn't have the means to provide for her the way you provided for Nell. Because of your generosity, Nell got to go to college and become a nurse. You made sacrifices for my daughter that no other white woman I knew back then would've made. You ignored your friends when they talked behind your back. You always took up for Nell. You treated her like your own."

"Because I thought of her as my own." Willa paused, willing herself to continue despite the tightness in her throat. "Especially after you were gone. Please believe me when I tell you I tried, May May. Even after her graduation, when she told us she no longer wanted to be a part of our lives, I tried to stay in touch. I sent cards and letters to the last address I had for her in Atlanta. Those cards and letters went unanswered for a couple of years, until one day a birthday card came back with one of those stamps showing Return to Sender, Forwarding Address Unknown."

"Those years were hard for her." Mavis draped one arm across her ample chest. "She got lost. In some ways, she still ain't found her way."

"Do you know why she cut us out of her life?"

"I do, but I'm not at liberty to say. I can tell you this much—figuring that out is the first step to finding your closure."

"According to what Regan said in there," Willa began, pointing at the teapot, then, realizing the absurdity of talking about people she'd seen in a teapot, she quickly retracted her finger, "Booker claims that Daniel acted inappropriately toward Nell at Lady's sixteenth birthday party. Which makes sense, since that's around the time Nell began to act strange."

"That's as good a place to start as any."

"It's not just me, you know. Now that Booker and Regan have been dragged into this mess, we need closure for the sake of the whole family." Willa fell back in her seat. "I should just quit while I'm ahead. I don't have the energy for this. I'm a dying woman. Let them figure it out on their own after I'm gone. Or not. I can't force them to make nice. They adored each other when they were girls. Maybe their relationship isn't important to them."

Mavis pushed the teapot in front of her. When Willa opened the lid, Nell's and Lady's angry voices escaped. "Folks don't argue unless something means something to them."

"I guess you're right, May May." Willa sighed. "If I don't die now, how much longer do I have to live?"

"You'll know when your time's up." At the snap of her fingers, the walls and floor returned to the kitchen. Standing, Mavis loaded a tray with the dishes and carried them to the sink. "If I may, I'd like to ask a favor," she said with her back to Willa as she rinsed the dishes.

"Name it," Willa said, coming to stand beside her.

"I'd like for you to meet my grandson. He seems like a fine boy. I want you to tell him about his grandmama."

CHAPTER TWENTY-EIGHT

LADY

During summers as a young girl, Lady used to sneak into her mother's room while she was napping in the afternoons. Stretched out on the green velvet chaise longue in front of their home's only air-conditioning window unit, she'd kept one eye on her mother, watching for signs that she might be stirring, and one eye on her novel, usually the latest in the Nancy Drew series. Her mother's planned activities for the late afternoons were the high points of Lady's days, a bike ride to the market or a trip to Peoples Drug for a Coca-Cola float at the soda fountain. Despite all those long summer hours of waiting for her mother to wake up, Lady had never been as excited to see Willa blink her eyes open as she was that day in the hospital.

Lady moved to the edge of her seat, closer to the bed. "Welcome back, Mama."

Willa grabbed hold of Lady's hand. "You have no idea how glad I am to be here. I feel like I've been to heaven and back." She let out a girlish giggle. "I love you, my darling child. I'm here to support you if you're ready to quit drinking."

Her eyes grew wide. "Are you saying you heard me?"

"I heard every word—the important stuff anyway. I learned a lot about my loved ones while I was away on my little journey." Willa struggled into a sitting position. "Now help me get up. I have work to do. And I'm starving. Is the food any good around here?"

"I don't know, but let's find out," Lady said, retrieving the room service menu off the rolling bed table.

Willa approached her recovery with more determination than Lady had seen from her in years. By noon the next day, a physical therapist—a brunette named Natalie with a sweet smile that reminded Lady of Regan—was called in to determine the next phase in her recuperation.

"I don't need you to tell me what I already know," Willa snapped at Natalie. "I'm ready to go home. How soon can the doctors sign the release papers?"

Natalie smiled at her. "I wish it were that simple, Mrs. Bellemore. We have certain procedures we're required to follow."

After assessing her physical condition in the room, Natalie strolled alongside Willa as she maneuvered her walker down the hall.

"She did well," Natalie reported when they returned to the room. "But her trip to the end of the hall wore her out, which is understandable after an illness as serious as hers." She helped Willa get settled in the lounge chair and then sat on the edge of the bed in front of her with her iPad. "Now, I need to ask you some questions." She two-finger typed on her iPad. "Do you have a first-floor bedroom at home?"

"My bedroom's at the top of the stairs," Willa said. "I can get to it just fine."

"You'll need to continue using the walker until you build up your strength." Natalie directed her next question at Lady, who was standing at the foot of the bed. "Do you have a room on the first floor you can convert into a bedroom?"

"No," Lady said, "but I'm sure we can figure—"

Willa's face grew red. "I refuse to have my home turned into a hospital. I'll be just fine in my own room."

Natalie's body grew rigid. "I don't think you understand, Mrs. Bellemore. If conditions in your home don't meet certain requirements, I'll have to recommend you be released to a step-down facility."

Lady and Willa looked at each other and then asked in unison, "What's a step-down facility?"

"A rehabilitation facility, an extended-care program. You have several medical concerns we must address. Your mobility challenges and oxygen needs are at the top of that list."

Lady gulped. "You mean she'll be on oxygen when she goes home?"

"At least for a while," Natalie said. "It's up to her pulmonologist to decide how long."

Lady noticed her mother sinking farther down in her seat. "Will someone show us how to use it?" she asked.

"Of course. It won't take you long to adapt." Natalie closed the cover on her iPad and set it on the bed beside her. "I understand you're eager to be in your own surroundings, and a first-floor bedroom isn't a requirement, but the only way we can consider sending you home is if you hire private home care."

"That'll cost a lot of money I'm not willing to spend," Willa said. "My daughter lives with me. She'll take care of everything."

Lady clasped her hands together to keep them from trembling. Quitting drinking was much harder than she'd imagined. Since pouring her vodka down the drain fifty-two hours ago, her cravings were becoming more difficult to ignore. She'd experienced many of the typical withdrawal symptoms, although they came and went in no consistent pattern. She had a constant headache, and the nausea had taken away her appetite.

"Do you mind, Natalie?" Lady asked. "I'd like a moment alone with my mother."

"Certainly." Retrieving her iPad, she rose from the bed. "I'll wait out in the hall."

Lady dragged an armchair near the bed. "I'll be frank with you, Willa. Your medical needs have risen to a level I'm no longer comfortable in managing. I'm sure that with time, I can figure out how to use the oxygen, but there's no shame in asking for help in the interim."

Willa set her jaw in determination. "Regan's a smart girl. She'll know how to use the oxygen."

Lady's thirst meter shot up ten degrees. "I'm sorry, Willa, but I have to put my foot down. I want Regan to enjoy these last months of her senior year in high school. She can't do that if she's taking care of her sick grandmother. I'm a smart girl too. But I'm exhausted. I've been waiting on you hand and foot for weeks. I pay the household bills. I know how much you have in your bank accounts. You have enough money to hire round-the-clock care for the next hundred years. You live like a miser. Why not enjoy your money while you can? It's what your parents would've wanted and why Daddy purchased such a considerable life insurance policy."

In the span of seconds, a host of expressions crossed her mother's face—doubt, followed by contemplation, and finally acceptance and elation. "You're exactly right, Lady. I am a miser. I've scrimped and saved all these years, worried that one day I'd run out of money. But I'm not going to live forever, and I can't take it with me to heaven." She threw her hands in the air. "Hire the nurses. And when I'm well, we're gonna have ourselves a grand old time. We'll buy new wardrobes, redecorate the house, and eat out at every fancy new restaurant in town. Maybe we'll even go on a Mediterranean cruise. I've always wanted to see Greece."

~

The hospital recommended two private home health-care companies, but only one met Lady's approval after interviewing them on the phone. Penny Yates, clinical manager at Lowcountry Home Health Care, intimidated Lady at first. Even though they were about the same age, Penny was everything Lady was not. Attractive, with her dark hair cut man-short in a style that complemented her thin face. Fit, dressed in tailored gray slacks and a trim-cut white cotton blouse. And professional, efficient but warm and compassionate with her clients.

Penny personally escorted them home from the hospital late Thursday afternoon. The certified nursing assistant, Monique, whose quiet confidence set Lady at ease, and a therapist from the oxygen supply company were waiting for them when they arrived. After helping Willa get settled in bed, Monique and Penny reorganized her suite of rooms to accommodate the walker.

As Lady was unpacking Willa's suitcase, she caught a glimpse of a framed photograph of Mavis. She'd seen the photograph a thousand times, but it had been years since she'd really looked at it. Lifting the frame, she inspected the image of the nanny she'd loved as much as her own mother. She touched the tip of her finger to Mavis's right cheek dimple. *Was it possible Mavis was the woman in the chapel?* She set the frame back down. *Great, so now I'm seeing ghosts. I must be hallucinating.* She'd read online that confusion was not uncommon in alcohol withdrawal.

After they'd finished rearranging the furniture, Penny pulled Lady aside. "Is there somewhere you and I can speak in private while these two get acquainted?" She gestured at the bed, where Monique was plumping Willa's pillow and Willa was rattling on about her granddaughter giving the valedictorian address at her upcoming graduation in May.

Lady's legs felt wobbly, and she braced herself against the bedpost. "Is something wrong with my mother?"

"Oh no. It's nothing like that." Penny waved away her concern with a flick of her wrist. "I just wanted to go over her medications and our schedule of workers for the next few days so you'll know what to expect."

"In that case, why don't we go downstairs and have a glass of tea," Lady said and led the way down to the kitchen.

Lady poured two glasses of sweet tea, and they sat down at the kitchen table.

Penny spread Willa's prescription pill bottles out on the table along with a folder of information about their services. "Monique is one of our top CNAs. I wanted her here when Willa got home to assess her needs and help her get situated. She'll stay for a while tonight, until the night-duty gal arrives, and then, starting at seven o'clock tomorrow morning, she'll work the day shift going forward."

"Whatever you think best," Lady said, and for the next few minutes, they discussed Willa's medications and general care for the coming days.

"Here's my card." Penny attached her business card to the folder of information with a paper clip. "Do not hesitate to call me night or day with any concerns whatsoever."

"Thank you, Penny. I feel like we're in capable hands."

Penny gathered her things, and Lady saw her to the door. "I hope you don't mind me asking," Penny said, "but have you ever worked in health care? I was watching you with your mother, and you're a natural. It takes a special kind of patience to deal with the elderly."

Lady bit down on her lip to keep from laughing out loud. She was the least patient person she knew, particularly in her current state of alcohol withdrawal. "Thanks for the compliment, but I'm not a nurse."

"I don't mean as a nurse. If you ever consider a career change, you might want to think about becoming a geriatric aide."

No longer able to hold back her laughter, Lady let out a loud hoot. "I'm just a stay-at-home mom taking care of my elderly mother. I would need to have a career first before I could consider changing it. But I'm curious. What exactly is a geriatric aide?"

"Someone who aids elderly people. They perform a wide variety of services. Some help with an individual's physical care while others provide transportation and companionship. With people living longer these days, the demand for this type of help has grown. The work is rewarding. Like your mother, so many of our clients are charming. You'd be a great fit."

Lady felt a glimmer of hope stir deep within her. She wasn't interested in changing bedpans, but she relished the idea of helping an older person keep up their quality of life. "What kind of training is required?"

"None, unless you want to work with the critically ill. Common sense, honesty, and reliability are key job requirements. I'd be happy to offer guidance or recommend you to some of my clients."

"I appreciate your vote of confidence." Lady opened the door for Penny. "I need to get my mother back on her feet first, but I'll give it some thought."

CHAPTER TWENTY-NINE

BOOKER

The library was buzzing on Thursday evening with excitement over the senior prom. Most of Booker's classmates had already been accepted to their college of choice and had given up on academics for the year. He wondered why they were even in the library when they weren't studying. He wished they'd go somewhere else to run their yaps. Who cared about the prom anyway? He had better things to worry about, like getting into Harvard. He'd managed to control his stress level these past few days by tuning out everything and everyone except his schoolwork. But his two best guy friends, Stuart and Owen, were goofing off at his table, enjoying their last days as boys before they were cast into the real world and expected to become young men. They picked at each other, which led to pushing and shoving, which led to Owen wrestling Stuart down on top of the table. Where was the librarian when he needed her?

Booker moved his notebook out of harm's way. "Stop it already, you two! Go somewhere else! I'm trying to study for our calculus test tomorrow. Some of us still care about our grades." He saw Regan, alone at a table across the room, with earbuds in her ears, oblivious to the ruckus around her. At this rate, she would get an A on their calc test, and he would fail. He gathered up his books. He'd have to finish his work at home.

"Where're you going, Book?" Stuart asked. "Don't leave. We're just having a little fun."

Owen added, "Yeah, man. You're taking this whole getting-into-Harvard thing way too seriously."

"Chill, dude." Stuart elbowed Owen in the ribs. "We get how important Harvard is to you. What we don't understand is why you won't take one night off from studying to go to the prom."

They'd been harassing him for days about getting a date to the prom. "Okay, Einstein, why don't you tell me who I'm gonna ask?" Booker said. "All the girls in our grade already have dates."

"Not all of them," Owen said, a mischievous smile on his lips as his hazel eyes traveled across the room to Regan.

Booker raised his hand in protest. "No way, man. Not Regan. She's my best friend. And she's mad at me anyway." He pushed back from the table. "I'm going home. I'll see y'all tomorrow."

Stuart snatched Booker's calculus book away from him so he couldn't leave.

"Give that back!" When Booker grabbed at the book, Stuart sat on it. "I'm not kidding, Stu. You're pissing me off."

"I'll give it back after you ask Regan to prom. No one misses their senior prom. It'll be like anti-American or something if you don't go. Even Broadbottom's mother got a date for him with some girl from his synagogue. I promise, you'll regret it for the rest of your life."

"That's true, dude," Owen chimed in. "And Regan is the perfect date for you. No strings attached. Like you said, she's your best friend. The two of you communicate on an IQ level none of us can touch. Y'all can sit in the corner and talk about chemistry and calculus all night."

Booker rubbed his chin as he considered the arrangements he would need to make in order to go. "Nah, man, no can do. I'm trying to pull my grades up. I don't have time to worry about renting a tuxedo, making dinner reservations, and buying flowers." He opened his notebook and flipped through the homework assignments he needed to study.

Owen slammed his notebook shut. "How can your grades possibly get any higher than they already are?"

"You don't have to worry about making plans," Stuart said. "We have the whole night figured out. Janie's parents are having everyone over for dinner before the prom. Our parents will drive us to the dance in shifts. Then afterward, we'll go to my house for breakfast." He rubbed his hands together. "That's when the real fun will begin."

Janie and Stuart lived two doors down from each other at the bottom of King Street. Not only were their parents longtime friends, Janie and Stuart had been boyfriend and girlfriend since middle school.

Owen held his hands out, palms up. "How easy is that, dude? All you have to do is rent your tuxedo and have your mom order a corsage or flowers or whatever."

Stuart and Owen sat on the edge of their seats, elbows planted on the table and eyes glued on him as they awaited his decision. They were late bloomers like Booker. All three would be hard-pressed to grow a full beard if their lives depended on it. He studied their eager faces, etching the details in his memory for next year when they traveled to different corners of the country for college. Their lives were about to change forever. When he saw them at Thanksgiving, he might not recognize them. He would cherish his time spent with them these past twelve years. And snapshots from prom night would make his memory bank complete.

Besides, his mom had been nagging him to get a date. He'd love to see her happy for a change.

"All right, I'll go. But only if Regan says yes. And don't be surprised if she shoots me down."

He got up from the table, summoning his nerve as he walked toward her. She was too lost in her own world of classical music and calculus to notice him approaching. He waved his hand in front of her face as he slipped onto the seat opposite her.

She tugged the earbuds out of her ears. "Hey, Booker. What's up?"

Her warm greeting gave him courage. "Not much. Trying to study for this calc test. How's your grandmother?" he asked in his most sincere tone of voice.

Her face brightened. "Better. Thanks for asking. She came home today. I'm going to leave here soon and go see her."

"That's awesome! I'm glad to hear it. So . . . um . . ." He glanced behind him at Stuart and Owen, who nodded their support in unison. "A little birdie—two little birdies, actually—told me you don't have a date for the prom. As it turns out, I don't either. And I was wondering if you wanted to go with me." He paused and then quickly added, "As friends, of course."

"Oh." She dropped her chin. "I'm not going to the prom."

"To be honest, I wasn't planning to go either, until I found out that even Arthur Broadbottom's got a date. I don't know about you, but I don't want to be the only loser in the senior class who doesn't show up for the prom."

Regan shrugged. "I don't consider myself a loser. I have an excuse. My grandmother's been sick."

"That may be true, Regan, but this is it for us. We'll never get a chance to go to prom again. And I'm not going if you don't go."

She looked away, her attention captured by a group of her girl-friends leaving the library together.

Out of the corner of his eye, he saw Stuart and Owen spying on them from behind the bookshelves and waved them away.

"Come on, Regan. This is our senior year. We don't want to miss out on the fun. Our friends have the plans all figured out. Janie's parents are having everyone to dinner beforehand."

Regan rolled her eyes. "I know. I've heard."

"See! It won't be like a real date. We'll all be together as friends."

"You make a good argument, Booker. Have you considered becoming a lawyer instead of a doctor?"

He grinned. "Funny you should mention it. I've been thinking a lot about that lately. Does that mean my persuasion is working on you? Will you go with me to the prom?"

She giggled. "Yes, it means I'll go with you to the prom." She held up a finger to signal a warning. "But I reserve the right to cancel if I can't find a dress."

"How hard can it be to find a dress?"

She laughed. "You have no idea."

"I'm sure you'll find something. I'll have to go stag if you bail on me. Then I'll look like a loser, and it'll be all your fault."

"No pressure. Geez."

He eyed her calculus book. "How's the studying coming?"

"Good! The material's easy for a change. Are you finished studying?"

"I haven't even started. It's too noisy in here for me. I'm going home where it's quiet."

When he moved to get up, she said, "Wait, Booker, before you go, there's something I need to ask you."

He sat back down. "What's that?"

"It's about this thing with my father and your mother." She leaned across the table and lowered her voice. "I need to know the truth. Did he rape her or not?"

Booker shook his head adamantly. "Your father did not rape my mother. He . . . well, let's just say he mistreated her. I don't feel like it's my place to discuss the details. I'm sorry for misleading you. I was in a bad mood that day, and I took it out on you. That's a sorry excuse, I know. Bottom line—I was wrong."

Her face was stricken with remorse. "Maybe I'll never know what happened."

"Trust me, you're better off forgetting about it if you can. Look on the bright side. Maybe we can use our prom date as a way to get our mothers together again."

"I wouldn't count on it," she said as she fidgeted with her earbuds.

"Don't be such a negative Nancy," he said, chucking her chin. "Where's that spunky Regan spirit I admire?"

She sucked in a deep breath. "You're right. We should keep trying. I'll talk to Mom. Maybe we can invite your mom to come over for pictures beforehand."

"That's a great idea," Booker said, standing. "I need to get back to the books. We'll talk more about the prom later."

When Booker returned to his table, Stuart and Owen were gone, and the noise in the library had dropped a few decibels. He decided to try one last time to focus. He was finding his place in his calculus book when his phone lit up on the table with a call from his father. *What the heck does he want?* Booker wondered as he turned the phone facedown.

CHAPTER THIRTY

REGAN

Regan burst through the front door and dashed up the stairs to her grandmother's room, throwing herself across Willa in the bed. "I'm so happy to see you! I was so worried."

Willa stroked Regan's hair. "I'm fine, child. You can't get rid of me that easily."

Regan felt a hand on her shoulder, pulling her off the bed. "Careful now, sweetheart," Lady said. "Your grandmother's still very weak."

"Stop your fussing, Lady. I'm getting stronger by the minute. Regan, I'd like you to meet my new best friend, Monique." Willa gestured to the stranger sitting near the foot of the bed.

Regan turned to the striking young woman of Asian descent. "Nice to meet you," she said, and quickly returned her attention to her grandmother. "Guess what, Willa! I got asked to the prom. Do you think you'll be well enough by Saturday to go shopping with me for a dress?"

Willa chuckled. "I'm afraid that would require a miracle." She shifted her gaze to Lady. "How about if I stay here with Monique and let your mother take you shopping?"

Regan creased her forehead. "I guess that'll have to work."

"What's with the long face?" Willa lifted Regan's chin. "You can text me pictures if you find something you like. I'll give you my credit card. It'll be my treat."

"Thank you, Willa. That's really nice of you." Regan looked at her mother standing next to her. "Do you mind going shopping with me? I know it's not your favorite pastime."

Lady beamed. "I can't think of anything I'd rather do. We'll make a day of it. Who's the lucky guy taking you to the prom?"

Regan had been dreading the question. Her mother was not exactly keen on Booker's mother at the moment. "Oh . . . you know . . . he's nobody. I mean, he's somebody. He's just a friend. I'm going with Booker."

Lady dropped her smile. "I see."

Willa snapped her head back. "Since when do you have a problem with Booker? He's been Regan's study buddy for as long as I can remember. Which isn't saying much, now that I think about it, but you know what I mean."

"Since now that I know he's Nell's son," Lady said. "For obvious reasons, I was hoping we could avoid further contact with their family."

"Those reasons aren't so obvious to me," Willa said. "Do you care to elaborate?"

The color rose in Lady's cheeks. "Can we talk about this another time?"

"We need to talk about it now, Mom," Regan said. "I was thinking we'd ask Nell to stop by for pictures when Booker comes to pick me up."

"I'd rather not." Lady glanced at the clock on the bedside table. "Would you look at the time? Nine thirty already. Come on, you. Let's get out of here so Willa can get some rest." She placed a hand on Regan's back and steered her to the door.

"Did something happen with Nell that I don't know about?" Regan asked her mother when they were alone in the hallway. She hadn't seen Lady since Monday at the hospital, and the few times they'd spoken on the phone, they'd discussed only Willa's health. "The last time Nell was here, you seemed happy to see her. I know she broke her promise to visit Willa, but she got called into work at the last minute. She can't help that."

Lady slumped against the wall. "We had a little run-in at the hospital. Two run-ins, actually."

Regan recognized her mother's exhaustion. For the four days Willa was in the hospital, Lady had left her bedside only long enough to come home to shower and change. "I'm sorry, Mom. I know you're tired. We can talk about this another time."

"I need to get this off my chest now," Lady said. "I know Booker is your friend, sweetheart. And that's fine. I don't want to get in the way of your friendship. But nothing good will come from having his mother in our lives."

"How can you say that, Mom? You saw how excited Willa was to see Nell when she visited last week."

"And Willa's health tanked when Nell didn't show up or bother to call after she promised to visit on Saturday. Our relationship with Nell is volatile at best. And Willa needs stability right now. Let it go, Regan. For all our sakes." Before Regan could press her further, Lady pushed off the wall and disappeared down the stairs.

~

Regan and Lady hit the stores bright and early on Saturday morning. They took an Uber to Upper King and worked their way down. They stopped in every shop that held promise. At the Copper Penny, she found a dress she loved with a black top and pink high-low skirt that was four sizes too big. The store clerk called the rep, but because the dress was last season's design, they were out of stock.

"You might try online." The clerk jotted down the designer and style number on a scrap of paper and handed it to Regan. "Good luck."

Regan was hungry by the time one o'clock rolled around. "I give up, Mom. Let's go home. I'm starving."

"And spoil this delightful weather?" Lady tilted her head up to the bright blue cloudless sky. "There's a restaurant with patio seating a block away."

Regan raised an eyebrow. "What restaurant?"

"I don't know the name of it, but I've driven by it a thousand times. Where's your sense of adventure?"

"Where's *my* sense of adventure?" Regan aimed a thumb at her chest. "This coming from a woman who hasn't been out to lunch in six years."

"I've been cooped up in a stuffy old house with a sick woman for months. I need fresh air." Looping her arm through Regan's, her mother dragged her down the sidewalk to the Kitchen 208 restaurant, where they were seated at the last available umbrellaed table on the patio. After a quick glance at the menu, they both decided on the smoked turkey wrap.

"Something's different about you," Regan said to her mother after the waitress had taken their orders. She'd been noticing the change all day, but she couldn't put her finger on it.

Pink spots appeared on her mother's cheeks. "I decided to start wearing some makeup. I'm amazed at how much a good concealer and a little foundation can hide."

Regan leaned closer and narrowed her eyes as she inspected her mother's skin. "Oh, right. I see it now. Makes you look ten years younger." Her eyes grew wide. "Oops. I'm sorry. I didn't mean to make you sound old."

Lady laughed. "No need to apologize. I am old. I have a daughter going off to college in the fall."

Regan couldn't remember the last time she'd been on any kind of outing with her mother. Something shifted in their relationship throughout their lunch. Away from Willa and the distractions at home, they were able to speak openly about themselves. They didn't share any deep, dark secrets but kept the conversation light. They talked about the twenty pounds Lady was planning to lose and the nannying job Regan was hoping to get for the summer. Although Lady never admitted it in so many words, Regan realized for the first time how hard her parents' divorce had been on her mother. She left the restaurant with a better understanding of Lady, not only as her mother but as a person.

They passed a swanky hair salon a block away from the restaurant on their way home. Regan stopped to peek in the window. "I should probably do something about my hair before the prom."

"You know, I've been thinking about getting a new hairdo myself. Let's go in." Lady held the door open for Regan. "I bet they accept walk-ins."

"I doubt it. This place looks expensive," Regan said under her breath as she brushed past her mother.

The receptionist, a sophisticated woman with fabulous hair, informed them in a snooty manner that they did not accept walk-ins.

"In that case, we need to schedule appointments," Lady said, undeterred. "My daughter's prom is next Saturday. Can you fit her in for a trim sometime this week in the late afternoon?"

The receptionist's attitude changed at the mention of the prom. "Let me see what we can do." After checking for an available time, she smiled and said, "Becky is available next Saturday at three o'clock. Would that work? She's one of our top stylists. After she cuts your hair, she'll style it any way you like." She came around from behind the desk to examine Regan's hair. "Perhaps some soft curls around your face would be sweet."

Regan nodded her head eagerly. "I like that idea."

The receptionist turned to Lady. "What did you have in mind for your hair?"

Lady ran her fingers through her stringy, mousy hair. Her mother was way overdue for a haircut.

"I was thinking about cutting off several inches and adding some layers," Lady said.

The receptionist lifted a strand of Lady's hair and rubbed it together between her fingers. "I would suggest adding some highlights as well. A lot of highlights, actually."

Lady clapped her hands together. "Let's do it!"

Returning to her computer, after a lot of scrolling and clicking, the receptionist found an opening for Lady on Wednesday afternoon at three.

"What gives, Mom?" Regan asked when they were back on the sidewalk. "Something is different about you that has to do with more than makeup and a new diet."

"All right," Lady sighed. "If you must know, I quit drinking. It's been only a few days, and I didn't want to say anything just yet in case I end up giving in to temptation. And believe me, the temptation is huge."

"Wow, Mom, that's awesome!" Regan stopped on the sidewalk, and in the midst of a throng of Saturday strollers, she gave her mother a hug. "I'm so proud of you." She drew away from her. "But you can't give in to temptation. You have to go to AA."

"How do you know about Alcoholics Anonymous?" Lady asked, surprised.

"Give me a break. Everyone knows about AA. But I have firsthand experience." She hooked her arm through her mother's and started walking. "Janie's mom is a recovering alcoholic. She hasn't had a drink since July 4, 2005."

Lady cast a sideways glance at her. "You know the exact date she quit drinking?"

"Yep, I was with them at their condo in Wild Dunes that night. She was a mess, and that's being kind. Mrs. Jensen is very open about her problem. She talks to Janie and me about drinking responsibly all the time."

Her mother was quiet for a minute before she asked, "Have you ever had anything to drink, Regan? You've never given me any reason to ask before."

Regan lifted a shoulder. "I've had a few beers here and there. Nothing major. UNC is a big party school, Mom. I hear horror stories about freshmen who've never had alcohol before making fools of themselves the first week."

"I guess that makes sense," Lady said in a reluctant tone. "Just as long as you keep it under control. I don't want you to turn out like me."

"You don't need to worry about that." Regan had no intention of following in her mother's wobbly footsteps. "I don't really like alcohol that much anyway. But seriously, Mrs. Jensen has sponsored lots of people for AA. She'd be happy to help you too, if you decide you want to try it."

Lady nodded. "I'll keep that in mind."

They walked for a block in silence, lost in their own thoughts. "About the dress," Regan said. "I gave myself an out. I warned Booker that I won't be able to go to the prom if I can't find a dress."

"You're going," Lady said. "How do you feel about vintage clothing?"

"I don't have any feelings one way or another. Why?"

"Because I have an idea." Lady increased her stride, dragging Regan along beside her.

When they arrived home, they stopped in to check on Willa—who, with Monique's help, was getting dressed after taking a bath—before moving down the hall to Lady's room. Her mother had two small closets, one that housed her everyday clothes and the other reserved for cocktail and evening wear. Regan had played dress up with her fancy taffeta and ruffled dresses as a child, but she'd never dared to explore the contents of the zippered garment bags at the back of the closet.

"I wore this to my senior prom," Lady said, removing a black garment bag from the closet. "I'll never forget the night. I took my best friend's brother as my date. He was a freshman at USC at the time."

Her mother rarely talked about her high school days. "Was he your boyfriend?"

"We had a thing, but it didn't last long. Hank and Mindy, his sister, were Irish twins, only eleven months apart. She was my best friend, and he was like a brother to me."

"Have I ever met her?"

"Once, when you were a baby. We fell out of touch after she divorced her first husband. But enough about Mindy." She unzipped the garment bag. "I loved this dress more than I loved my own wedding dress."

Regan recognized the dress as a Lilly Pulitzer by the floral print, bright blue-and-green hydrangea-like flowers, and signature white embroidery around the neck and down the front.

"It's beautiful. It's so . . ."

"You." Lady handed the dress to Regan and spun her around to face the full-length mirror on the back of the closet door. Regan held the dress up to her body. "I can't believe it. How old is this dress? It's like an antique, but it looks brand new."

"Now you *are* making me feel old," Lady said, laughing. "Lilly Pulitzer's designs never go out of style. It's fresh and youthful and—"

"Just what I was looking for." Regan fingered the fabric. "What's this fabric?"

"Piqué, a heavy cotton with a raised pattern."

"Here." She handed the dress back to her mother. "Help me try it on. I'll die if it doesn't fit." Regan stripped off her clothes and stepped into the dress.

"No need to worry. It fits perfectly," Lady said as she zipped up the dress with ease. "I can't believe I was ever as tiny as you."

Regan admired her reflection in the mirror. With bare arms and slits up both legs, the dress showed off enough skin without being provocative. "What kind of shoes would I wear?"

"A low-heeled strappy sandal, which shouldn't be hard to find this time of year."

"I can't wait to show Willa." Noticing the look of dejection on her mother's face, she threw her arms around her. "Thank you, Mama, for letting me wear your dress. I just love it. I promise to be careful. Maybe one day my daughter will wear it to her prom."

Lady's lips broke into a wide smile. "Wouldn't that be something."

Regan lifted the bottom of the dress as she headed for Willa's room.

"You realize, at some point, we'll need to talk about your father."

Her mother's words stopped her in her tracks, while all her excitement over the dress escaped her like air deflating from a helium balloon. She'd gone all afternoon without thinking about him. "Can we please not spoil the day?"

"I agree. Not today, but soon."

CHAPTER THIRTY-ONE

NELL

Nell kept tabs on Willa's recovery through a friend who worked as a nurse on the fourth floor. But by the time she got up the nerve to visit Willa again, she'd already been released from the hospital. After their recent confrontations, she felt obligated to ask Lady's permission before visiting Willa at home. She texted and left messages on Lady's cell phone, but on Monday, after several days with no response, she gave up and called the house line. She summoned the number from memory with ease, as if she'd been dialing it every day for the past thirty-seven years.

A voice she didn't recognize answered on the fourth ring. "Bellemores' residence."

She cleared her throat. "Yes. Hello. I'm calling for Mrs. Bellemore. This is Nell Jackson," she said, using her maiden name for the first time since Desmond left her. It sounded both foreign and fitting to her ears.

"One moment, please." Nell heard a rustling noise, as though the woman who'd answered the phone was pressing the receiver against her body.

Willa came on the line. "It's so wonderful to hear from you, Nell. How are you?"

"I'm fine, Miss Willa. More importantly, how are you?"

"Better now that I've heard your voice." Willa broke into a fit of coughing that prevented her from talking.

The woman came back on the line. "I'm sorry. Miss Willa's having a bit of a spell. I'm her home-care nurse, Monique. May I have her call you back?"

"Actually, I was hoping to stop by for a visit sometime this week if she's feeling up to it. Wednesday afternoon would fit my work schedule."

"Just a minute." She heard a pause and more rustling. "Wednesday afternoon is fine. Miss Willa is usually up from her nap around three."

"Three it is, then. Please tell her I'm looking forward to seeing her."

~

Nell fretted over what to take an elderly woman recovering from a life-threatening bout of pneumonia. Remembering how much Miss Willa once loved to work in the garden, she decided on flowers. She purchased a spring bouquet from Sweetgrass Flowers in Mount Pleasant and arranged them in a cylinder vase along with fresh greenery she cut from her yard. She left her house at two o'clock on Wednesday afternoon, allowing extra time in case of traffic. She arrived downtown in a record twenty minutes. To kill time, she cruised the neighborhood streets, remembering afternoons with Lady spent riding their bikes to their friends' houses. *Their* friends. Hers and Lady's. Their friends had not rejected her. Nell had shut them out of her life after the snowy night in 1981.

She was on Rutledge Avenue, heading back toward the seawall, when she noticed a tiny two-story salmon-colored house for sale. A handsome man wearing a blue sport coat and gray slacks stood beside the Realtor's sign, shifting from one foot to the other and casting frequent glances at his watch. She spotted a brochure box attached to the sign, pulled alongside the curb in front of the house, and got out.

She smiled at the man and said, "Excuse me," as she removed an informational flyer from the box.

"It's a great house," the man said. "Not a lot of room, as you can see, but it's priced accordingly, which makes it attractive if you're looking for something in this area."

Nell scanned the flyer. The home offered two bedrooms with two full baths on the second floor, and a kitchen, living, and dining room combo on the first. "Has it been on the market long?"

"Long enough. I'm Bennett Calhoun, listing agent." He extended his hand to her. "And you are?"

"Nell Jackson."

"Care to take a look?" He glanced at his watch one last time. "My two fifteen appointment is officially thirty minutes late. I have time to show it to you if you're interested."

"I'm not exactly in the market for a new home, Mr. Calhoun, and I have to be somewhere in fifteen minutes."

Bennett Calhoun's blue eyes twinkled with mischief. "This house is so small, it'll only take ten." He unlocked the front door and held it open for her to enter. "I feel obligated to warn you that if you're not already in the market for a new home, you will be after you see this little gem."

Calhoun walked her through the house and then allowed her a few minutes to explore on her own. She stood at the window of the front bedroom watching pedestrians walking and jogging around Colonial Lake. Her home in Mount Pleasant had views of the Wando River from nearly every room. She realized with a jolt that she wouldn't miss it. Nell had poured her heart and soul into designing that house, but she'd never felt about it the way she felt about this dollhouse. She couldn't put her finger on it. Something just felt right. She would thrive in the heart of downtown Charleston. She felt a sense of calm here, a place for her to heal. She would fill the rooms with her most beloved possessions, things she cherished that had nothing to do with Desmond.

"So what do you think?" Bennett asked when they were outside once again.

"I think I'm going to be late for my three o'clock appointment." She walked to her car, and he followed her. "You never gave me a straight answer, Mr. Calhoun. How long as the property been on the market?"

He looked her square in the eye. "For six months now."

"So the buyers are motivated to sell, in other words," she said, opening her car door and tossing her bag onto the passenger seat.

"We'll have better negotiating power, Ms. Jackson, if I represent you. That is, if you don't already have a Realtor." He fished a business card out of his wallet. "Give it some thought. Perhaps fate brought us together today," he said with that twinkle she was starting to warm up to.

Noticing the wedding band on his ring finger, she said, "I feel sorry for your wife."

He cocked an eyebrow at her. "Oh really! Why's that?"

"Because I imagine she has a hard time saying no to you."

He laughed out loud. "I'll be sure to tell Midge that when I get home tonight. She'll get a kick out of it, because the truth is, Ms. Jackson, I'm the one who has a hard time telling her no."

~

Nell was walking up the sidewalk from the street when Willa called down to her from the piazza outside her room. "Come on up. The door's unlocked. My aide is in the kitchen making a fresh pitcher of sweet tea."

She let herself in the front door and hurried up the stairs, relieved to find Lady nowhere in sight. She walked through Willa's room and out onto the piazza. "These are for you," she said, presenting her with flowers and a kiss on the cheek. "I must say, you're looking well, much better than when I saw you in the hospital."

"Not my best moment, for sure." Willa sniffed the flowers and placed the vase on the table beside her. "These are lovely. Thank you." She motioned Nell to the love seat next to her. "Sit down. Monique will be up with our tea in a moment."

Nell settled herself in. "Miss Willa, I owe you an apology for breaking my promise to visit you. I got—"

Willa held her hand up to silence Nell. "You already apologized." Nell shot her a questioning look, and Willa added, "While I was in the hospital. I heard your apology."

"Oh." Nell's face grew warm. "Then I suppose you heard everything."

Willa nodded. "Out of respect for your privacy, I'm not going to ask what happened with Daniel. He's Regan's father, and truthfully, I'm not sure I want to know. I'm also not going to ask you why you and your husband are getting a divorce. But if you ever want to talk about it, I'm here for you."

"I'll remember that. Thank you. And thank you for respecting my privacy."

A woman wearing a uniform printed with cats and hearts stepped onto the piazza with a tray bearing a pitcher of sweet tea, two glasses, and a plate of cheese straws.

Willa introduced Nell to Monique. "Monique claims that hers are the best cheese straws in the South, but I've assured her that no cheese straw could possibly compare to your mama's cheese biscuits." Willa held the plate out to Nell. "Will you do the honors of performing the taste test?"

Nell laughed out loud. "That's a lot of pressure, Miss Willa." She took a cheese straw from the plate and broke it in half. She tasted the savory goodness of aged sharp cheddar with a peppery bite. "I have to say, this is pretty darn good."

"Let me try one." Willa grabbed a cheese straw and stuffed it into her mouth whole. "Not as good as May May's, but they'll do." She winked at Monique, who smiled and scurried off.

"Now, where was I? Oh right, the hospital. I want you to know, the things you said while I was in my fever delirium meant a lot to me. Did you mean what you said about us being a family again? I'd really like to know my grandson."

Nell busied herself with pouring each of them a glass of tea. She'd mentally rehearsed what she wanted to say to Willa, but given the opportunity, she questioned how her words would be perceived. "There's nothing I'd like more than for you to meet my son. You'll have an opportunity to do that on Saturday when he picks Regan up for the prom."

"Oh yes, the prom! My granddaughter is so excited." Willa's face took on a dreamy glow. "She's wearing her mother's dress. Do you remember that floral Lilly Pulitzer she wore to her senior prom?"

"I remember," Nell said. She would never forget the sight of Lady in that gorgeous blue-and-green gown with her blonde hair cascading down her back in ringlets. Or the way Hank looked at her when he came to pick her up, as though he'd never seen anyone lovelier. Nell's brief crush on Hank had long since ended by then, but that night had been difficult for her just the same. She remembered how left out she felt when all her friends went off to their prom together with smiles on their rosy lips, nails polished and hair groomed, small bouquets of sweetheart roses attached to their wrists. Watching them go had been yet another reminder to Nell that she didn't belong. She'd gone to her own prom, dressed in her own lovely gown, at her own school. But it hadn't been the same.

"I know Regan will be as lovely as her mother was in that dress," she said. "Now that I can envision it, I'll know what flowers to order for her bouquet. Be sure to take lots of pictures."

"I'd have to talk it over with Regan and Lady first, but I'd love for you to come over to the house with Booker. That way, you can take all the pictures you want. You can stay for supper after we see the kids off."

There it was—the invitation she'd been hoping for. Oh, how she hated to decline. "I'm not sure Lady is ready to let me back into your lives. And honestly, I don't blame her. The last thing I want to do is cause your family more pain."

"*Our* family, Nell. You are a part of that family." Willa's shoulders sagged. "But I'm afraid you're right about Lady. She's sorting out her own life right now and needs some time. Both of you are on the cusp of a whole new life with your children going off to college."

"Don't I know it." Nell crossed her legs as she sipped her tea. "I'm scared to death, if you want to know the truth. I've lost my husband, and now I'm losing my child. I've never really been on my own before, except those first few years out of college. And I wasn't exactly single then either. Desmond and I were practically living together, already talking about getting married. I'm not sure I know how to be on my own."

"Good thing you're a quick learner," Willa said, tilting her glass to Nell. "Look at it as an opportunity to reinvent yourself. There's so much to see and do in Charleston. I'm sure you have plenty of girlfriends who'd want to explore all the trendy new restaurants and cultural events with you."

"Most of my friends are my husband's friends' wives," Nell said with a pang of sorrow. "Which means they were never really my friends to begin with."

They sat for a few minutes, listening to the foghorn of a cruise ship coming into port. Nell stared out across the neighboring houses while the smell of the harbor summoned pleasant memories from her childhood. So many good things had happened to her while she lived in this house. It hadn't been all bad like she'd convinced herself over the years. She felt at peace sitting on the piazza with Willa, as one might when coming home after a long absence.

"A funny thing happened to me on my way here today." Nell launched into a description of her encounter with the Realtor and her walk-through of the dollhouse for sale. "I connected with that house like one connects with a new friend. Until now, I've been adamantly opposed to selling my house, trying desperately to hold on to my old life. I realized today that what I truly need is a fresh start. And even though it will be at least a year before I have a divorce settlement, I have enough in my personal savings account to make a down payment."

"Where is this dollhouse?"

"Not far from here on Rutledge Avenue, overlooking Colonial Lake."

Willa pounded the table beside her. "Then what're you waiting for? Get over there now and make your best offer before someone snatches it up. We would be neighbors. I would love having you close to me."

Nell smiled. Willa's enthusiasm was infectious. "I'd like that too, but I can't do anything without talking it over with Booker first. He'd have to approve of the property. Maybe I'll take him to see it on Sunday."

"That's the spirit! Let me know how it goes. Now." Willa rubbed the top of her nearly bald head. "Did you bring your razor with you?"

Nell lifted her purse off the floor. "I did. And I brought you a turban as well." She removed a pair of scissors, a razor, and a mint-colored cancer beanie from her purse and set the items on the table between them. "My patients love these beanies. They're made of bamboo rayon and fit snug to your head. They come in a variety of different colors. Say the word, and I'll order more for you."

Willa fingered the beanie's fabric. "This one should do nicely. Now that the treatments are behind me, I hope my hair will start to grow back."

"And you'll be surprised how quickly it comes back in." Standing behind Willa, Nell trimmed her remaining hair down to a stubble, then ran the electric razor lightly over the top of her scalp. "There. All done," she said, raking the hair droppings into a pile.

Willa's fingers felt the top of her bald scalp. "Would you be a dear and get my handheld mirror out of the bathroom for me?"

Nell took the hair clippings to the bathroom, dropped them into the trash can, and returned to the porch with the mirror. She let Willa hold the mirror long enough for her to get a glimpse of herself and then took it away. "Let's put this on." She tugged the beanie down over Willa's head and handed her the mirror again. "See, you look glamorous."

Willa smiled at herself in the mirror. "I do, don't I? Like Elizabeth Taylor. Perhaps I'll have you order more colors after all. One for every outfit."

Nell laughed. "Next time I come for a visit, I'll bring my laptop with me, and we can shop the website."

"You will come again, won't you?" Willa said in a pleading tone.

"Of course. But I won't promise a specific date until I look at my work calendar."

Willa suddenly looked exhausted.

"Let's get you inside. I'm afraid I've worn you out." Nell helped Willa up from the chaise longue and into bed. "Do you have a cell phone, Miss Willa? I'd like to call before my next visit."

"I hardly ever use it. I couldn't even tell you where it is at the moment." Willa pulled the covers up under her chin. "Call me on the house line. Lady never answers it."

Nell placed her business card on the nightstand. "Here are my numbers. Do not hesitate to call me if you need anything."

With heavy eyelids, Willa smiled and nodded.

Nell nestled the comforter tight around Willa's body and tiptoed out of the room. She waved to Monique, who was watching TV in the drawing room, and let herself out the front door. She was halfway down the driveway when Lady pulled in.

Lady slammed on the brakes and threw open her door. "You again. Did you come to make more promises you can't keep?" She was wearing makeup and a new hairstyle, her appearance drastically improved from the last few times she'd seen her.

"Lady, I—"

"Spare me, Nell. I thought I made it clear the other day—you are not welcome here. By your own choice, you're no longer a part of our lives. Now, please leave. And don't come back." She slammed the car door and drove to the top of the driveway.

Nell started toward her car on the street and then changed her mind. She strode up to Lady, who was removing groceries from the trunk. "For your information, Willa and I had a nice visit today. You can't stop me from seeing her. She wants me here. If you don't believe me, ask her yourself." She spun around, and as she hurried down the driveway, she called over her shoulder, "By the way, your haircut looks nice."

CHAPTER THIRTY-TWO

BOOKER

Booker was crossing the Ravenel Bridge late Friday afternoon, on his way home from school, when his smartphone rang. He snatched the phone up from the center console and answered without so much as a glance at the screen. He realized his mistake immediately when he heard his father's voice.

"Booker! At long last! I've been trying to reach you for a week."

Duh, Dad, Booker thought. *I've been avoiding you for a week for a reason.*

"What's up, Dad?" he said with zero enthusiasm in his voice.

"I miss you, son. It's been way too long since I've seen you. Can we have lunch tomorrow?"

"Sorry, but I have to study tomorrow."

"Surely you can take a few minutes away from the books for your old man."

As far back as Booker could remember, with the exception of the rare vacation, he'd never eaten lunch in a restaurant with his dad. He understood his father's motives all too well. A week of nonstop calls meant he wanted something. And Booker was curious what that something was.

"Fine," Booker said. "As long as we meet somewhere close to the library with fast service."

"Name the time and place."

"Brown Dog Deli at noon," he said, and hung up without saying goodbye.

As he turned off the highway toward home, Booker rolled all his windows down, hoping the fresh air would cleanse his mind of the brief exchange with his father. He was almost home when he realized he'd forgotten to pick up his tuxedo. He banged his palm on the steering wheel. He'd either have to go back out now, in the late-Friday-afternoon traffic, or pick it up tomorrow, which meant more time away from studying. Agreeing to go to the prom was turning out to be a big mistake. Of all weekends, his teachers had loaded them down with homework. He was marching headlong into doomsday. On May 1, National College Decision Day, he would have to submit his deposit for next year to one of the four schools that had accepted him. The probability of him actually attending that college increased with every day that passed with no word from Harvard. If only he knew which of those colleges to choose.

He circled the cul-de-sac in front of his house and headed back toward the highway.

~

Booker was up at dawn the following morning and seated at a desk in a secluded corner at the back of the library by eight. He was so engrossed in his studies, he completely forgot about the lunch meeting with his father until his phone vibrated on the table beside him at quarter past twelve.

His father sounded irritated when he accepted the call. "Where are you, Booker? I'm waiting for you at the Brown Dog Deli. Are you on the way?"

"I'm leaving the library now," Booker said, pulling on his windbreaker.

"Hurry. I'm holding a table for us."

Booker left his books spread out on the desk. The library was practically empty, and he didn't plan to be gone long. He jogged down the block and around the corner to the deli. His father rose to greet him when he entered the restaurant, but Booker dodged his hug and slid into the booth opposite him. Before he could look at the menu, the waitress, who was about his age and wore thick glasses, approached the table for their drink orders.

Booker nodded at his father's glass of tea. "Sweet tea, please. And I'd like a grilled cheese with bacon for lunch. I'm kinda in a hurry. Can you put the order in as soon as possible?"

"Sure. What kind of cheese would you like on your sandwich?" she asked, pen poised above notepad.

"Yellow," Booker responded, not caring what kind of cheese they put on his sandwich.

She turned to his father. "And you, sir, would you like to place your order now?"

"No, he's gonna wait until I'm finished eating to order," Booker snapped.

His father offered her an apologetic smile. "I'll have the same."

"You didn't need to be so rude, son. I've never known you to be unkind. What's gotten into you?"

Avoiding his father's gaze, Booker reached for the container of sugar packets, separating them by color in neat stacks on the table in front of him. "Suffice it to say, I'm having a bad year. For starters, my father cheated on my mother and ruined our family."

"I'm not here to discuss my marriage to your mother."

"That's right. I forgot. You let Mom handle the unpleasant family talks." Booker stuffed the sugar packets back in the container and slid it into place beside the napkin dispenser. "Why are you here, then, Dad, if not about the divorce? Are we planning a family vacation sans Mom?"

"Be serious, son. We need to talk about college." His father folded his hands and placed them on the table. "May first is approaching fast. Not counting today, you have exactly nine days to make a decision about college. I've spoken with the head of admissions at Duke, who happens to be a classmate of mine, and he's offered to personally give you a guided tour of the campus at a mutually agreed upon time next week. I know you've already visited once, but it wouldn't hurt to see it again."

He looked his father in the eye. "I'm not going to Duke, Dad."

"As difficult as it may be, I think it's time to face the reality that Harvard may not be in the cards for you."

Booker glared at him. "I face that reality every single day. Did you not hear what I just said? I'll decide on one of the other schools by May first, but I promise you it won't be Duke."

"Then I promise you I won't pay for it," Desmond said, his body perfectly still despite his flaring nostrils.

Booker's mouth fell open. "That sounds like a threat to me. Either your school or no school. Is that what you're saying?"

His father shrugged. "Pretty much. You're too young to make this decision on your own. Your future is at stake, and you need my guidance. The relationships you'll make at Duke will serve you well for the rest of your life. None of those other schools will afford you the same opportunities as a school of Duke's caliber."

"Cut the admissions crap, Dad. I'd rather not go to college than go to Duke." He scooted to the edge of the bench seat. "I should've known you'd pull something like this. I won't let you control my life like you've controlled Mom's."

The waitress approached the table with their food at the exact moment Booker stood abruptly, nearly knocking the tray out of her hands. "Cancel my order. I lost my appetite," he said, and stormed out of the restaurant.

He walked back to the library in a stupor and wasted the afternoon staring blindly at the empty tables and chairs around him. His classmates were spending the day getting ready for the prom—the girls bronzing their skin by their backyard pools, having their nails done and their hair styled in elaborate updos. He didn't know what his guy friends were doing that afternoon. They were certainly not in the library. Their college decisions were made, their deposits submitted. The fat lady had sung. The party was the only thing left for them.

Meanwhile, Booker had no clue where he'd go to school, *if* he could even afford to go to school. His mother would help him, if she was financially in a position to contribute now that she was single. He'd accumulated a small savings account, money he'd earned working the snack bar at his neighborhood pool during the summers. Was it too late to apply for financial aid? Scratch that idea. He wouldn't be a candidate, considering his father's income. He'd have to find a higher-paying job this summer in order to afford even one semester at the least expensive school. Maybe he could work construction. One of his friend's fathers was a residential contractor. Not only would he earn a better salary, working hard labor would benefit his physical appearance. He smiled at the image of himself going off to college looking buff for the ladies.

~

Hours later, however, the sight of his scrawny tuxedo-clad body reflected in the mirror erased any hope of him ever developing muscles. His mood darkened from stormy gray to pitch black. He'd accomplished absolutely nothing that afternoon. He'd stayed at the library until he could no longer stand the silence and the walls began to cave in on him. After dumping his backpack in his car, he walked down to the waterfront and spent the rest of the afternoon pacing up and down the seawall trying to make sense of this new development in his life.

His mother had been waiting for him when he arrived home. She was so proud of the flowers she'd purchased for Regan from the florist.

"I thought girls wore flowers on the wrist," Booker said when he saw the small bouquet of blue and white flowers with matching satin ribbons wound around their stems.

Nell shook her head. "Apparently not. I asked Stuart's mother, and she assured me the girls prefer a nosegay over wearing a wrist corsage."

Booker shrugged. "Moms know best."

He felt sorry for his mom. She was being a good sport, but he could tell she felt left out. He'd been disappointed when an invitation for Nell to join them at the Bellemores' home for pictures before the prom never materialized. His mother's confrontations with Lady at the hospital were no doubt responsible. Still, he viewed his prom date with Regan as an obvious first step toward reconciliation.

Booker didn't understand grown-ups. If Regan's mom was upset with Nell for shutting them out of her life all those years ago, why wouldn't she be thrilled when Nell begged to be let back in?

Before he left for the prom, his mother insisted on taking pictures of him outside on the patio. He felt silly standing alone, dressed in his tuxedo and holding Regan's nosegay, but he forced a smile on his lips to humor her.

As he drove through the streets of downtown toward Regan's house, Booker's palms sweated, his chest ached, and he worried he might vomit all over his rented tuxedo. He was one racing heartbeat away from having a full-fledged panic attack. Under normal circumstances, he would've been ecstatic to meet his mother's adopted family, but considering Lady Bellemore's hostility toward Nell, he wondered if he'd even be welcome in their home.

CHAPTER THIRTY-THREE

REGAN

Regan backed out of her room and into the hallway when her mother came after her with a can of hairspray. "Mom, stop! You'll mess it up." After evening up the length, the stylist had fastened her bangs back with a rhinestone hairpin, letting the rest of her hair fall in soft curls around her face.

Grabbing hold of her wrist, Lady took aim at her hair with the can of spray. "I'm just going to spray a little to hold it in place."

"I'm not kidding, Mom, stop it! The stylist already coated it with spray. It's glued into place for life." The doorbell rang, offering her an escape, and she ran down the stairs to answer it.

The look of approval on Booker's face brought a smile to Regan's lips. "Wow! You look amazing. These are for you," he said, presenting her with the small bouquet of flowers that matched her dress perfectly.

"Thanks!" She took the flowers from him. "You look pretty darn good yourself."

And he did look handsome, despite how nervous he seemed. Regan could tell he was worked up about something, something that probably had nothing to do with meeting her family, but he did a good job of hiding it when she introduced him to Lady and Willa. To her relief, Lady was pleasant, although somewhat reserved, while Willa babbled on about her own prom night as she pinned his boutonniere, a single white rose with a sprig of greenery, to his lapel.

When Lady suggested they go outside to take pictures, Booker offered Willa his arm for support. He walked patiently by her side as she carefully put one foot in front of the other on the way down the porch steps to the small walled garden behind their house. Willa, determined to rid herself of the walker, was growing stronger every day. She'd dismissed the nursing services the day before and had spent an hour working in her garden that morning.

Regan and Booker posed in front of a row of pink rosebushes while Lady snapped a continuous stream of pictures with her smartphone.

An awkward silence fell over them when Booker held his phone out to Lady. "Do you mind? I'd like to send one to my mother."

Lady hesitated, and Willa took the phone from him. "Here, I'll do it." She took several pictures and handed him back the phone. "Your sweet mama came to see me this week. We had a lovely visit. I hope she'll come again."

Booker's faced glowed. "Yes, ma'am. She's planning on it."

Regan tugged on Booker's tuxedo sleeve. "We should probably go." She sniffed the flowers she was holding. "Am I supposed to take these with me?"

"I would think you'd want them with you for the photographs," Lady said.

"Of course," Regan said. "I didn't think of that."

Arm in arm, Lady and Willa followed them out of the garden. Regan turned and waved as she and Booker continued down the driveway to his car.

She waited until they were on the way to Janie's before asking, "Is something wrong, Book? You don't seem like yourself."

He hesitated, then said, "My dad's being a jerk about college. I'll tell you about it later. I don't want to think about it tonight."

"As long as you promise we can talk tomorrow. We've had this tension between us lately that has everything to do with our mothers and nothing to do with us. I've missed our friendship. Do you think it's possible for us to get back to the way we were?"

"I do," he said, nodding. "I'm spending the night at Stuart's tonight. Why don't we go to brunch tomorrow and talk?"

"I'd like that," Regan said with a smile.

Janie's parents had planned an elaborate dinner for their friends. One long table, flanked by white folding chairs, draped in white linens and set with silverware and china, extended across their small backyard. Small bouquets of green hydrangeas in square mirrored vases were spaced intermittently with hurricane lanterns bearing cream-colored pillar candles down the center of the table. A dark cloud loomed in the distance, but Mrs. Jensen assured her young guests that the rain wasn't forecasted until later.

Popular tunes played on low volume from outdoor speakers as her classmates mingled among themselves. Most sipped soft drinks from red Solo cups. Some had spiked their drinks with alcohol, but when Stuart offered Regan a splash from his flask, she declined.

"I'll wait until the after-party," she said. She had too much at stake to get into trouble before graduation. Her grandmother was determined to attend the ceremony, and Regan, in turn, was determined to honor her by delivering the valedictorian address.

Shortly before they sat down to dinner, Regan was snapping selfies with a group of her girlfriends when she noticed Booker pluck a tiny object from Owen's palm and pop it in his mouth. Regan knew he was stressed, and assuming he was taking an Advil to relieve a headache, she thought nothing of it until later when they got to the prom.

"The band is awesome. Let's dance," she said after they'd been at the prom for a while. They were sitting together in a corner watching their classmates on the dance floor. Booker was a great dancer, which was one of the reasons she'd agreed to go with him to the prom. But he'd sulked all throughout dinner and barely spoken a word to her since they'd arrived at the school's auditorium.

"I'm not in the mood to dance, but you go ahead."

"Right, Booker. Everyone's here with a date. You're the only one here who will dance with me." She shifted in her seat toward him. "Are you on something, Booker? I saw Owen give you a pill."

His head shot up. "I'm stressed out, Regan. He gave me a sliver of Xanax to take the edge off. And don't go getting all sanctimonious on me. I have no intention of becoming an addict."

"What's gotten into you? You're—"

"Save it, Regan. You have no idea what it's like to have an asshole for a father." He turned away from her, lost again in the movement on the dance floor.

She stared, mouth agape, at the side of his head. He had no clue what he'd just said to her. Whatever his father had done paled in comparison to what her father had done.

She'd made a mistake in coming. All of their friends were coupled together, either with longtime boyfriends and girlfriends or with someone they had a crush on. She had no desire to go to the after-party. She would have Stuart's father drop her at home after the prom.

"Fine. You keep pouting. I'm going to get something to drink," Regan said and left him in search of refreshments.

She was in the bathroom thirty minutes later when she overheard a group of girls talking about her. "Regan is killing it in that dress."

She peeped through the crack in the stall door. The group of girls congregated at the sink counter were part of the popular crowd from the grade below.

"Did you hear the rumor going around about her?" said a pretty blonde as she smeared on a slutty shade of red lipstick.

"That rumor has been confirmed," one of the others said. "Regan's father raped Booker's mother."

"And his mother got pregnant," a third girl chimed in. "Which makes Regan his half sister."

"Ooooh," the slutty blonde said. "She's his date tonight. Isn't that like incest?"

The shrimp and grits Regan had eaten for dinner threatened to come back up. How ignorant of them to even think the last part of the rumor could be true. That would make Booker thirtysomething years old. How did the rumor get started in the first place? She certainly hadn't told anyone. Booker must've blabbed his mouth to one of his friends. Why would he do such a thing? He'd used the word *rape* instead of *assault*, but that was just a technicality. Either was unforgivable.

She waited for the girls to leave the bathroom before exiting the stall. Biting back tears, she opened the door slightly to make certain the hallway was empty before fleeing the restroom. She darted to the end of the hall, flung open the exit doors, and took off on foot into the stormy night. She didn't care that her beautiful dress was soaked through within seconds. All she wanted was to go home. She considered calling an Uber but decided she'd get there quicker if she ran.

With tears blurring her vision and hair clinging to her face, she stepped off the curb and into the path of an oncoming motorcycle.

CHAPTER THIRTY-FOUR

BOOKER

Booker had been staring at the couples on the dance floor for so long, his eyes had grown tired and blurry. The crowd had dwindled as prom attendees had headed off to various other festivities. The band played a series of slow songs for those few couples remaining, most of whom were shamelessly making out. Owen's magic pill had succeeded in taking away his anxiety, but Booker felt drowsy, like he could sleep for a week. He didn't trust himself to drive home to his own bed. As soon as he got to the Dixons' house for the after-party, he'd sneak up to Stuart's room and crash. Hopefully, Regan would understand. He would find her and explain.

He circled the auditorium, but she was nowhere in sight. As he walked down the hallway toward the restrooms, the beat from the band grew dimmer, and the faint sound of sirens drifted toward him. He opened the exit door at the end of the hall and peered out into the foggy night. A light drizzle fell, and the air was thick with humidity. The storm that had threatened earlier had finally moved through, leaving the lawn and sidewalks and trees saturated. Red and blue lights flashed from a number of emergency vehicles parked near the crosswalk in front of the school. Booker let the auditorium door close behind him and joined the group of onlookers gathered along the curb. When a pedestrian in front of him shifted, he caught a glimpse of the body lying motionless in the street. Several excruciatingly long seconds passed before his mind registered where he'd seen the blue-and-green floral pattern on the victim's dress.

Regan! He pushed and shoved his way through the onlookers. "Move! Please!" he repeated over and over. "That girl is my friend."

By the time he made his way through, the EMTs were carefully lifting Regan's body, her head supported by a neck brace and her honey-colored hair matted with blood, onto a stretcher. She looked so fragile and wounded. This was all his fault. He'd been so self-absorbed in his own problems, he'd let her wander off on her own.

One of the EMTs, a middle-aged woman wearing designer tortoise-shell glasses, pulled him aside. "Do you know her, son?"

"Yes, ma'am. Her name is Regan Sterling. She's my date to the prom tonight. We got separated. I don't know why she would've left the auditorium. What happened to her? Did she get hit by a car?"

The EMT shook her head. "Not a car. A motorcycle." She gestured at the biker standing nearby, helmet in hands, his motorcycle a crumpled heap of metal at his feet.

The biker noticed Booker staring at him. "I'm sorry, man," he said, his face contorted with remorse. "She came outta nowhere. I couldn't stop in time."

Booker looked away, unsure of what to say to the biker.

"I'm trying to get contact information for her family. Her phone won't power on." The woman held up a mangled iPhone. He recognized the pink glittery case as Regan's.

Booker was grateful for the Xanax, which enabled him to remain calm. "I can get in touch with her family," he said, removing his phone from the front pocket of his tuxedo trousers.

Booker stepped aside as the EMTs loaded the stretcher into the ambulance. He placed the call to his mother, who answered on the second ring. "I didn't expect to hear from you tonight. Are you having a wonderful time?"

"Mom, listen, I don't have much time to explain. I'm not even sure how it happened. But Regan's been in a bad accident. She was hit by a motorcycle in front of the school."

Nell let out an audible gasp. "Is she okay?"

"I don't think so. They're taking her away in an ambulance. I don't know her mother's number. Can you call her?"

"Of course. But I need to know where they're taking her. This is important, Booker. Make sure they're taking her to MUSC. They have the only trauma center in the area."

Holding the phone away from his face, he asked the EMT with the glasses, "Are you taking her to MUSC?"

"That's correct," the woman said, slamming the back doors of the ambulance. "We have room up front if you want to ride with us."

He nodded at the EMT and returned the phone to his ear. "They're taking her to MUSC. I'm going with them. I'm scared, Mom."

"Hang in there, son. I'll call Lady and meet you there."

Booker climbed into the passenger seat, and they took off, sirens blasting through the rain-soaked streets of downtown. As the ambulance dodged cars and flew through red lights, Booker gripped the dashboard with one hand while using the other to shoot off a text to Stuart, explaining the situation. He closed his eyes and said a silent prayer, promising the Lord he would go back to being a nice guy if he saved Regan's life.

"Will she be okay?" he asked the EMT as she backed the ambulance up to the emergency unloading area.

"I don't know, bud. I certainly hope so. She took an awfully bad hit to the head."

～

Booker saw Regan's mother and grandmother arrive at the emergency room within minutes of the ambulance. Lady walked down the hallway ahead of her mother, who limped along after her with a cane. Lady confronted Booker outside the examining room where a team of doctors and nurses worked on Regan. "Where's my daughter?"

"In there." He aimed his thumb over his shoulder at the cubicle behind him. "They told me to wait out here."

"Do you know the extent of her injuries?" Lady asked, slightly out of breath with a film of sweat covering her face.

"Only that she took a bad hit to her head," he said, tapping his forehead.

"How did this happen, Booker?" Lady asked. "She was in your care. What was she doing outside in the rain in the middle of the street?"

"I don't know, Ms. Bellemore. We were watching the band, and Regan went to get something to drink. When she didn't come back, I went to look for her. That's when I heard the sirens."

"How long was she gone?" Lady asked, her face red with anger.

Booker shook his head. "I have no idea. Maybe an hour."

"You left your date alone at the prom for an hour?"

"I didn't think it was a big deal." He looked up and down the hall, praying his mother would arrive soon. "I just assumed she was talking with one of her friends."

"Why would she have gone outside?"

"Calm down, Lady," Willa said in a warning tone. "He already told you he doesn't know. How this happened is not important. I'm more concerned about her condition."

Lady stepped closer to Booker, her legs planted wide. "Unless you were doing something you weren't supposed to be doing." She gave him the once-over. "You're acting strange. Are you on something?"

Booker's mouth went dry. "I'm sorry, ma'am, but I don't think you know me well enough to make that judgment."

"Why you rude—" Lady stopped in midsentence at the sight of Nell hurrying toward them. She shifted her anger toward his mom. "I told you on the phone not to come."

"I'm here for my son's sake. Like it or not, he and Regan are close friends." Nell kissed Booker's forehead. "Are you okay?"

"I'm fine. I'm just worried about Regan."

Nell started off down the hall toward the examining room, but Lady stepped in front of her. "Don't you dare go in there. I don't want you anywhere near my child."

"Lady, for heaven's sake." Willa whacked her daughter's leg with her cane. "I understand you're upset, but there's no reason to be rude when Nell is only trying to help."

Nell turned to face Lady. "I worked in this trauma unit for several years when I first moved back to Charleston. I still know many of the doctors and nurses on staff. I wouldn't be here if I didn't feel I could be of use to you. But if you want me to leave, I'll go. It's your call."

Lady started to speak, but Willa hit her again with the cane. This time Lady called out in pain. "Ouch, Mom! That hurts."

"We'd like for you to stay," Willa said to Nell. "We need you here."

Nell handed her purse to Booker and approached the nurses' station across from them. The nurse gave Nell a sterile paper gown to put on before entering the curtained cubicle.

Lady asked one of the nurses to find her mother a seat, and while the two Bellemore women huddled together, whispering, Booker leaned against the wall, with his mother's purse slung across his body, texting with Stuart. Word of the accident had spread throughout their classmates. According to Stuart, no one remembered seeing Regan during the dance.

Regan's cubicle buzzed with activity as doctors and nurses came and went, wheeling a host of different medical devices in and out. Fifteen minutes passed on the wall clock before his mother emerged.

"Regan has suffered a severe head injury," she explained to Lady and Willa. "They're doing a CT scan now to determine the extent of her injury. She'll probably need surgery to repair the damage. The neurosurgeon on call is already in surgery with another patient and likely to be a while. With your permission, I'd like to call a friend of mine who is on the neurosurgery team. In my opinion, David Summers is the best."

"That would be wonderful, Nell," said Willa. "Thank you."

"Hand me my phone, please, son," she said with an outstretched hand.

He dug in her purse for the phone and handed it to her. She located the contact and pressed the phone to her ear. "David, it's Nell. I'm sorry to wake you in the middle of the night. I have an emergency, and I need your help. A young woman"—her eyes settled on Booker's face—"a special friend of my son's, was in a horrible accident tonight. I'm here with her at the emergency room. Dr. Powers is in surgery with another patient. He's going to be a while."

Nell paused, listening. "Would you?" Her shoulders slumped in relief. "That'd be awesome. I owe you one." She ended the call and slipped her phone into her back pocket.

"He's on the way. Fortunately, he lives downtown. He'll be here in fifteen minutes."

～

True to his word, the neurosurgeon, a large black man whose immense size commanded attention, arrived thirteen minutes later. He kissed Nell on the cheek and nodded at the Bellemores before entering the cubicle. His expression was impassive when he emerged a half hour later.

Nell provided the brief introductions. "Your daughter suffered a severe head injury," Dr. Summers said to Lady. "She has significant bleeding on the brain. We're preparing her for surgery now."

Booker broke out in a cold sweat when Lady asked, "Is she going to die?"

Dr. Summers squeezed Lady's shoulder. "I'll do everything I can not to let that happen." He turned to Nell. "I'm having a member of my team prepare a private waiting room for you on the third floor. You know the drill. We'll keep you updated as we go."

"Can I see my daughter, Doctor?" Lady asked with a trembling chin.

Dr. Summers nodded. "But only for a minute. We need to get her to the OR, stat."

CHAPTER THIRTY-FIVE

LADY

Lady's gut ached and her skin itched and her brain throbbed against her skull. Sweat seeped from every pore in her body. Once they were shown to the private waiting room Dr. Summers had promised, she went into the restroom, locked the door, and vomited her dinner into the toilet. She flushed the vile contents of her stomach, and then—with knees on floor, elbows propped on toilet seat, and fingers intertwined—she prayed to God with every fiber of her being to let her daughter live. She would gladly trade places with Regan, her sweet baby girl. She'd felt like her heart was being ripped out of her chest as she watched Regan's body, so fragile and still, being wheeled into a surgery she might not survive. She sat back on the cold floor and sobbed, her voice echoing off the tile floor and walls. "How is this even fair? She's only seventeen years old. She has her whole life ahead of her."

She buried her face in her hands and cried like she'd never cried before, mournful howls from a woman possessed. She'd lasted thirteen whole days without alcohol, but she couldn't face the worst crisis of her life without a drink. She needed to get out of the hospital, away from Nell. Surely there was a restaurant or bar nearby where she could get a glass of wine. Or a bottle. She forced herself to get up. At the sink, she blew her nose several times, the cheap toilet paper rubbing it raw, rinsed her mouth out with cold water, and patted her face dry. Despite her new haircut and makeup, her reflection in the mirror frightened her. She couldn't go out in public looking like Carrie. She'd have to find booze from somewhere else.

She considered whether to call Daniel but opted to wait until she knew more about Regan's condition. She was stressed enough without having to defend herself to her ex-husband, who would undoubtedly accuse her of being responsible for the accident.

Three sets of eyes stared at her as she emerged from the restroom. Two small sofas and rows of comfortable armchairs were positioned in front of a large window overlooking the darkened city of Charleston. Willa, her face pale and drawn, sat on the edge of one of the sofas with Nell and Booker seated to her right.

Lady went to stand in front of her mother. "The doctor said the operation could take hours, maybe all night. Why don't I take you home? I'll put the phone by your bed and call you the minute we know something."

Nell jumped to her feet. "I can take her home, Lady. You need to stay here."

"I should be the one to take her." Not only did she feel her mother, in her fragile state of health, would be better off getting a good night's sleep in her own bed, but she also had an ulterior motive for wanting to go home. She hoped to find there a stray bottle of liquor or wine she may have missed when she'd cleaned out her stash last week.

"Nobody's taking me anywhere!" Willa said, her voice raised. "I'm not leaving this hospital until I see my granddaughter smile again."

"In that case, I'll go see if I can find some pillows and blankets," Nell said with a smile before disappearing from the room.

Lady admonished herself. *You can't leave the hospital while your daughter is fighting for her life in the operating room.*

She checked her purse for some sort of relief, but all she found was one bent and broken cigarette at the bottom. Moving to the refreshment station, she investigated the offerings of K-cup beverages and the assortment of cold drinks in the refrigerator. But there were no minia-ture bottles of wine or vodka. *Man up, Lady. Regan needs you now more than she's ever needed you before.* Abandoning the search for booze, she brewed two cups of Earl Grey tea, handing one to her mother, and sat down on the sofa opposite her.

Willa took a sip of tea and then placed the cup on the table beside her. "Come sit with me, young man," she said, motioning Booker to join her. "I want to tell you about my guardian angel. I feel her presence here with us tonight."

Booker appeared skeptical but did as he was told.

Willa settled back on the sofa. "I want you to know about your grandmother. Mavis was the best person I've ever known. With the exception of my Regan, of course."

Lady felt hurt that she hadn't made her mother's List of Best People. Then again, a washed-up alcoholic didn't deserve the honor.

Booker's lips curled into a soft smile. "Regan is a really good person. She's considerate of everyone."

"Your grandmother was like that too—always thinking of others. She died way too young. She left a great big hole in all of our lives. I, for one, was never able to fill that hole. I don't think Lady and Nell ever did either."

When Lady felt their eyes on her, she shook her head.

"What did Mavis look like?" Booker asked.

Willa drew her head back in surprise. "Have you never seen a picture?"

"No, ma'am."

"I have plenty of pictures at home. I'll show you sometime." Willa tapped her chin in thought. "Let's see. Mavis was dark skinned with warm brown eyes. And she was plump. She squished me with her big bosom every time we hugged."

Lady's mouth fell open. "Mom! I don't think Booker wants to hear about his grandmother's bosom."

Booker snickered. "It's fine. Clearly, my mom didn't inherit her . . . um . . . you know."

"No, I guess she didn't," Willa said, shaking her head. "Mavis had the greatest laugh, a deep throaty cackle. We didn't hear that laugh often, but when we did, it reverberated throughout the house."

"Why didn't she laugh much?" Booker asked.

Willa angled her body toward him. "Mavis was a serious woman most of the time—quiet and shy but devoted and hardworking. She started out as my housekeeper, but we quickly became friends. The best friend I ever had. And let me tell you, she could cook. Man alive, how that woman could cook. And she worshipped your mama to pieces."

Booker grinned. "What can you tell me about my grandfather? I've asked my mom, but she either doesn't know or doesn't want to talk about it."

"I suspect she doesn't know, son. That's the way May May wanted it. She told me about your grandfather once. Not the particulars, not his name or anything like that, only that he was not a good man and she was lucky to escape him. She begged me never to tell Nell. And I haven't. May May had her reasons for not wanting her daughter to find her father, and I've respected that all these years."

Nell returned with her arms piled high with blankets and pillows. She positioned a pillow behind Willa's back and tucked a blanket around her.

Booker leaned forward, his eyes aglow. "Will you tell me more about my grandmother?"

Willa reached for his hand. "In due time, my boy. I'll tell you every-thing you want to know. But we're in for a long wait. We should all try to get some rest." She closed her eyes and was snoring softly within seconds.

Lacking the strength for idle conversation, Lady set her teacup on the table beside her, relaxed her head against the back of the sofa, and closed her eyes, tuning out their murmured voices. She wouldn't sleep until Regan was out of surgery. Maybe not even then. Maybe not until Regan went home from the hospital or off to college or on her hon-eymoon. Provided, of course, that all those things were in the cards for her. This accident was a reminder of the fragility of life. If she got another chance with her daughter, she'd do things differently. She would make Regan proud of her. And Willa too. She would not stop trying until she reached the top of Regan's and Willa's Best People lists.

She was lost in her own thoughts, remembering how lovely Regan had looked in her prom dress, when she heard Booker say, "Mom, I did something tonight I shouldn't have."

Lady listened, her interest piqued.

"What's that, son?"

"I took a Xanax. But not for the reasons you might think. I wasn't trying to get high. I wanted to get rid of the stress." Lady heard sniffling and assumed he was crying. "For once, I just wanted to get rid of the stress."

A moment of silence passed before Nell responded. "I was wondering why you seemed so calm. Taking pills and drinking alcohol are no way to relieve stress. What's bothering you, son, that's making you so uptight? You know you can always come to me with your problems. Is this about Harvard?"

"Yes'm. I've been stressed out for weeks. I even had a full-fledged panic attack one day at school."

"Why didn't you tell me?"

"I was handling it on my own until I had lunch with Dad today," Booker said. "He's refusing to pay for college unless I go to Duke."

Nell gasped. "Why, that rotten . . ."

"I know, right? What a jerk. I was such a mess when I got to Regan's. I'm surprised I didn't have a panic attack right there in the yard while we were taking pictures. When we got to Janie's, Owen could tell something was wrong and offered me a Xanax. In a moment of weakness, I took it. It relieved the stress, but I hated the way it made me feel. I've been in a funk all night. I ruined the prom for Regan."

"Does this have anything to do with Regan getting hit by a motorcycle?"

"I honestly don't know why she was outside. She was irritated at me because I wouldn't dance with her. Nothing against Regan. I just didn't feel like dancing. She went to get something to drink and never came back. I don't know what I'll do if something happens to her."

A long period of nose blowing and throat clearing followed. Lady felt guilty for eavesdropping on such a private conversation, but if she revealed herself now, she risked making Nell angry.

"I'm glad you told me about the Xanax, sweetheart. You shouldn't have to go through this alone. Will you promise to come to me if your stress gets out of control again?"

"I promise," Booker said, sniffling.

"What did you and your father decide about college?"

"Ha! That's a joke. There's no deciding anything with Dad. It's his way or no way. I've seen how self-centered he can be by the way he's treated you all these years, but he's never given me an ultimatum before. I'm going to take a gap year and save my own money for college."

"Your father isn't the only breadwinner in this family, you know. I have some money saved, maybe not enough to afford Harvard—"

"Harvard's off the table. Even if I get off the wait list, I'm not going there. The idea that I was smart enough to even apply to Harvard got the best of me. And you know me—I never shy away from a challenge. So I've been thinking that South Carolina makes more sense. They offered me good scholarship money. They really want me there, and it feels good to be wanted. Plus, I'd be much closer to you."

"Don't give up on Harvard just yet, son. I was going to tell you tomorrow." Nell paused. "I guess it *is* tomorrow. I've decided to sell the house. Your father and I own the house outright, with no mortgage, and we've agreed to split the equity. I can afford to send you to whichever college you decide."

"But, Mom! I don't want you to sell the house because of me."

"I'm not, sweetheart. I'm selling it because of me. I have plenty of happy memories from that house but plenty of sad ones as well. With you leaving in the fall . . . well, I don't want to live in that big house all alone. I think it's time for me to make a fresh start."

"But where will you live?"

"I stumbled upon this adorable house on Rutledge Avenue. It's tiny, barely big enough for you and me, but I prefer to think of it as cozy."

"I can totally see you living downtown, close to work. You should buy it if you really like it. I want you to be happy, Mama. You deserve it."

~

Lady experienced a newfound respect for her old friend. Nell obviously worked hard to maintain a close relationship with her son. The middle-aged Nell was not so different from the serious, wise-beyond-her-years girl she'd once known. Lady had more in common with Nell than she'd realized. Nell, too, had married a jerk. Lady knew all too well how difficult divorce can be, not just on the man and wife but on their children.

Even when they were growing up, she'd never thought much about Nell's life outside of how it affected her own. Nell had been her playmate, her companion, her best friend. But only on Lady's terms. She'd always had the upper hand. She'd been the leading lady, and Nell had played the supporting role in every scene. How wrong she'd been about so many things.

She suddenly remembered what she'd forgotten about the disturbing dream she'd had—the one where Daniel raped Nell and a baby girl named Regan with Booker's face was born nine months later. She'd forgotten the haunted look on Nell's face when she'd emerged from the closet. How utterly terrified she must have been after what Daniel had done to her. How alone she must have felt. Lady had condemned Nell for not confiding in her, for shutting her out, but who's to say she wouldn't have reacted the same way?

Lady's heart went out to Booker. Like Regan, he was a conscientious kid with dreams of conquering the world. He was just a boy, someone else's child, who obviously cared about Regan a great deal. And Lady had been unforgivably rude to him in the emergency room.

When she sensed movement in the room behind her, Lady opened her eyes and saw a nurse in blue scrubs standing in the doorway, her surgical cap damp with perspiration and her mask pulled down around her throat. Lady's heart pounded against her rib cage as she jumped to her feet. "Is she okay? Is my daughter alive?"

"Yes, ma'am. She's alive." The nurse approached her. "I'm here to give you an update. The surgery will take several more hours, but everything is going as well as the doctor had hoped. So far, he hasn't encountered any unforeseen complications."

With her hand gripping a fistful of shirt, Lady asked, "That's good, right?"

The nurse smiled. "Yes, ma'am. That's a good sign."

Nell waited for the nurse to leave before rushing to Lady's side and embracing her. "See! Sweet Regan's gonna be okay."

Lady collapsed in her arms. "Thanks to you, Nell. If you hadn't been here to take charge, to call in Dr. Summers . . ." Her breath hitched. "I can't even bring myself to think of what might've happened to my baby."

"I'm just glad I was in a position to help."

Lady locked eyes with Booker over Nell's shoulder. "I owe you both an apology. I treated you unfairly tonight." She pushed Nell away and dropped to the sofa. "You see, I'm an alcoholic. I've been on the wagon for less than two weeks. I'm not handling withdrawal very well, I guess."

Nell sat down next to her. "There's no playbook when it comes to quitting drinking, Lady. You're under a lot of pressure here. Your daughter was in a terrible accident tonight. But you're managing to hold it together." She smiled as she placed an arm around Lady's shoulders. "A little grumpy perhaps. But you didn't reach for a bottle, and that's the important thing."

Lady's cheeks burned. "Oh, I reached for a bottle all right. Fortunately, there's no booze around here." She gestured at the refreshment station. "I'm sure of it because I've checked."

Nell snickered. "This is hardly the place to enjoy a cocktail."

Lady stared up at Booker, who was standing awkwardly nearby. "I was pretending to be asleep when I heard you talking with your mother. She's right. Don't turn to pills or alcohol to relieve your stress. Believe me, Booker, once you start, it's nearly impossible to stop."

He gave her a sympathetic smile. "Yes, ma'am. And I'm sorry for your troubles."

Lady nodded. "And I'm sorry for yours."

Booker leaned down close to his mother's ear. "Is it okay if I go outside? I need some fresh air."

"Of course, sweetheart. Just be sure to take your phone with you."

He held his iPhone up as evidence.

Lady waited for him to leave. "That night, the night of my sixteenth birthday party, was the first time I ever got drunk. During the months that followed, when you shut me out and I didn't know why and nothing I said seemed to get through to you, I turned to booze for comfort. And that was the beginning of my addiction. You've always been stronger than me, Nell. You were the victim, but you didn't become an alcoholic because of it."

Nell sighed. "Instead, I blamed the ones I loved for things that were not their fault. I hurt you, Lady. I never understood how much until recently. I'm sorry for so many things. If I had trusted you enough to tell you the truth, you never would have married him. Was he awful to you?"

She shook her head. "At least not until the end. Daniel was destined to be part of my journey in life. In a weird way, I knew that when he came to my party that night. If I'd known what he'd done to you, I would never have married him. But then I wouldn't have Regan. And I would go through all the hardship again for her."

"This may be asking too much after everything I've done." Nell reached out to touch Lady's arm and then pulled her hand back. "More than anything in this whole wide world, I'd like to put the past behind us once and for all. Do you think it's possible for us to be a family again?"

"I'd like that." Lady set her eyes on her sleeping mother. "There's nothing that would make her happier. Having us together as a family again could give her the strength she needs to beat this cancer. If we're lucky, we'll get a few more good years."

Nell rested her head on Lady's shoulder. "We have a lot of time to make up for."

When she kissed Nell's hair, she found her scent familiar. The years fell away, and they were children again, snuggled up in Lady's bed reading *Doctor Dolittle*. "Yes, we do."

They remained that way, with Nell's head on Lady's shoulder, for a good while. When Lady realized that Nell had fallen asleep, she eased out from beneath the weight of her body and moved to the other end of the sofa to rest her head against the cushions. She eventually dozed off, and when she woke again, the first rays of dawn were streaming through the window. Booker had returned and was curled up like a cat on the sofa beside his grandmother. Tugging her phone out of her pocket, she saw that she had a string of text messages and five missed calls, one of them from Janie's mother. She retreated to the hallway for privacy to return the call.

Kate Jensen answered on the first ring. "Lady, thank goodness! We've all been so worried. How's Regan?"

They spoke for a minute about the accident, the surgery, and the kids in the senior class who were beside themselves with concern for her daughter.

"You'll let me know as soon as she's out of surgery?"

"I promise." Lady inhaled a deep breath as she summoned her nerve. "I have another matter I'd like to discuss with you. I was wondering if you'd consider being my sponsor for Alcoholics Anonymous."

CHAPTER THIRTY-SIX

REGAN

Regan opened her eyes wide and then shut them tight against the glaring light. "Hurt," she muttered through parched lips. Seconds later, she slipped back into the abyss. Fuzzy faces surrounded her when she came to again. Blinking her vision into focus, her gaze traveled from one person to the next—Booker, Nell, Lady—before landing on her grandmother. "Where am I, Willa?"

Willa stepped forward. "You're in the hospital, sweetheart. You were in an accident and hurt your head."

She remembered something bad happening to her but couldn't recall what. She noticed Booker's wrinkled tuxedo shirt, and it all rushed back to her—the prom, the girls in the bathroom, the rain. When her heart began to race, blaring alarms pierced the air from somewhere over her head. A nurse rushed to her side. "Clear the room," she ordered as she injected a clear liquid into Regan's IV.

"Am I gonna die?" Regan asked the nurse.

"Not on my watch you're not. But you're recovering from major surgery. You need to remain as calm as possible and get lots of rest."

Regan felt like she was floating on a cloud, and seconds later everything went dark. The next time when she woke, her mother was the only one in the room with her.

Lady righted the lounge chair and came to stand beside the bed. "Welcome back, beautiful. You gave us quite a scare. I called your father. He's trying to book a flight."

"Call him back and tell him not to come. I don't want to see him. Ever again. I need to talk to Nell. Is she still here?"

A look of surprise crossed her mother's face, but she didn't argue. "She's out in the waiting room. I'll get her."

When she started out of the room, Regan called after her, "Wait! Mom, before you go, did the doctor say . . . Did they shave my whole head? Am I bald now, like Willa?"

Lady laughed. "You'll be happy to know they only shaved a patch about the size of a tennis ball at the back of your head. Once the incision has healed and the bandage is off, the rest of your hair will cover the bald spot."

Her mother disappeared, and Nell entered the room a minute later. "How do you feel, sweetheart?"

"Like the Warriors have been playing basketball with my head."

Nell smiled. "That's expected. You're gonna feel that way for a while. At least you have good taste in basketball teams."

"I need to know, Mrs. . . . ," Regan stammered, unsure how to refer to Booker's mother in light of her pending divorce.

"Please call me Nell. After all, we're related, at least by law."

"The law is good enough for me," Regan said, wincing when she tried to smile. "It's important for me to know the truth. Did my father rape you?"

Nell exhaled a gush of air. "No, Regan. Daniel got rough with me, and he said some hurtful things, but he did *not* rape me. I made a mistake in talking to Booker about what happened that night. I thought that by telling him, he would better understand the choices I've made in my life. More importantly, I saw an opportunity for him to learn how a man should never treat a woman. The last thing I wanted was for you to get hurt. Did your accident have anything to do with any of this?"

"Sorta, although I don't blame you. I overheard some girls talking about me in the restroom. Somehow a rumor got started that my father is a rapist."

The news that her father wasn't a rapist failed to bring the relief Regan had hoped for. Even if he hadn't raped Nell, he'd assaulted her nonetheless. And that abuse had cost her dearly. Cost all of them dearly. Nell had made choices based on his actions that had affected her whole family, from Willa on down to Booker. Regan never wanted to see her father again. And she would never forgive him for what he'd done.

Regan opted not to tell Nell the other part of the rumor, that Nell was the victim and Booker the result of the rape. It was too ridiculous to even consider.

"Oh, honey, I'm so sorry. For you and for Booker. I imagine this rumor will make its way back to him. Neither of you should have to deal with this."

"Is Booker here?" Regan asked. "I'd like to be the one to tell him."

"He's in the waiting room, hoping for a chance to see you. He won't leave the hospital until he knows for certain you're out of the woods."

Nell exited the room, and Booker appeared in the doorway almost immediately.

"You can come in, Booker. I won't bite. Are you okay?"

A slow smile crept on his lips. "Typical Regan, worried about me when you're the one lying in the hospital bed with your head bandaged up like a mummy."

She lifted her fingers to her head dressing. "Now that you mention it, my head does kinda hurt."

He approached the bed with caution. "What were you doing in the street? Were you just going to leave the prom without telling me?"

"Some girls in the grade below us said some things that hurt my feelings," she said, and then told him what she'd overheard.

"That's ridiculous. That would make me"—he stared up at the ceiling while he counted the years—"like thirty-seven years old."

"How did they hear about it, Booker? That's what I want to know. I certainly never said anything to anyone."

He thought about it, his brow furrowed, and then anger crossed his face. "Owen and Stuart. They were eavesdropping on us in the library when I asked you to the prom. I waved them away, but they must have overheard us when you asked if Daniel raped my mother. I'm sorry, Regan. If I had known . . ."

"Don't worry about it. There's nothing we can do to stop the rumor now."

Booker's face brightened. "But there's good news in all this. Our mothers have forgiven each other. There's talk of us being a family."

"Yay! That is good news. I guess that makes us cousins." She patted the mattress. "Sit down for a minute, coz. I want to know about you. What did your father do that upset you so much?"

He sat down gently on the edge of the bed. "He refuses to pay for college unless I go to Duke."

"He can't do that!"

"Actually, he can. It's his money. He can do whatever he wants with it."

"But what's going to happen? You've worked so hard. You have to go to college."

"Oh, I'm going to college. I won't give Dad the satisfaction of knowing he has control over me. Mom and I have talked about it. We'll find a way to make it happen. I just have to figure out which college. Harvard's out of the question. Even if I get off the wait list, which I doubt will happen, we can't afford it. My dad's decision not to pay reinforced what I was starting to figure out on my own."

Regan cocked her bandaged head to the side. "And what's that?"

"That it doesn't really matter which school I pick. I'll make the most of my academics no matter where I go. I'm not really the fraternity type, and I'm not into sports, although it'd be fun to have a winning football team to pull for. Main thing is, I'd like to be close to my mom, especially while she's going through the divorce."

Regan toyed with the IV attached to her arm. "I've been thinking the same about college lately."

"How so? I thought you were dead set on going to Chapel Hill."

"I'm beginning to wonder if I applied to UNC for all the wrong reasons. I wanted to make my father proud by going to his alma mater and becoming a successful attorney like him. Now I'd rather chart my own path to the end of a cliff than follow in his footsteps." She turned the IV loose and looked up at him. "How did we both end up with such jerks for fathers?"

"Luck of the draw, coz. Same way we ended up with amazing women as mothers."

Regan caught a glimpse of her mother standing sentry beside the door out in the hallway. She'd been hard on Lady. She'd condemned her for being an alcoholic when she should've encouraged her to quit drinking. Despite her mother's flaws, Regan could always count on her love, which was more than she could say for her father.

EPILOGUE

The late-morning sun beat down on the families and friends gathered on the lawn in front of All Saints School. The long sultry days of summer were upon them. Willa sat between her daughters in the front row, a proud grandmother watching her beloved grandchildren graduate from high school.

Regan's grades had slipped in the weeks following her accident, allowing Booker to take the lead in the race for valedictorian. Since making his decision to go to USC, he'd stopped worrying so much about his grades, but with Regan missing nearly two weeks of school, he'd inched ahead of her anyway. The head of All Saints had called Booker into his office ten days prior to graduation. "I'm officially awarding you the honor of being valedictorian of the class of 2018," Mr. Long had said.

"I'm sorry, sir, but I decline the honor," Booker had said. "Regan's GPA has been higher than mine for the past four years. It's not fair for me to take that honor away because she was in an accident."

"I'm delighted to hear you say that, young man. While I stand by my belief in healthy competition among students, this is one time I'm willing to bend the rules. Regan's GPA has been only a fraction of a point ahead of yours throughout your high school careers. You deserve to share the honor of being valedictorian."

Draped in their hunter-green caps and gowns, Regan and Booker delivered their valedictorian addresses with grace and eloquence. Willa knew Regan's speech by heart from listening to her practice. And she'd also heard a preview the previous afternoon of Booker's address when he'd stopped by the house with his mother, requesting an audience to rehearse.

Afterward, Nell had commandeered the kitchen and taught Regan and Booker the secret to making May May's delectable cheese biscuits. "It's all in the cheese," Nell said. "Cracker Barrel's extra-sharp cheddar is the key." But she showed Regan and Booker a special way of rolling out the dough that Willa and Lady weren't privy to.

One bite of biscuit brought back memories for Lady, Nell, and Willa, and they'd spent the next two hours drinking sweet tea and telling Regan and Booker tales of old times.

Regan spoke to the graduation audience about the importance of family while Booker encouraged his classmates to never let anyone or anything deter them from following their dreams. His was a message intended for his father, who sat two rows back and whom Willa met briefly after the service but did not invite to the celebratory lunch she was hosting at her home in honor of the graduates.

A week after the accident, when her headache had finally dulled, Regan had called her father and confronted him about his mistreatment of Nell. To no one's surprise, he'd denied any knowledge of any impropriety. At his daughter's request, Daniel had agreed not to come to her graduation. He'd sent a gift instead, a shirt box covered in silver paper that remained unopened on the dining room table. There was a lot Willa still didn't know about the night of Lady's sixteenth birthday. Things, she'd decided, it was best for her not to know. Whatever Daniel had done to Nell had shaped all their lives for the last thirty-seven years, and Willa would never forgive him for depriving her of the chance to spend that time with her daughter and grandchild.

Tears sprang to Willa's eyes—not the first or the last of the day—as she gathered with her family around the table on the piazza. She'd never dreamed this day was possible—not only to have Nell back in her life but to be blessed with such a loving grandson.

Everyone contributed to the celebration. Lady made a hot chicken salad casserole, and Nell brought a honey-baked ham and mixed green salad. Willa ordered a Lady Baltimore cake from Sugar Bakeshop and helped Lady set the table with linens, china, and the season's first blue hydrangeas from their garden.

The conversation over lunch was lively. With the exception of Willa, who was grateful to be alive and momentarily cancer-free, they were all embarking on a new path in life. At the eleventh hour, Regan had changed her mind about UNC and decided to join Booker at USC in the fall, where they would attend the Honors College together.

When she announced her decision, Booker had jokingly said, "A new race is on for valedictorian. And this time, Regan, I'm not cutting you any slack. May the best man, or woman, win."

With the guidance of her two new mentors, Lady was charging full steam ahead with her life. Kate Jensen had agreed to be her sponsor for Alcoholics Anonymous, and they met a couple of times a week for meetings. And Penny Yates was guiding Lady toward a career as a geriatric aide. She'd formally offered Lady a job with Lowcountry Home Health Care, but Lady declined. She wanted to pick and choose her clients. She preferred driving them to doctor's appointments and social functions over taking care of their physical needs. So far, she'd had business cards printed and converted the old upstairs apartment, where Nell and Mavis had once lived, into an office. Penny had sent her several referrals, and she was networking with friends and acquaintances to get the word out about her services.

Of those gathered at the table, Nell beamed the brightest. She'd put her house in Mount Pleasant on the market and made a down payment on the Rutledge Avenue dollhouse. She was all set to move in mid-June. She'd confided in Willa that she'd never been happier in her life. "I finally feel free to just be me."

Lady was slicing the cake when Booker waved his phone in the air and let out a whoop. "Guess what! I got off the wait list at Harvard!"

Regan's face fell. "Congratulations, Booker. That's what you've always wanted."

Booker sent an elbow to her side. "I got off the wait list, silly. That doesn't mean I'm going."

"If this is about money, sweetheart, we can figure something out," Nell said, her face pinched in concern.

"And I'd like to help," Willa said, smiling at him from across the table. "You're my grandson, Booker. I would be privileged to pay your tuition."

Booker's jaw dropped. "Wow, Willa, that's awfully generous of you. But I can't accept. And it's not because of the money. Harvard is not the right choice for me. Don't get me wrong, I'm thrilled I got accepted. I mean, seriously, think of the bragging rights. But I'd rather be at the top of my game at Carolina than struggling to stay afloat at Harvard. That's not to say the curriculum at the Honors College won't be rigorous. But I don't think the admissions office would've awarded me scholarship money if they didn't have faith in me." His eyes traveled the table. "Besides, I don't want to be that far away from my family."

"You've made a fine choice, Booker. But I'm going to pay your tuition anyway." Willa shifted her gaze to her granddaughter. "And yours too, Regan. Your mother reminded me recently that my parents, who bestowed this wealth upon me, would've wanted me to enjoy it while I'm still alive. And paying your tuitions will make me very happy indeed. As will helping the two of you."

She locked eyes with Lady first and then Nell. "Lady, I want you to fix this house up any way you'd like. It'll be yours one day. We might as well make the improvements now so we can enjoy them while I'm still alive. And, Nell, I want you to own your dollhouse free and clear. I'm going to reimburse you the money you spent on the down payment and pay the balance on your mortgage."

Exchanging glances, Lady and Nell started to object, but Willa cut them off. "Hush! It's all been taken care of. I already met with my accountant, and he's working out the arrangements. Who knows how much longer I have to live, but I'm blessed to be able to spend my dying days with the four of you."

After dessert, when Regan and Booker headed off to a round of graduation parties that promised to last through the evening, the three women retired with coffee to the upstairs piazza.

Willa lay back on the chaise longue and listened to Nell and Lady talk.

"I've been meaning to ask you, Lady, how's Mindy? Does she still live in town?"

"She got married right out of college, divorced two years later, and now lives in Seattle," Lady said. "I understand from mutual friends that she's remarried with children."

"What about Hank?"

"He still lives in Charleston. On Tradd Street, I believe. He's married to a really nice girl. They have a son two grades below Regan and Booker."

"I had a crush on him, you know," Nell admitted.

Lady laughed out loud. "Didn't we all?"

Nell and Lady talked on about their divorces and how quickly the years had flown, Nell's nursing career and Lady's new career endeavor, the kids and how strange it would be when they left for college.

"But you'll be living so close," Willa said to Nell. "We'll get together at least once a week for dinner."

"I'd like that very much." Nell set her coffee cup down on the table beside her. "I know we're trying to move past everything that's happened between us. But I feel like I need to say it one more time. I am so sorry for the way I behaved. I was trying to find my way, but now I realize

I was never really lost. My place has always been right here with you." She took both of their hands in hers.

Lady swatted at a tear. "And I'm sorry too, Nell. You were right. I truly was a brat back then."

Nell cocked an eyebrow. "Back then?"

"I admit it!" Lady threw her free hand in the air. "I've always been a brat, and I'll always be a brat."

They all shared a laugh.

Nell squeezed Willa's hand. "Thank you, Miss Willa, for never giving up on me."

"We're together now," Willa said. "That's all that really matters. I can live out the rest of my days a happy woman."

"Forever . . . ," Nell said, and Lady joined her in reciting their pact. "Together, forever. Let nothing or no one ever come between us."

ACKNOWLEDGMENTS

I'm grateful to the many people who helped make this novel possible. First and foremost, to my editor, Patricia Peters, for making my work stronger without changing my voice, and my agent, Andrea Hurst, for her guidance and expertise in the publishing industry and for believing in me. To Danielle Marshall and her team at Lake Union Publishing as well as Mariette Franken at Kindle Press. A big thank-you to my beta readers—Alison Fauls, Mamie Farley, and Kathy Sinclair—for taking interest in my work and providing invaluable feedback. I'm always appreciative to Tim Galvin, Richmond architect, for answering my many questions about architecture, and Leslie Rising, of Levys of Richmond, for offering fashion advice for my characters. To Betsy and Moultrie Dotterer and Catherine Kresken for location information about the Charleston area. A heartfelt thank-you to the staff at MUSC for taking amazing care of my mother during her recent extended stays. The nurses who work grueling hours and tend their patients with compassion provided inspiration for Nell.

I am blessed to have many supportive people in my life who offer the encouragement I need to continue the pursuit of my writing career. I owe a huge debt of gratitude to my advanced review team for their enthusiasm for and commitment to my work. Love and thanks to my family—my mother, Joanne; husband, Ted; and the best children in the world, Cameron and Ned.

Most of all, I'm grateful to my wonderful readers for their love of women's fiction. I love hearing from you. Feel free to shoot me an email at ashleyhfarley@gmail.com or stop by my website at www.ashleyfarley. com for more information about my characters and upcoming releases. Don't forget to sign up for my newsletter. Your subscription will grant you access to exclusive content, sneak previews, and special giveaways.

ABOUT THE AUTHOR

Photo © 2018 Maguire Neblett Photography

Ashley Farley is the bestselling author of the Sweeney Sisters series as well as the stand-alone novels *Sweet Tea Tuesdays*, *Magnolia Nights*, *Beyond the Garden*, and other books about women for women. Her characters are mothers, daughters, sisters, and wives facing real-life situations, and her goal is to keep readers turning pages with stories that resonate long after the last word.

In addition to writing, she is an amateur photographer, an exercise junkie, and a wife and mother. While she has lived in Richmond, Virginia, for more than two decades, part of her heart remains in the salty marshes of the South Carolina Lowcountry where she grew up. Through the eyes of her characters, she captures the moss-draped trees, delectable cuisine, and kindhearted folks with lazy drawls that make the area so unique. For more information on the author and her work, visit www.ashleyfarley.com.